A
Resolute
Child

Jacqueline S Harvey

ISBN:979 8 6514385 0 1

Cover design
Pixel Studio

Acknowledgements

I thank Sarah Wise for her interest. Her book 'The Blackest Streets' was invaluable in setting the scene for May's life and it has been an education for me.

Thanks also to Lori Oschefski, CEO of 'British Home Children in Canada'. The site has been very useful for researching experiences girls like May had and her interest is also appreciated.

May's story grew from an idea planted when I lived close to Barnardo's Head Office in Barkingside – the site of Mossford Village. There is now a road called Thomas Barnardo Way in recognition of the role the organisation still plays in aiding children.

Foreword

May's story is fiction but many of the persons mentioned are real and events where dates are given are based on fact. Where possible, descriptions of these events are from reports in newspapers of the time.

I do not attempt to decry or commend the child migration as arranged by Thomas Barnardo that became an important part of May's life. I am aware of its contentious nature and the background to some of the events - both good and bad – is sourced from contemporary accounts.

The snow of October 1880, although unusual, did occur. The Waterloo Road Workhouse and Doctor Barnardo's opinion of it were lifted from his history. The Netley Hospital no longer exists and has been replaced by the Royal Victoria Country Park. The slum called Old Nichol was eventually cleared and is now The Boundary Estate.

The name of the police inspector may be familiar but if not a quick Google search will explain.

May was a child resolute in her desire for justice and goes on to be passionate in seeking a fairer political system – not only for women. How would she view the inequality that still exists today I wonder?

Jacqueline S Harvey

One

"Oi you, child, get away from my stall you thieving little cow. I can see you - just about to nick me prime fish."

"I ain't no thief mister. I'm a 'spectable gel about to be goin' 'ome after me honest day at work."

"No you ain't, you're a perishing little thief. What honest work could a dirty mangy looking creature like you do round here? Only thieving more like. Get back to that filthy slum where you belong, you're scaring me poor horse, look."

"Blimmin cheek, I ain't that mangy, there's worse round 'ere than me mister, that scraggy looking 'orse for a start." snorted the child, May, as she tossed her rather matted and infested hair, brushed down her grey shift that was stiff with street grime and pulled her fraying shawl around her narrow shoulders.

"Anyway I got boots, look. Most round here ain't got no boots or shoes at all. Good uns they are an' all, theys good leather they are."

May turned around and pulled a face at the stallholder before petulantly kicking one of his pots of vinegar over - something she couldn't have done with bare feet so she was pleased she had those boots. No doubt they had serviced many a pair of tiny feet, both of girls and boys, before they eventually reached her. They had been good boots once but that was long before she had acquired them. She couldn't remember how but only knew she had something to protect her grimy feet and lots of others did not - although they were not even an actual pair. Gradually the one brown and one black - luckily one left and one right - had become the same colour, that of grime and dirt. If boots could talk then the tale they told would surely document the journey of degradation from those who lived a reasonably comfortable life to those, like May, who barely even scraped a living.

As she backed away, May, as usual, had the last word.

"What would I want with your rotten ole fish anyway? I'm off home to a lovely stew made for me by my dear ole mum. Best stew in London she makes, we even 'ave some meat in it sometimes y'know. Better than your 'orrible smelly fish you miserable ole devil."

She scurried off into the nearby alleys leaving the man to pick up his pot, which luckily for him had been almost empty anyway. He shook his head and tutted.

The stallholders didn't mind the odd bit of pilfering, they had kids too and they knew what hunger meant. Some kind ones kept the less saleable wares that were left over to give to the poor little blighters - when they could. Trouble was, if they seemed too much of a soft touch, hordes of the little perishers would swarm around them so their stock didn't stand a chance. It was useless to try to chase after them because, like wraiths, they could evaporate in an instant down the passages and back alleys. What they couldn't eat they pinched to flog, because they had to live somehow and often it was the only way.

The truth was, though, May was not on her way home after a day's honest work to be welcomed by a loving mother with a bowl of steaming hot stew. She wished it was but hadn't been for half a year or so - since her mum had been suddenly taken ill with a fever and died. Even before her sad death, such a meal was very much a fantasy; a warm comfortable home was a fantasy also, as reality was one small, poky room. A meal that consisted of any more than bread and scraps was an occasional treat when mum had enough sewing work coming in and it was sufficient not just to pay the rent but also to eat comparatively well. And May *was* a thief - since her mother had passed away thievery was often the only way to get by. Unfortunately, unlike some she knew, she was not a very good one.

Since her mum was taken from her she managed as best she could and actually counted herself fortunate compared to some other children she knew. At least she had once had a mum, and a good one at that; at least she had had a home for most of her short life if even though it was just a simple room. That was more than many other children had - they didn't know what it was like to be cuddled, to be put to bed on your own palliasse and to be loved. She did so she felt she was lucky. She never knew her father; mum didn't talk about him but May never missed having one anyway and there were plenty of others who were fatherless also.

It was all right if you had a good one. Some she knew did but others, well, their fathers were the sort you were much better off without. May remembered when Freddie's was killed at the docks; he fell and was crushed between the dockside and a big ship that he was working on unloading - drunk probably as he was very often drunk. The money he sometimes earned and sometimes gave to Freddie's mother (but mostly spent on cards and beer - so Freddie said) was gone but so were his beatings so he didn't really care much. Anyway, he got a new dad soon enough, someone who his mum had known before his dad went. He was much better to Freddie and taught him useful stuff like woodworking - he could even make a chair now.

No, May didn't need a father. She'd had her mum and her mum was kind and her mum had taught her to read a bit as well as sending her to school when she could manage it. May's mum had always struggled to do her best and she loved her. These were May's thoughts often and she managed to find some comfort from remembering better times. She would never stop missing her.

Things were very different now. May survived as best she could on discarded leftovers and the kindness of some of the neighbours who had little to spare but tried, when they were able, to help and if they had space she could squeeze in, would let her stay to sleep. Sometimes she acquired, either by stealing, begging or, and her mum had told her this was best if possible, by honest means like selling bit and pieces, the cost of a meal and sleeping space in a hostel.

The unsavoury hostels were not the sort of place a young girl would wish to spend the night - not the sort of place anyone would really but at least they were dry when the rain was falling. When the weather was dry though, a place out of the way with other children like her for company and warmth would be preferable - and safer. Her favourite place to stay was with Posh Peg and it was to Posh Peg's room that she was headed this fateful day.

She had encountered Peg one day at a Rag Stall where clothing, second, third or even fourth-hand, could be bought for pennies. Peg held herself different from most of the women round there. May couldn't put her finger on what was different but Peg seemed to have something about her. She had seen May looking at a tatty shawl. All of the clothing had obviously seen better days but one that caught May's eye had not lost its entire colour to fading yet and she obviously admired it. Peg held up the shawl to May.

 "Do you like this, child?"

"Yeah, I do missus. This is the only one I've got and its fallin' to bits it is. I think this is right lovely I do."

"*Would* you like it?"

"Yeah, missus but I ain't got nothin yet cos I ain't managed to earn nothin see."

"Where is your mother? Is she working?"

"Ain't got no mother no more missus - my poor darlin mother got took by fever so I've been on me own since then but I'm a tough kid I am. I don't take no nonsense from no-one I don't."

Peg looked at the skinny but defiant girl and was instantly taken with her. She wished she could take her in and perhaps could from time to time but if the agents knew she had another person, even a little child, living with her the rent would be increased. It was a struggle already and an increase would not be something she could cope with.

What she could do was, using a few coppers that were to be used for herself, make the child happy by buying the shawl for her. May left the stall with her gift, twirling round and posing to show off what, to her, was one of the best things she had ever owned. Both she and Peg left the stall with much more than a shawl; they both left with a new friend.

May needed a friend; she didn't have any aunties who could have taken her in. Her mother had a sister, called Violet, because her mother had often talked about her. Violet had died of the big illness a few years before May was born so May never knew her. The coral or something like that was what she thought the illness was called and loads of people were taken by it. She looked like Violet her mum had told her.

'You were both pretty like flowers so that's why she was called Violet and why I called you May, like the lovely spring blossom in the month you were born.' May had actually never seen the blossom that bore her name so just had to imagine its shape, colours and sweet smell.

She did have an uncle – George – but he left for the army before her mum died so he wouldn't even know about her passing. If she had had a father then she would have wanted him to have been like Uncle George – kind and strong. Perhaps he would come back for her one day. He used to help her mum when he had any spare money and would give them treats like cake and sweets when he was flush. May never really knew what else he did but he often had black eyes and sometimes his hands were bound up so he must, she thought, have been a fighter, a boxer. A good one too because it was usually after he had the bruises that he managed to give her and her mum a few coppers or the treats. She knew he joined the army

7

because he never had a wife and children and he wanted, once again – as he had travelled before, to see something more than 'round here'. This was all May knew. It was as if the world was flat and that if she ventured too far from what was familiar she would disappear over the edge into nothingness.

The furthest beyond what May knew as 'round here' was the not too distant Victoria Park and the big river. She had been as far as the park with her mum one lovely day the summer before mum passed away and to the river with her uncle before he joined the army. That fine day with mum was one of the best in May's short life and one that she would always remember. Some plain cake wrapped in paper and a cup of lemonade from a stall while in the park with her mum were all it took to make it so wonderful and for just one day the sun shone on the two of them. The slum that was the Nichol – and their home - seemed a million miles away.

Victoria Park was how she imagined the countryside would be with endless carpets of bright green grass. Grass was something that was rarely seen in the colourless labyrinth of the slum – occasionally the odd, resilient tuft fought its way through the dirt between the cobbles. Where light managed to reach down to the ground, breaking the grey monotony and the soul-sucking blackness, the occasional splash of green would break through. Yes, May imagined the countryside would be like Victoria Park, only it would be far bigger, with lots of wonderful animals she had never seen and was never ever likely to see. There might be wolves and bears and maybe even dragons. The thought scared her but excited her also as did the thought of all the strange things that existed in faraway countries like one she had heard of called China.

She had seen Chinamen with their funny clothing and little pigtails around the markets. She wondered, and tried to imagine, what faraway China was really like. There was a strange building on an island in the park that was, her mother had told her, a Chinese structure called a pagoda. Perhaps there must have been Chinese people that lived there but maybe they only came out at night, as she did not see them there. Someone told her they came out at night to feed the ducks and geese that lived on the lake. The fowl there were the only ones she had ever seen that weren't already dead or in the towering cages down Sclater Street. The cages were several stories high – like tenements for the unhappy birds and May thought how lucky were the free birds on the lake in comparison to those poor, confined creatures. The caged birds would never know freedom, just as most of those who dwelled in the Nichol probably never would. Perhaps they wouldn't know what to do if they were suddenly set free – perhaps those who had the misfortune to live in the slum wouldn't either.

With her uncle, she had seen the huge ships that journeyed all over the big, wide world. There were so many ships with towering masts, creamy white sails and tall round things, called funnels, that it was impossible for May to see where they ended; they seemed to stretch for miles and the sight amazed her. George had already travelled far away on such sailing ships as a very young man, just a boy really, and had told her thrilling tales, that she wondered if were true, about his travels on the high seas.

It was a surprise to him, on his return, that his baby niece May even existed as his seafaring had taken him away for over a year and the last he knew of his one remaining sister was that she was working in service somewhere much 'posher' than the Nichol. He had pressed her for information about the circumstances of May's birth but she was resolutely silent and determined to get by without help from any other quarter. Perhaps May inherited her stubbornness from her mother.

As May stood that day gazing at the ships she could not conceive how big the world was or how different all the far off places were from the only one she had ever experienced. She wondered if she would ever, like Uncle George, see any of these far off lands. Would she ever journey far away on a big ship? In the present, she often wondered where her uncle was now and wherever he was if he was fighting. Did he have to fight very hard? Would she ever see him again? Was he even still alive?

So the park and the river; these were the limits of her world and for now, the only place she was concerned about was where she would sleep tonight. The woman who May called Posh Peg had been her friend ever since she bought May the shawl and she would let her sleep in the corner of her room sometimes. It was the place, over all others, May liked best. Peg's room was not as damp as some others she had stayed in and she even had two chairs though there was only one of her. She had a stove that was small but always had a pot of something on. Usually, it was something tasty that May looked forward to and she could smell as she climbed the stairs.

To make the room more homely there were covers that Peg had made from the rags she had gathered and washed. There was a faded picture of a lady with curled hair. She wore a low-necked dress that showed her shoulders. Her neck was set off by a choker that partly concealed a small cross beneath it. Peg kept the picture behind glass that was always polished - despite the glass being cracked. May had asked who the lady was. Was she a toff? But Peg would only chuckle and say nothing. May called her Posh Peg as she spoke differently to all the others around there. She said head instead of 'ead like May and all the others did. Maybe she had been a toff once thought May but she wasn't now or she wouldn't be living in one room in the crumbling tenement in Half Nichol Street.

May's mother had warned her about toffs. 'Never trust a toff my darling. They look better than us with all the fine stuff they wear but they're no different underneath and surely they are no better. Why, if you had the chance to live in a fine house instead of round here you would look much lovelier than any of them. No, my darling, never trust a toff; trust your mum because she knows. Your mum knows.'

If May had known the word 'wistfully' and what it meant it may have occurred to her that these words were spoken by a woman with good reason to feel the way she did about toffs. If Posh Peg had been one and they couldn't be trusted, her mum must have meant men. Perhaps ladies were different; perhaps they could be trusted. At least some of them - like Peg.

Having had no success with getting anything to eat from the fish stall man and with the evening starting to draw in May headed back along the still busy streets picking her way through the grey slimy puddles and horse dung. Her thinking was that she would rest at Peg's tonight then go off to the school – the Ragged School it was called - for breakfast in the morning. She continually looked down just in case there were any discarded scraps of food or something that was not too disgusting that could be sold or given to Peg as a thank you. Last time she had found a piece of ribbon just before she went to Peg's and Peg was pleased with it so she was pleased as well. She was hungry. But then she was always hungry - even when she had eaten she remained so.

The light, such as it was in the labyrinthine streets, was starting to fade as she turned the second from last corner before the narrow street where Posh Peg lived. She cried out an oath, for she had stepped in a steaming pile of dog dung and the odious sludge had oozed through the holes in her left boot and squeezed between her already dirty toes. Looking down at her feet she screwed up her face as she considered the state of her precious boots. May needed to clean her foot before she got to Peg's tenement, as she couldn't take filth like that into Posh Peg's room.

Her mum had always tried to keep their place clean when she could and it wasn't easy but Peg was even more particular. She told May 'just because it's old it doesn't have to be dirty.' Sometimes, this just couldn't be true when the only water came from a pump shared by so many people and had to be carried up flights of disintegrating stairs or through dank narrow passages. In these streets, both cleanliness *and* godliness were often in extremely short supply.

Peg's lodgings were on the second floor of the tenement block and despite the climb, May liked this. When she lived with her mum they were on the ground floor and the cellar room ran underneath so there were always comings and goings all hours. The room was noisy with frequent visits from rats. May hated the rats and remembered how pleased she was when the Gradys moved into the next room. They bred little terriers and although they could be snappy little creatures, they made short work of the perishing rats so that was, at least, a blessing. Another thing about the ground floor was that some people even had the cheek to pinch window rags as well. She recalled her mum plugging up the holes in the broken windows only to find someone else had nicked them for their own use.

On the first floor it wasn't so bad but could still be noisy. The second floor was further away from the noise so was better still. Also not so many tried to sleep on the landings up there because the steep stairs with broken and rotting treads were hard for the cripples, drunkards or both, to manage. The windows had less chance of getting broken as well although many were. Those that weren't broken were so dirt-encrusted they hardly let in any light anyway. Despite this May liked it up there and hoped that Peg would be at home (but where else would she be?) and that she would let her stay (why wouldn't she?)

Two

In the more open streets, the shadows were lengthening as the pale watery light disappeared behind the grimy buildings. This was how May knew roughly what the time was but in the narrow alleys, it made no difference as they were always in shadow - even in the summer, as the buildings were so close together and claustrophobic. Light, even if there was any, struggled to be able to penetrate to ground level. The only other way to try to tell the time was by what the people of the neighbourhood were doing. If the stallholders were packing up it must be time to look for a place to bed down. If the men were going into the pubs or beerhouses and the women were loitering outside then it was time to go to settle at whatever place could be found, hopefully with some mates, and try to sleep. If you could find the odd scrap to help fill your belly then that would be good. Just a bit of bread would often be the only food she had.

As May was considering her disgusting foot, a nearby shopkeeper was sluicing down his frontage. He took pity on May and let her rinse her foot and boot which ended up only marginally cleaner because the water itself was already grey and murky. It meant her boot was wet and soggy thus speeding up its inevitable disintegration but she tried, as best she could, to dry it, and her foot, with some rag She remembered Peg's words about cleanliness so wouldn't turn up with a foot that was stinking and filthy.

As well as cleanliness, innocence was at a premium in the slum too. The sights and sounds that were part of everyday life were not conducive to innocence. Somehow, despite the cursing and often lewd behaviour that went on around her May had managed to retain the purity and innocence her mum had sought to protect. So far - except for some cursing, but of course cursing was simply another part of everyday life.

If Peg wasn't there (but where else would she be?) then May might move on to another friend of her mum – but she didn't really want to. She had stayed with her straight after mum went but the problem was that shortly afterwards she had taken up with a new man and May wasn't keen on him. She thought he looked at her funny so she didn't feel comfortable around him – he was, she thought, shifty. Her other option was to seek out Ernie, (poor Ernie he had been on the street for a long time now and didn't look too well anymore – right haggard she thought) and Nick (dead sharp was Nick - always managed to find food from somewhere) and Aggie (Nick's sister who came and went depending on how much she had earned – from flower selling May thought; although she couldn't be sure.

Aggie always seemed to have many men friends so perhaps she did some work for them.)

It was getting a bit late for any of these other options really because of the time it had taken to sort out her foot but none of this mattered because Peg would be there and Peg would let her stay. May spotted a lone apple on the cobbles; it wasn't too bruised and dirty so May picked it up quickly before another street urchin could grab it. She wiped it on her shift despite it being marginally dirtier than the apple and took a bite. The rest she would save for Posh Peg. She trusted Peg. Peg deserved the apple for being kind to her

May arrived at the tenement where Peg lived just as the watery light turned to shadow on the pavement and in the dusk the business of the day was turning into a different kind of business of the evening. In the dimness of the hallway, there were already two old, smelly men huddling down. May thought they looked very old, at least sixty she thought but it was hard to tell, especially through the grime, and May wasn't even certain of her own age. She thought she was born in 1870 but really wasn't sure. She was pleased to get to the sanctuary of Peg's block and almost skipped up the steep staircase to Peg's room. There was no light but she could just see, from under the door, the glow of a candle. This was good because it meant that Peg was there. (But where else would she be?)

She knocked.

"Peg, Peg, it's me, little Maisie. I got an apple for you. It ain't too bruised an' I only 'ad one bite from it. The rest is for you cos I know you like apples."

Peg didn't come and May was confused. She could hear other voices. Who did Peg have there? She must be there because where else would she be? However, Peg wasn't there. The door opened and a much younger woman with a tired face and a harassed expression came out.

"Yeah, who are you? What do you want?"

"Peg lives here, I'm looking for Peg."

"Not no more she don't. We lives here now. Me, me kids an' when he's around me perishin' husband."

"But she was 'ere only a coupla days since. Where's she gone?"

"Look kid all I know is that we is 'ere now and if you're on the cadge we ain't got nothing. Nought to spare at all, barely enough to feed me own brood 'ere."

"It's getting dark missus. I was gonna stay with Peg. It's too late to find somewhere else now. Ain't you got room for another little 'un, just for one night? On the floor is all I want, I won't be no trouble missus honest I won't."

"Sorry, you poor little scrap, me baby's crying. Gotta go."

With that, the woman slammed the rickety door and May could hear her shouting at the squawking baby. She stood for a moment not knowing what to think or what to do. She trusted Peg, why had she gone? Perhaps you couldn't trust any toff - even ladies that had once been toffs. Couldn't trust any of them. She turned to go back downstairs just as the door opened again.

"Oi gel is you May?"

"Yeah, missus."

"This was left for you." The woman thrust a folded piece of paper into May's grubby hand. "Oh, an' this an' all."

It was the faded old picture that Peg kept in pride of place. It was no longer in its frame and written on the back in faded ink was a name - Maud. Underneath was written 'but always Peggy to me'; a date – 1858 - and the words 'will always remember you.'

May had wondered about the woman in the picture and now she knew it was Peg herself. Peg had been a very beautiful woman and someone must have cared for her very much all those years ago. What had happened in Peg's life that had brought her to the awful slum? May's eyes filled with tears as she tried to read the note.

17th October 1880

My dear May

I fear that I may not see you ever again. It is Sunday evening as I write this by the light of my last remaining

19

candle. The oil for my lamp ran out the day after I saw you and I did not have the means to obtain any more. Black Monday surely and regrettably follows Sunday and it is then the agents of my anonymous landlord will come to demand my rent. Alas, I do not have it and have no way to remedy my unfortunate situation. So, as no credit is given - although as I am a proud woman I would never demean myself to plead for it - my time here will be at an end. The House is most likely to be the place where I live out my remaining years and sadly I am reconciled to it.

I have welcomed and enjoyed your all too brief visits. Your irrepressible spirit, despite what has been dealt to you in your short life, has brought much needed cheer to my lonely room. I know not whether you will be able to read every word I have set down here but you are a bright child with some reading I know, so I hope you will understand the meaning. It gives me great sorrow that I cannot bid goodbye to you in person as I was hoping we would meet again at least once. You must believe that I will think of you fondly and often. Please remember me as a good friend. I hope and pray to our dear Lord Jesus that you will find a place to keep yourself safe and that one day the sun shall shine on you.

P

May couldn't understand all that Peg had written but could make out enough to know that she had not left willingly and would always count her as a good friend. May did not like to think of Peg (why was she called Peg anyway if her real name was Maud she wondered?) in the House because she had heard stories about it and no poor soul who went in there ever seemed to come out again except in a coffin.

May stuffed the note from Peg into her deep and only pocket so anything that May owned (which was usually nothing) and had to carry, was borne in that one pocket. She then wiped a tear from her cheek thinking of her friend Peg in the House but also for herself – where would she sleep tonight?

By now there were two more figures huddled in the hallway downstairs. It was turning colder in the evenings as October marched steadily on towards winter. May's mum had been taken just after her birthday on a warm sunny day when, at any other time, it would be good to be alive despite the hardships of their existence. How she wished her mum was saved but no doctor who would attend in the Nichol could be found in time - and there was no money for payment even if they had. Her mum just quietly slipped away with May holding her hand and pleading through tears with her not to go.

May left the building and hesitated, not knowing which way it would be best for her to go. She chose to head towards the lay at the viaduct arches, as it was the quickest place to reach in the gathering gloom. She had seen some of the other children meet up there when they had nowhere else to go so hoped she wouldn't be alone. She was cold now, having only her shawl, and wondered how she would manage when the winter set in; a slight, innocent girl with no-one and nothing; nothing but some good memories. Yet May was a trier. She knew nothing other than the claustrophobic world that comprised these streets and would make her way the best she could. That was all she could do, perhaps until her Uncle George came back from the army for her. He would come back, wouldn't he?

As she trudged onwards, a familiar voice called to her from behind. She spun around and was pleased to see a friendly, but gaunt face. It was her pal, Ernie. May hadn't seen him for a while and his appearance was even worse than she remembered. The laboured way in which he breathed and the pallor of his skin, despite the dirt, startled her.

"That you May? I thought you'd be going off to that Posh Peg's place cos it's right cold t'night."

"Peg ain't there no more Ernie. She 'ad to go to the Work'ouse, so I won't be able to stay round her place no more - I'm going to the arches to see if I can sleep there. Is that where you are going an' all?"

"Ain't got nowhere else to go, so, yeah, that's where I'm going."

The two grimy children were pleased they were no longer alone and headed off through the maze of alleys towards the precarious sanctuary of the arches.

On the way, their route took them past the sights, sounds and foul odours of a regular night in the slum. The pubs and beerhouses were filling up as those with a few pence in their pockets looked forward to an evening where they could forget their troubles for a while or, as often happened, end up in more trouble. Many an angry wife would berate a drunken husband who had 'pissed the rent money up the wall', many an eye would be blacked in a brawl and many a woman would live to regret a sordid fumble in the shadows. In contrast, those with not a penny to spare, with strong family bonds to get them through their harsh existence, or with work still to do, shut themselves away in their often overcrowded rooms until morning.

As May and Ernie made their way through the dusk they happened upon what was becoming a common occurrence 'round here' and they wondered why. They had to live there but why others who had no *need* to venture into the slum would choose to do so was very strange indeed to them. These well-dressed toffs would come, their bellies full after the sort of dinner the likes of May and Ernie could only dream of, and be guided as they gingerly picked their way through the fetid streets. They would hold handkerchiefs over their noses and even have the cheek (May thought they had a *bloody* cheek!) to peer through windows at the lowly residents. May had heard about zoos where lovely animals were caged and it seemed to her that being stared at by curious people peering in through your windows must be similar to those poor animals in the zoo.

Sometimes troupes of unkempt children would play to their fine audience - dancing and clowning or even pretending to be 'simple' in the hope that a few coppers may be forthcoming. However, whilst some made pretence of affliction, others, sadly, did not have to. A reaction to this 'entertainment' from the well-dressed voyeurs was one of amusement or disgust or often a combination of both. May had even seen a woman swoon at the sheer horror of what she had witnessed and have to be comforted by her dashing male escort. Yes, sometimes life 'round here' was like being in a zoo. Nevertheless, it was all she knew, and all, she thought, she was ever likely to know.

On they went deeper into the oppressive alleyways. At first May thought she had imagined it but then another flake fell, then another. It was snow. It was only October but incredibly there was snow falling faster and faster and heavier and heavier. This was not the only way that tonight was different. This night would turn out to be very different. This night would be the night that May's life changed forever; when any shred of innocence and naivety was stripped away and cast down onto the foul cobbles. She would experience firsthand just how cruel the world could be; crueller even than the hunger she had grown accustomed to.

Three

At the bottom of Slats Alley, just visible in the weak light and another faint lamp or candle glow coming from some broken windows, May and Ernie saw a figure. He was obviously a toff because of his tall hat and long coat. He was looking up at the buildings, scrutinising them, and then looking down as if at a book. He had not seen them at this point but as he turned towards them they caught his eye. In the background, maybe just around another corner, May and Ernie could hear a horse neighing. Possibly the horse that would pull the carriage to take him back to somewhere posher; somewhere that was warmer; somewhere that was cleaner. Somewhere that was definitely not 'round here.'

"He might 'ave something for us May. He might give us a few coppers. He ain't 'ard up is he. Dunno what he's doing round 'ere."

"Leave 'im Ernie. I don't like the looks of 'im. An' my mum told me never to trust a toff an 'e's a toff right enough he is."

"Nah, 'e'll give us something 'e will."

And so Ernie hurried, as best he could, towards The Man. "'ere mister, you got a couple of coppers you could spare us? We ain't got nowhere to sleep an' it's right freezing – you could 'elp us, mister, find somewhere warmer like."

But no help would come from this wealthy interloper to their world.

"Be off with you, you filthy little wretch. If you want money you must work for it as all decent honest people should."

"I do when I can mister but I ain't bin well see. I have a right bad cough. All I want is a few coppers. That's nothing to a fine gent like what you are".

The Man turned to head towards the direction of the horse neighing. There was no one else around; just The Man, Ernie and May. No one other than May saw what happened next and May would not forget it.

Ernie followed The Man, reached out and touched his coat. May called to him to leave The Man alone but again Ernie pleaded.

"Please mister I ain't hurting you. Just a few coppers that's all."

"I said leave me alone you disgusting creature. You are after my wallet. I know about all the common thieves around here."

"I ain't after your wallet mister, I just..."

"Let go of my coat! Your filth will surely contaminate me...let go."

"Please mister..."

Ernie's words were cut short as The Man raised his cane and brought it swiftly down catching the weak boy on the side of his head. He fell to the ground reaching up for help as blood ran down his face.

"Stop it mister. Stop it. You'll kill 'im, 'e's my friend, leave 'im alone!"

May flung herself towards The Man but there was nothing she could do; a small girl and a frail boy against a well-fed adult with a large stick. A stick topped with a shiny silver knob. A stick that was designed and made especially for The Man and cost him a fortune; a fortune to May and Ernie but to him not so – just a trifle.

He rained another blow down on Ernie as he cried for help and tried to stand but none came and the alley remained eerily silent as the snow quietly continued to fall.

Ernie did not move any more. May felt frozen with shock and fear hardly noticing the numbing cold. Briefly, her eyes and those of the cowardly attacker met. May was out of his reach and as she backed away she called,

"I seen you mister, I seen you and I'll know you."

To go to Ernie would only mean she suffered a similar fate so she could do nothing but escape into the warren of passageways and get herself quickly to safety.

"And I've seen *you* girl. I will remember you." The Man's voice was cold, completely devoid of emotion. And yet he had just murdered a helpless boy.

With barely a glance at the prone body of poor Ernie, which was already beginning to be obscured and unrecognisable under the increasingly heavy snow, The Man disappeared rapidly towards the sound of neighing horses.

May ran, slipping and sliding through the snow. It hit her face mixing with the tears that were streaming down her ashen face. She didn't know where she was going; she wanted her mum. But she had no one, not even Peg, to run to. The Man's face was still in her head; she knew it would always be there. By the time she stopped running the snow had transformed the dank streets.

Instead of blackness, there was a white carpet that, despite what had just happened, made the alleys appear less threatening, less suffocating. The beer houses and pubs spewed forth their customers into the night. Shocked and disorientated by the snow and with no shortage of oaths and cursing, the ragtag crowds lumbered off to whatever shelter they had lined up for the night - be it home or doss house or street. Those who were resigned to a night on the streets were those who would be most affected by the unseasonal weather. And May was one of them. She was still in shock when she finally reached the arches under the viaduct. There were already some children huddled under an old tarpaulin, that whilst it shielded them did not provide any warmth. Nick was there but not his sister. He called to May, intending to make light of the snow until he saw her drawn, disconsolate face. She couldn't tell him, she couldn't say anything. In silence she settled down to try, as best she could, to sleep. Maybe she would dream of happy things and, just for a while, be transported away from her abject misery.

For the rest of the night, the snow fell steadily. It would continue to do so until around noon the following day. The cold had taken many of the destitute by surprise and some would not survive to see the snow melt or turn to black slush as the business of the slum resumed at dawn. Ernie was just another casualty of the unexpected snow. What would be said about his death? Very little, if anything - especially as he would be one of many, no doubt. Perhaps he had fallen, slipped and sustained his head injuries when he did so. His face may have appeared to have been struck but most likely he must have slammed his face into the wall close by where he lay. Only two people knew the truth of what really happened and they would say nothing.

May had seen violence in her short life. Rival gangs, beatings, bloody faces and broken limbs were part of slum life. May had seen death too but not like this. Never like this. She had previously viewed violence as if shielded by an invisible bubble of optimism (although that was not a word she knew) and innocence. It was just the way things were; that was it, it could be worse. That night she found out how much worse it could be and the worst thing that she had ever seen was not caused by the gangs, the drunkards or the muggers – the 'low lifes' as they were described by more genteel folk of London. It was caused by a toff. That unseasonably cold night changed May. The sight of a grown man, and a toff at that, beating to death a frail, helpless boy, trampled anything she had seen as good in her slum – the friendships, the sharing and sometimes even fun and laughter. October 19th 1880 was the snowy night when ten-year-old May determined she would never trust another toff as long as she lived. Her mum was right and she would never - ever.

Four

Just over four miles away the carriage discharged its patron into the entirely different, much more salubrious surroundings of Belgrave Square; it was an area in which the wealthy and influential resided.

During the journey, as he wiped blood and filth from the shiny silver knob of his stick, The Man considered the events that had occurred in the snowy slum. Each year, around this time, he would reluctantly deign to visit his assets and contemplate how best he could maximise his income. Of course he had agents to collect the rents for him and deal with the lowly scum who inevitably were his tenants. Of course a fine gentleman such as he would not, indeed could not, as such a busy important person; sully himself with such unsavoury matters on a regular basis. But the problem was that others could not always be trusted and he needed to see his domain for himself. Surely it was his essential duty to his family and his responsibility to them to ensure no one managed to elude paying what they owed and that what they paid was not too little.

He had arrived later in the day than he had wished or intended hence the reason why he was still there when Ernie and May encountered him. His earlier engagement was important and could not be delayed – not if he wanted to realise his ambition of becoming a

Member of Parliament with ultimately a government post. Other vital business would take up his time for the remainder of the week so he could not postpone his visit until another day. Thus, fate had contrived for his path and that of Ernie and May to cross.

Of course he regretted what had happened to the boy – he was a father himself and one who, whilst believing in a firm hand, (perhaps too firm his wife secretly felt) felt love for his two children - but the child had brought it on himself. The boy had been warned to let go and he was surely about to steal his wallet. Was the boy fatally injured? The Man thought not; he was frail certainly but these street children were much tougher than they looked. They were used to hardship and most were beaten by their parents anyway so were no doubt hardened to it. He probably got up afterwards, wiped away the small smearing of blood from his head and went on his way. Did he really believe this was what happened? In his heart, if indeed one did lurk somewhere in his well-nourished body, he knew the boy was unlikely to have got up nor would ever do so again.

As for the girl, well, he said he would know her - but would he? From what he had seen, the girls of her type and station all looked the same. They were all devoid of colour; they all had the same matted filthy hair; they all had the same grubby faces and lacklustre eyes. Maybe he wouldn't know her if he ever did see her again but felt this was unlikely to happen anyway. Yet, and he couldn't deny this even to himself, there was definitely something about the girl that might make him remember her, something even slightly familiar.

The Man climbed the steps to his imposing house. A house that was, in stark contrast to the blackness of the tenements he owned – purest white. The door was opened by one of his many housemaids who curtseyed, dutifully, took his wet hat and coat then placed his stick with the shiny silver knob, no longer sullied by Ernie's blood, in the elaborate hallstand by the grand entrance. He was then greeted by his gracious and fragrant lady wife who commiserated with him on being out on such a frightful night. The sweet smell of her eau de cologne finally eradicated the foul stench of the slum from his grateful nostrils. After enquiring about his children, who were safely tucked up in beds comprising deep feather mattresses, fluffy pillows and finely stitched counterpanes, he entered the drawing-room to warm himself with a nightcap of fine French brandy. Having downed his brandy in front of the glowing fire that burned in the ornate marble fireplace he retired to his bed that was warmed, not only by his wife but also a highly polished copper warming pan.

The events of the night did not prevent him from slipping into a deep slumber but just before he did so May's face flashed briefly into his mind. At the same time, a world away, his face was also on May's mind but would remain there much longer. When he awoke the following morning, The Man, now fully invigorated from the rigours of the night before by a dreamless sleep, watched from a finely dressed window as their governess took his two children into the white garden. They were wrapped against the cold by cosy hats and coats and stout boots. He smiled as they squealed with laughter as snowballs flew between them. He smiled then turned away to get on with the business of the day knowing they were in safe hands.

Five

After a fitful night's sleep under the arches - managed despite the bone-chilling cold, May stretched and felt severe hunger pangs. She had barely eaten yesterday and the overwhelming desire for food, for a few seconds, blocked out the events of the night before. After these few seconds without those thoughts, thus almost blissful despite the hunger, the horror came flooding back.

Nick woke and, rubbing his eyes, reached to May.

"May, May you alright? You looked right fearful last night you did, like you'd seen an 'orrible phantom or sumfink. What was it May, what 'appened?"

"I'm alive Nick, that's all, so I reckon I'm alright although I'm perishin freezing. There's plenty that ain't...won't be after last night."

Nick thought she was just referring to the snow; May wouldn't tell him about Ernie. She wanted to keep the horror to herself; didn't want anyone else to share the pain she felt. Not only that, but the more who knew, the more likely it was for her whereabouts to filter through to The Man - he might find her. He would surely want her gone so she might be in danger. Thus May kept silent, except to say she was hungry and was heading off to the free school to try and get some bread and porridge for breakfast. Was Nick coming?

She wondered what had happened to Ernie. Had he been found or did his poor little body still lie where it fell? The route to the school did not take in the alley so May had no reason to go through there. She didn't want to go there. What would be the point? Ernie was beyond help. He was in heaven now; maybe he would see her mum there and she would look after him. Maybe he would be much happier in heaven than he was down here. May tried to use this thought to comfort her but it didn't work. Even if heaven did exist and it was good, no one should reach its peace and goodness in such a terrible way. A lump formed in her throat and she fought back the tears she felt for Ernie- not wanting Nick to see her weeping.

The snow was still falling as May, Nick and a few others peered out of the meagre shelter provided by the viaduct arches into the bitter cold. During the night their huddled bodies had generated some warmth but now, with no decent clothing to protect them they felt the full force of the biting wind. May at least had boots but others, including Nick, didn't.

"I ain't going out there May, I can't do it. Me feet'll freeze an' me bleedin toes'l drop off I swear."

"Nah, May we ain't going neither." Some other voices piped up from the shadows. "Perhaps when the snow stops but we ain't goin yet."

May was grateful for her shabby boots although without stockings the protection they actually afforded was minimal and she too felt her toes would fall off, but the hunger was such that she had to try. She silently waved to her friends and tried to smile despite feeling strange and unwell. Then, doubling up the fraying shawl as best she could, she began the trek to the school where, hopefully, hot porridge would be provided. There wasn't much that the likes of her were given free but this school was such a place and she had been there before although she knew little about it. What else she did not know was that her life was about to change and she would not see Nick or his sister again. Well, not for a long time anyway and certainly not in circumstances she could possibly have imagined.

As May traipsed solemnly through the snow the sounds of the business of the slum seemed to become suffocated by it; somehow it was enveloping everything like a silent white shroud. She could see the school and its steps before her but then the buildings faded away to shadows until they disappeared completely. Then May heard a voice. It was a soft, gentle voice; a familiar voice but one she had not heard for a long while. It seemed to be coming from the whiteness in front of her but the source of the voice was not yet visible. Then gradually the figure took shape and called her name.

"May my darling girl, it's your mum. Where have you been my girl? I've been looking for you. Come on Maisie, come home with me. Come with your mum."

"Mum, mum. Is it really you? Have you really come back for your little May? Oh, mum, I missed you ever so much I did. You're too far away mum. I can't reach you."

"Come May, look who else is here with me. Look, it's Ernie; he wants you to come with us. Come on May, come to us and we can be together again. I can look after you like it used to be."

May could not see anymore; the whiteness engulfed her and she closed her eyes while still calling out to, and reaching for, her mum.

Six

"May, May come on May, wake up now, come on. You can wake up now dear."

The voice May heard as she opened her eyes was not her mum's; it was a voice she had never heard before but it was calm, kind. No longer was she in the bitterly cold street but in a place that was the warmest she had been for a long time. She looked briefly at the face that was smiling at her then closed her eyes again and drifted off once more, but this time it was to a different kind of sleep - a much better kind.

The woman looked down at the now peacefully sleeping child. She did not know her but heard the girl utter the name May when she appeared to be calling, in her delirium, to the mother she could see but who was not there. The girl was pale and dirty; her small frame barely protected against the dreadful weather by the grey shift and somewhat shabby shawl. Her feet, when the boots that were close to falling apart were removed, were ingrained with grime except for an area of one foot that looked like an attempt had been recently made to clean it.

The child had no money. All she had, in her pocket, was a crumpled note and a photograph. Judging by the contents of the note the woman deduced that this May was a good child who was utterly alone in the world.

As well as sadness for May, the woman felt pity for the lady, as she surely once had been, who signed the note P. She seemed a decent person also and one who did not deserve to live out her life in the dire conditions of the workhouse.

Syrie Barnardo had seen many such children even before marrying her husband, Thomas, seven years previously. She compared their plight to the comfortable lives of her own cherished children, the most recent of whom, a little girl named Gwendoline, had only been in this world for fifteen months. They had travelled some ten miles from their Village Lodge home today as a direct result of the snow. The many trees of the Village with most of their leaves, although turning brown, still clinging on, were an unusual picture covered as they were by the unexpected snow. The Village girls were delighted by the sight and had nothing to fear from it, giving as it did an almost magical quality to their already sylvan surroundings. This Village was in a place called Barkingside that May had never heard of – never knew existed - but a place that would come to play a major part in her life.

In contrast to the Village, the slum was devoid of trees. The initial whiteness was now replaced by foul black slush as it mingled with the dirt and manure that clogged gutters and coated the cobbles. It appeared even more forbidding than before. The Barnardos knew that such uncommonly wintry weather would mean even more casualties than could usually be expected at this time of year so they would endeavour to rescue as many of the poor freezing creatures as they could. To encounter the thin child who collapsed in the street just outside the school confirmed they were right to make the journey from Barkingside that day.

In May, Syrie saw a candidate surely deserving of salvation from her pitiful plight. Even her name resounded with Syrie as just this year a new cottage home at the Village opened and duly named 'May'. Surely this dreadful day could be redeemed by little May's liberation from the hopelessness of the slum, the dangers of its streets and its disgusting lodging houses. All of these presented dangers to a young girl that would be removed by her deliverance into the cottage that already bore her name.

After sleeping for several hours, May opened her eyes again. This time she awoke properly and, as before when she wakened under the viaduct arches, the rumbling of her empty stomach was the first and most urgent thing she thought of. There had been an attempt to offer her hot broth when she was taken in, by both cup and by spoon, but she was in no condition to take it. Now she pushed herself up on the mattress; the mattress that was, despite its thinness, the softest thing she had ever slept on. She looked around the room - small but clean, with windows that were not dirty or broken and filled with rags. She wondered if she was dead and in heaven. Would she be an angel? Would she see her mum soon?

"I can't be dead though, can I?" she muttered to herself. "Angels don't get bellies rumbling, angels don't 'ave to sleep I don't think. No, I ain't dead; I'm alive and blimmin 'ungry that's what I am..."

Her thoughts were interrupted as just outside the open door May heard ladies' voices.

"Our little urchin should wake now to eat. Fetch her some soup Annie and then we must bathe her before replacing those filthy rags with some more fitting attire."

"Yes ma'am, shall I bring her cake as well?"

"Indeed, I doubt the poor child has eaten cake for some time. I only fear her empty stomach will be unable to cope with such sudden sustenance. But we must risk this surely and pray she will not be overwhelmed."

"Where am I, at the school?" puzzled May. She remembered she was heading to the school, hoping for porridge so this place would most likely be there but a room she had not seen before. The strange encounter with her mother had been erased from her memory and the last thing she recalled was waving goodbye to Nick and the others at the viaduct.

"Hello child." said the owner of the younger of the two voices she had heard. "You are indeed at our school. We have rooms for children in distress and there are some others here who were caught out by the unseasonal weather. How are you feeling now? Better I hope and pray better still when you have eaten the soup and cake that our Annie is bringing for you."

"I'm alright missus but right 'ungry though. I ain't got no money so I can't pay you nothing."

May tried to push herself up to get off the bed but was gently eased back down.

"There is no need for payment dear. You will be fed, bathed and clothed then we will see what is to be done with you."

"I likes the sound of being fed missus but I ain't never been bathed by anyone but my mother an' I think that was only a couple of times right proper, an' the water wasn't nice an' warm then anyway, so I don't feel right comfortable about that bathing business I don't."

Before she had the chance to debate the matter further Annie arrived with the soup and cake. The steaming hot soup smelt wonderful and May sniffed in the aroma as deeply as she could. The cake, dark with currants, and smelling of spices, made her mouth water. The thought of bathing was forgotten as she tucked, with great relish, into the food. She even felt slightly guilty because this soup was far better than anything Peg had made for her.

"Slow down child, you will surely choke if you continue to gollop the food down so quickly."

May took no notice of Annie who, with her hands on her hips, shook her head but couldn't help smiling as colour trickled back into the child's wan face.

By the evening May had been suitably fed and even, despite her initial protestations, been bathed and dressed in the cleanest clothes she could ever remember. Her hair was washed, trimmed and brushed after the crawling lice and nits were duly removed.

As she looked in a mirror – the first unbroken one she had seen in a long time since even Peg's mirror had a crack in it – a different child stared back at her. 'Would The Man who cruelly murdered poor Ernie know me now?' She wondered. She thought he most likely wouldn't; that he could pass her in the street and not give her even a glance of familiarity and she was glad. Even though he may not know her, she would certainly know him.

Annie broke her reverie.

"Come young May, the Doctor wishes to see you now."

"I'm alright now missus. I don't need a Doctor. I was wondrin where my clothes have gone."

"The Doctor sees all the girls before they are taken from the squalid streets to the Village Home. He will listen to your story and tell you about the new life that awaits you – if you so desire it."

"What new life missus? An' who's this Doctor with a Village 'ome? I don't know no Village 'ome. I ain't got nothing' except my clothes – my shawl 'specially-and my picture. Where are they anyway?"

"Your clothes were beyond repair child. Your picture and the note from your friend are safe and will be returned to you. Now come along. You have already met Mrs Barnardo now you shall meet the Doctor."

"I want my own shawl missus. It might be not as grand as what the likes of you 'ave but my friend Peg gave me that; she got it special for me. It's all I got that's been given just to me an' I ain't gonna let no one – not even no Doctor – take it off me."

May was grateful for the food and the rest and the bath – the first proper one she had ever had – but was not going to have the only possession of value she had taken from her and discarded. That faded shawl was her link to Peg and she would tell this Doctor that she wanted it back!

"I'll see this Doctor an' I'll tell him so, I will."

Annie tried to take May's arm to lead her to the Doctor's office but May shrugged her away and stomped along, arms folded. Leaving the room May found that she was not alone. In the area outside this Doctor's office were several other girls of mixed size and age. Some were silent; some were sobbing; some were even cursing until given a withering glare by Annie. All looked hungry and of low fortune.

May looked for anyone she might recognise but did not see anyone familiar and caught the eye of a girl who looked a bit older and, she thought, right tough – right surly.

"Wot you looking at you cow?"

"I dunno what I'm looking at cos the label's come off." retorted May swiftly.

The girl went to move forward threateningly towards May but was prevented from doing so and was quickly ushered into the office.

She regarded this Doctor with curiosity. He appeared quite short but this was hard to tell as he sat behind a desk. He had spectacles, long side-whiskers, was well dressed and she wasn't quite sure if he was a toff. Were Doctors toffs? She didn't really know, as she had never encountered a proper Doctor before.

"Hello child, May isn't it? What is your surname child, your last name? Do you know it?"

"Course I know me blimmin name. I ain't feeble-minded mister. It's 'Arris."

"Do you mean Harris, May?"

"Yeah that's wot I said – 'Arris."

Not wishing to upset May further and being familiar with the manner of speech used by the east end slum dwellers, the Doctor indicated a chair to May before he continued.

"Sit down young May and let me find out more about you. My wife tells me you collapsed outside our school. Indeed the weather is truly awful for so early in the season but I trust you are feeling rather better now – having eaten."

"I'm much better now mister but I want my shawl back I do. It may not be much to you 'ere but it's mine and I want it back before I tell you anythin."

May sat in silence, arms folded. Her feet couldn't quite reach the floor and she swung her legs from side to side.

Doctor Barnardo summoned Annie and requested that the shawl be retrieved, if it was possible, and shown to May before removal for laundering rather than being discarded.

Still May sat in silence but she was thinking. Maybe this Doctor person could be trusted. Maybe she would listen to and talk to him. Maybe she would but she wanted to see the shawl first so still she sat in silence as he spoke.

"Will you, May, come to my Village Home in Barkingside where you will have nourishing food, a comfortable bed, be taught a domestic trade, learn to read and write and of course, follow the ways of our lord Jesus? You will have a 'Mother' to look after your physical and spiritual needs and you will become one of my 'Little Daughters'. We have a new cottage called May...." May looked up in surprise at this – hearing a cottage had her name. "...yes truly, we have a cottage named as you are. You could live there safely and happily away from the perils you face on the streets."

She wasn't going to speak but it was the mention of 'Mother' that changed her mind.

"I 'ad me mother. She was the best mum anyone could ever 'ave and I ain't going to call no one else mother mister. And I never 'ad no father so I can manage without one now but I like the sound of a comfortable bed and reading and writing..."

Just then the door opened and Annie stood with an arm outstretched. She was holding May's shawl by an edge between her thumb and forefinger.

"That's it!" shouted May. "That's the shawl Peg gave me."

Doctor Barnardo regarded the faded, frayed shawl and the child's reaction to it. The relief on her face; the emotion that such a lowly article could provoke revealed him more about the life she had led than she could ever tell him.

As May wrapped the grubby shawl around her clean shoulders she looked again, thoughtfully, at the Doctor.

"Are you a toff Mister Doctor?"

"Do I look like a toff?"

"Well, I don't rightly know. You talks posh like and you look right smart but well... are you one?"

"I don't think so child. Does it matter to you? I know many good gentlemen you would consider toffs but no, I do not regard myself as one. Why does it matter to you?"

"It do matter Mister... Doctor but I ain't, I can't, tell you why."

May sat again in silence. Still she wondered – what was this Doctor *really* like? Could she – should she – trust him? But... and this was what swung it for her-'The Man' wouldn't know where she had gone.

The Doctor watched her and waited.

"All right mister Doctor, I'm gonna come. Where is it – this Barkingside?"

Thomas Barnardo smiled.

Seven

"I ain't having it done! You can't make me. I've never had a picture and I'm not gonna have one done now. And why 'ave I gotta put rotten clothes on that ain't my own? You gave me right nice togs - all clean togs and I'm clean now I am. I don't wanna take 'em off for no blimmin photo."

May, like the other street girls, including the surly one, was required to have a picture taken to record, the Doctor said, their plight before being transformed into one of his 'Little Daughters'. Some were clad as they arrived but May, as she had been ill, had already been cleaned up. She had agreed to go to this Village Home in a place called Barkingside she had never heard of but was not sure, not very happy, with what would happen when she got there. What were these pictures for? Would they be shown somewhere where The Man might see them? Perhaps he would find her.

"I ain't 'aving it done. You can't make me and if you try I'm clearing off I am."

Some of the other girls, hearing May shouting, decided they wouldn't have their pictures taken either. The surly one, whose name May discovered was Lottie, looked impressed at May's stand. Maybe this skinny kid, bearing in mind they were all skinny, could be someone she could get on with. Perhaps even be a friend and friends were something Lottie had never really had. Her tough exterior was a screen, a barrier because she was fearful of letting anyone get too close. Lottie, unlike May, had never had even the briefest of times with love and with care. She wore her bravado as a defensive cloak.

The group was placated with the promise of some extra supper and all except May, who remained steadfast in her defiance, eventually filed in front of the photographer to be captured, in their grime, forever. They were captured not only to provide a record but also to induce sympathy and pity to elicit funding, which was always perilously short, from those touched by the children's plight. The cards produced from the photographs would indeed find their way to the home of someone who was connected to The Man. May's instinct, as usual, had proved right although she would not discover this for some time.

May, along with the others similar to her, entered the gates of the Village with some trepidation. What they found might as well have been another country: a country that could only previously have been imagined for the likes of May. It was a country that for many would prove to be their salvation. She had often thought of the countryside – dreamed of it even when confined in the squalor that was the Nichol. Now she was there – really there. There were trees but their leaves were dying and blowing down like small pieces of brown paper. The only trees she had seen in this number, so many, was that summer day in the park with her mum. She imagined trees were always like that. Always green and bright and alive and somehow friendly – these trees were different and whilst they scared her they fascinated as well. They were dead things that towered above her as the tenements had towered above her but there the similarity ended.

Where the recent snow had melted, the ground was sodden and the grass looked very different from the bright green field they had picnicked so happily on, but it was better than cobbles caked in mud and horse dung – much better. Any apprehension May had about living in this strange, unknown place were pushed aside in her wonderment and any fears, any doubts, would not be acknowledged. She had impressed the tough girl that was Lottie and was not going to let her confident, defiant mask slip. Not for a second.

"Cor bleedin 'ell!" exclaimed Lottie upon seeing the Village Green, which, even despite the mud, was a picture compared to the Nichol. The neat cottages were arranged around it and prompted Lottie to say, "I ain't never seen nuffink like this 'ave you May?"

"No, never and I never thought that I would. Is this a real place? Is this where we're gonna live?"

"It looks like it. I wonder if we ever get out. Will we be here forever?"

"Don't know. I don't want to be 'ere forever. I want to go on a big ship and see the world I do."

May considered the streets that had been her home. She felt guilty because she hadn't thought about Ernie. She had thought about The Man and how, here, she felt safe – shielded from him finding her. As for Ernie, for a short time, she had forgotten him. But only for a short time. His poor little face, covered in snow was soon back on her mind. She vowed to herself that whatever happened she would hold his memory in her mind forever. His face and that of the wicked Man.

"Where's my house – the one named like me?"

"You've got a house named like you 'ave you?"

"Yeah, I have. That Doctor told me. I'm gonna live in a house called like me."

Lottie looked impressed.

"Hope I can live there wiv you."

"Yeah, we're mates now."

"Yeah, we're mates right enough."

The two girls took each other's hand and filed forward ready to enter their new home.

In the reception hall the lady who had accompanied them from Stepney organised the new arrivals, allocating them to the cottage, which, from then on, they would call home. From now... until when? They didn't know; maybe given where they came from they didn't care.

May scanned the faces of the 'Mothers' waiting to receive their new charges. Some were young; some were older. Some looked kind some looked not so kind and others, to May, looked very scary. May hoped she and Lottie wouldn't get a scary looking one, but they did.

Their new 'Mother' eyed her new charges quizzically. Hetty Casey had been at Mossford Village for three years now. She had answered an advertisement asking for 'Good Christian Ladies' with education but no commitments that would affect their ability to dedicate themselves to ensuring the girls in their charge were brought up in the godly manner decreed by the Doctor. Hetty had never married and it was also a requisite that the House Mothers be spinsters. She had the chance to marry once and would have done so as her clerical gentleman friend was kind and appealing but this was not to be, as she was the only one who could care for her infirm mother. She had siblings. She had a sister but Laura had troubles of her own – a drunken husband – to contend with, whilst her older brother had long since emigrated to Canada.

Upon her mother's death, with her prospective husband now married to another and with no source of income or other avenues to follow, the park-like surroundings and clean air of Mossford Village were a godsend. Doctor Barnardo had transformed the area by instigating drainage systems and, by building a well that ran very deep, ensured his girls drank only clean, safe water. The memory of the last terrible cholera epidemic in East London some fourteen years before was still vivid in Hetty's mind. Indeed her family had not been untouched by it as her father had succumbed relatively early.

There was no salary paid to the Mothers but a small amount was paid yearly to those with no independent means, for them to clothe themselves. Hetty had no need for any other luxuries and her life, since entering the sheltered and feminine world of the Village, with no male-induced friction to complicate matters, was settled and for the most part, calm. It was a pity she was not really fond of children but this was a minor drawback and one that she had been, by and large, able to overcome. Her patience could sometimes wear thin and her manner be brusque but her heart was in the right place and the girls in her charge trusted her.

It wasn't that she didn't care – she did but her demanding mother had exhausted all her empathy, all her softness, and there was not much left. To interact too much with the girls was difficult but she couldn't show this to the Doctor. He also couldn't know about her condition – not yet anyway. It would get worse; she could feel it getting worse but the Village was her life now and so the girls to whom she was Mother and the Doctor could not know. Sometimes the pain was too much and she had to shut herself away. The girls thought she was being awkward. There was a time when one of the girls had asked for a bar of soap and instead of giving it to her personally, she left it on the hall table. 'Does she not want to talk to me? Have I done something wrong?' thought the girl.

The truth was that Hetty was often in pain and did not want the girls to see her that way; she had put the soap on the table while the girls were asleep and would not see her suffer. May didn't know what to make of Hetty. She wanted someone to trust; someone she felt cared about her. Someone like her mum, or someone, even, like Peg.

The Village was a strange place to May. She was not used to anything regular and ordered as it happened at May Cottage. In her previous lives – those with her mum and on the streets, she got through each day the best she could. Of course, with mum, there was some order, some constancy, but on the streets time had no meaning as the only things that ruled her life were what to eat and where to sleep when darkness fell. There was then, a kind of freedom but a different kind to that of the Village. There she was free from hunger, pain and fear – contrasting with the freedom to go wherever she was physically able that she had on the streets.

So which freedom was better for May? She missed her friends (and wondered what they were doing now) she even missed some of the excitement of pinching stuff and then running away. What she didn't miss was the grime that seemed to coat everything everywhere, the foul odours, the bone-chilling cold and the dark dreariness. She didn't miss the pain that accompanied the fearsome growling as her stomach cried out for food. A full belly was something she had longed for; something that was rare even when her mum was alive. Now her belly was full her thoughts could turn to other things. Things like learning – things like her future. The Village was better for now certainly and May was happy to be there, but she had ideas about her future and the Village, however safe and secure it seemed, did not figure long term. Young May was starting to grow in many ways.

The Mother was firm and perhaps, May thought, in her way she was kind but it was a cold manner of kindness, a kindness that did not come from shared experiences, of family bonds or was borne from genuine caring or even love. Mum was kind to everyone but especially to her because she loved her. Peg was kind to others as well but especially to her because...because... why? Could it be because she perhaps actually loved her? Not in the same way as her mum had – that could never be – but it was something more than just kindness. May had never thought of this before. She thought Peg would be a good mum. Did she ever have any children? What was she doing now in the Workhouse?

In that place, that was as far removed from the Village as the world inhabited by The Man, Peg often thought of May also. Of course, she did not know what had happened; did not know how May's life had changed, did not know about the horrible crime she had witnessed. Peg, stripped of any dignity by the numbing routine of the Workhouse, survived *physically* on the meagre rations served up with regular monotony but *mentally* on her memories. Her memories before her descent into poverty in the Nichol and those of happier times even there when a little street girl called May cheered her.

The first couple of months at the Village sped by for May. The days were full, not always fun, but full as everything was meticulously planned. She came to understand Mother Hetty and the other girls with whom she lived much better. She wondered why Mother was sometimes short with her charges and sometimes distant. Her face often looked pinched and strained. Was there something wrong? Did the Doctor know?

May had never been so clean or seen such cleanliness. The smell she liked best was that that wafted from the laundry. She never knew that a combination of hot water and soap and steam and warmth could be so all-enveloping and comforting. She breathed in the aroma from the laundry and it evoked everything that was clean – everything that was pure. Her mum had said she was pure so the laundry brought to mind her mum. The dirt, the stench and the often sordid events that were everyday life in the Nichol were not only banished from her nostrils but also, astonishingly, from her consciousness. The odour of the laundry was wonderful to May - like a conquering army of cleanliness sweeping away all the filth of the world in which she used to dwell. However, there was one thing it could not sweep away and she would never wish it so. That one thing was the poor, broken body of little Ernie gently and quietly being blanketed by the delicate snowflakes.

Eight

May's relationship with Lottie became closer and, although it had only been a short time, they grew to be firm friends. Often when the lamps were out and the other girls were sleeping they would quietly talk about their futures – and their pasts.

"I didn't like the look of you at first," volunteered Lottie. "I thought you looked stroppy like an' 'ard. That's wot I is so I thought we would fight for who would be top dog 'ere."

"Yeah and I thought you were rough cos you went for me till that Annie stopped you."

"Funny now ain't it cos we get on right well don't we? I ain't never really 'ad a proper friend before. I didn't 'ave a mum like you. Your mum sounds right smashing."

"Yeah, she was right smashing." May smiled as she thought of her mum.

"Ain't never 'ad no dad neither but nor did you did you May?"

"No, I ain't never 'ad one and I don't care neither cos dads ain't always that great anyway."

"You 'ad lots of friends though didn't you May? You had some good friends didn't you?"

"Yeah, yeah I did." Her face softened when she thought of Peg. "I did 'ave a right good friend – a lady she was. Her name was Peg. Look, I have a picture she left for me. It's when she was young. Right lovely ain't she? Course, that was a long time ago."

"Cor, yeah, I ain't ever seen a picture like that before."

"She talked proper and all. Like how I'm gonna learn how to talk one day. She said 'house' not 'ouse like wot we do."

May made a point of pronouncing the 'h' sound.

They laughed as May attempted to speak 'posh', but quietly so as not to disturb the other girls and wake Hetty who this evening really looked like she needed to sleep,

"What 'appened to 'er May? What 'appened to your Peg?"

"She couldn't pay her rent no more so now she's in the Work'ouse. I ain't heard nothing about her but it ain't gonna be much fun with Christmas coming up in that 'orrible place."

"Nah," agreed Lottie, shaking her head. "What about your other friends? What they doin?"

May had not told Lottie what had happened to Ernie and now seemed like a good time.

"I have some friends I'd kip down with under the arches sometimes. I suppose they're still gettin on as best they can but, but there was... Ernie..."

"Ernie?" asked Lottie. "What 'appened to Ernie? I think I've 'eard you mutter that name in your sleep sometimes an' I wondered who he was but thought you'd tell me when you's ready."

May looked at Lottie and appreciated her sensitivity, although that was not a word that she knew.

"Yeah, I'll tell you about poor Ernie an' what 'appened to 'im."

As May was about to relate her tale one of the smaller girls began to cry loudly. Hetty awoke and, looking pale, came in to see what was happening. The conversation between May and Lottie was cut short and they pretended the crying had just wakened them. Hetty attended to the girl who had a bad dream and then returned to her own room to try to sleep despite the pain she seemed to be feeling more and more often. May and Lottie, now past talking, floated off to sleep themselves. Ernie's story would have to wait until another day.

November had drifted, unnoticed by May, into December as Christmas at the Village drew near. This would be May's first Christmas without her mum. Mum had tried to make Christmas special and Uncle George had, for their last Christmas together, managed to acquire a goose – something May had never had before and found quite delicious. From where he had acquired it May did not know and her mum had certainly not asked. All May knew was that it was good. Carol singers were around in the Nichol attempting to bring some cheer to the place and most

63

of the inhabitants seemed to be in a better mood than usual – even if only for one day.

Mossford Village was getting ready for Christmas but Hetty was getting steadily worse. One morning, just two weeks before Christmas, the girls were surprised, as they got up to begin the usual business of the day, to see the Doctor and his wife hurrying through the cottage towards Hetty's room.

"What's happening Doctor, is something wrong?" asked one of the girls.

May and Lottie were getting the smaller girls ready and just caught his reply.

"My dear little daughters, I fear your dear Mother is very unwell and we have been summoned by Angela to attend to her."

Angela was the oldest girl in the cottage and it appeared she had discovered Hetty out of bed and slumped on the floor when she went to take her tea. She had hurriedly run to the Doctor's house then he and Syrie Barnardo had rushed quickly to May cottage.

The girls stood in silence and they waited for news. Then some of the younger ones began to fidget and ask;

"Wassamatter wiv 'er?"

"Is she dead?"

"Who will look after us?"

"Will we still get breakfast?"

The Doctor and Syrie emerged from Hetty's room looking grim-faced.

"I am afraid to tell you, my Little Daughters, that your dear Mother has left this world and will be residing in heaven in the arms of our good lord for Christmas."

There were gasps and some sobbing whereas others appeared unmoved

"It appears to me now that Miss Casey had been ill for some time but, being a strong Christian lady, she continued to undertake her duties until she could do so no more. You will all be excused from your regular tasks today as we make arrangements for Miss Casey. I am sure you will all join my wife and me in praying for her soul and thanking her for the commitment and care she has shown to you all."

Angela had been in Hetty's care since they had both arrived at the Village and was the most upset; May gently put her arm around Angela to comfort her.

"I lost my mother an' all. I know she weren't your real mother but the closest to I reckon so I know what you're feeling I do."

Angela turned to May and smiled weakly.

The next few days were hard at the Village and it was not just because of the heavy snow and severe frost. Without a Mother of its own, May Cottage's routine was disrupted. Mrs Barnardo spent more time there as well as other Mothers sharing their time and older girls from other cottages attending. This, however, was a situation that could not continue especially with Christmas advancing ever nearer. The Barnardos needed to appoint another mother- and quickly – but the usual procedure to do this could be a lengthy one as they were careful that the candidates chosen were of the necessary calibre.

"May," Lottie said, a few days after Hetty's death, "about another Mother. Wot about your friend Peg? She sounds she'd be right good as a Mother."

May looked at Lottie wide-eyed. She was right. She was very right! Peg would be a wonderful Mother and she could not believe she had not thought of it herself.

"Lottie you're right. I need to speak to the Doctor. I need to tell 'im to get Peg. I'm goin now, 'is wife's here so I'll see 'er first. You coming?"

"Yeah, I'm coming. Let's go an' get your Peg."

Nine

Mrs Barnardo was in Hetty's old quarters sorting through things when May and Lottie knocked at the door.

"Hello my young ladies and what can I do for you?" Lottie pushed May forward."Please do not be scared May. I know you are not afraid of speaking your mind."

Syrie remembered May from the first encounter and her obstinate refusal to be photographed.

"Well missus, it's like we know you need to find a new Mother quick like and well, I know someone who'd be right good. It was 'er who gave me the shawl. She's kind and clever an' she speaks posh an' all. You'd like 'er missus, both you an' the Doctor. I know you'd like 'er."

"May you know we have very high expectations of our Mothers here. What do you know of this lady and where we might find her – if indeed my husband judges her to be suitable enough to warrant consideration?"

"I still got my picture of 'er 'ere. Always got that."

May reached into her smock pocket for the picture she carried all the time. She had no pictures of her mum to hold on to so this was the next best thing.

"It's an old one but you can see what she was like."

Syrie took the picture and looked carefully at it. She had seen it before when May was brought in but May was not aware of this.

"This lady is very pretty May and I think she has a kind face. Do you know where she is child?"

"Well missus I don't rightly know but I do know she 'ad to go the Work 'ouse as she couldn't pay 'er rent no more. I ain't 'eard nothing' about 'er since afore I came 'ere. I still got the note she left me an' all." May again reached into her pocket, this time taking out the crumpled note and passed it to Syrie, "I kept this right through the time I was brought in. They saved it an' the picture for me when my dirty old clothes were took away. 'Cept my shawl o'course – they weren't chucking that. I still got that, missus. It's in the box under my bed."

Syrie also remembered the commotion when May was at the school and Annie had tried to take the shawl away from her. She smiled and read again the creased, grubby note, which she found, as upon first reading, moving.

"With your permission, May, I will take this to show to my husband. If he thinks the same as I do, and I am pleased to say that he often does, that this lady sounds the sort of person we would welcome into our family then I will come to see you this evening. I promise you will have the note, which is obviously precious to you, returned."

"Thank you, Missus. I know we can find 'er. I, I trust the Doctor I do, an' I trust you an' all.

Syrie squeezed May's hand and left, wondering what her husband would decide.

Thomas Barnardo paced thoughtfully around his drawing-room in Mossford Lodge on the other side of the Village. He was looking down and contemplating the wrinkled note that Syrie had passed to him. It was not something he had seen before. Finally, he spoke.

"I do not think we can do this Syrie. Of course I respect and value your opinions for without your support and strength I could not maintain this world we have created, but we have no references; no way of knowing whether this lady - kind and as caring as she appears - would meet our standards. The spiritual welfare of our charges is too important for us to be lax in our vigilance. I don't..."

Syrie cut her husband off.

"My dear, I know your conscientious nature. I know what a stickler you are for following careful procedures and I love you for it but time is short. Christmas will be upon us with much haste and to manage to provide the occasion our children deserve we desperately need more help. I fear for your own health if you work even harder than you regularly do."

Syrie paused and watched as her husband's thoughts became visible on his face - as they often did. She could see conflict between what he thought he should do and what needed to be done. After a silence during which he continued to pace, he stopped, looked at Syrie and spoke.

"You are right, of course. We owe it to our charges that their wellbeing is upheld and that they are properly supervised. I would not wish any child in my care to lack that which I could provide for our dear children. I will fetch young May tomorrow and we will endeavour to locate this apparently good lady, liberate her from whichever workhouse she dwells in and fetch her to reside among us – if she does indeed meet our standards."

Syrie smiled and Thomas slumped down in his chair seemingly still somewhat burdened by whether or not he had made the right decision.

From a window in May cottage May watched for the Doctor or his wife to return with her note and the answer she had hoped for.

"I'll get you Peg. They're good people they are. I dunno if he is a proper toff – ain't made my mind up yet but he's a good bloke right enough an' 'is wife an' all. It was them what found me an' I reckon I might 'ave been a goner if they 'adn't. I reckon they'll come for you an' all." May whispered this to herself as she looked out of the window and was pleased to see Syrie hurrying across the frosted green from Mossford Lodge towards the cottage. "Lottie," called May "I think he's said yes, it looks like I'm going. I'm going to get Peg."

Ten

It had been two months and two days since Peg had arrived unceremoniously at the Bethnal Green Workhouse on Waterloo Road. It was a place she had hoped never to see, but now a place she believed she would never leave – except upon her death. She would then spend eternity in a pauper's grave.

She had arrived with nothing other than the clothes she stood up in having wrapped herself up as well she could to save carrying the small amount of clothing she had and also as protection against the cold. Around her neck was the silver cross she had worn for many years - the only thing of any worth she possessed. There had been nothing else in the room that held any value for her other than the cross and the photograph. The cross she had close to her heart and the photograph, she hoped, would find its way to May.

Upon her admission, Peg had been assigned to sewing and mending duties. The bedding, clothing, sacking and everything else that could be worked with a needle had seen better days – much better - and their life was extended (indefinitely?) by the likes of Peg. She had given her occupation, or rather her former occupation, as that of a seamstress. Whilst she did indeed perform some sewing tasks as well as sorting rags and the like to earn whatever meagre income she could, she chose not to reveal to the Workhouse Master the role in society she held before her demise. It had been her intention, at some point, to reveal her story to young May; perhaps whilst they were sharing broth on an occasion when May was staying in her room as an alternative to another night on the street. She was not aware that May also had a story she would want to share; a story that, as yet, she had not shared with anyone.

When the inevitable knock upon the door came she had been ready. The two agents who delivered that knock were in no mood for compassion or sympathy. Their positions were dependent on them ensuring that their master's wishes were carried out to the letter - that all tenants were up to date with their rent. Those who dared to default, whether by tardiness or poverty, were given short shrift and sent packing immediately - regardless of their state of health or what dubious fate might befall them.

That day their vigilance was even more vital since the regular visit to the Nichol of their wealthy employer was due. The discovery of any discrepancies or shortfalls would certainly be punished by instant dismissal, probably precipitating their own rapid descent into destitution. Thus, Peg was speedily and discourteously removed.

"Come on you old baggage. We've got others here that can pay the fair rent that our benevolent master has set so you have got to move on to whatever hovel you can."

"It'll be the workhouse for this one by the looks of her."

Peg stood straight and proud as the men attempted to manhandle her to the rickety stairs to make her final exit from the building that had been her home, if it is possible to call such a place home, for longer than she cared to remember. On the way down she encountered a hassled looking woman clutching a baby, a surly man who was some sort of manual worker judging by his clothing and a rowdy child who was grumbling as he was dragged up the stairs by, it was assumed by Peg, his father.

The room, Peg thought, would by extremely cramped for a family and, she had no doubt, would cost them more than she had paid. Peg had, the night before, penned a note she wished young May to see so she would understand her sudden disappearance. As she met the woman on the stairs she held out the note.

"Mistress, I was the previous occupant of the room you are about to enter and that you will, for however long you are allowed, call... home." The woman looked at Peg quizzically and at the note she proffered. "I wonder would you take this? There is a child, a small girl, who may – no will, I'm sure – come seeking me. Please give this to her for me. I have no one else and, I think, nor has she."

"Give it here then and I'll give it to 'er if she comes. Course, if I remember like."

The woman turned back to hurry up the stairs as Peg went down. After a couple more steps Peg paused, reached into her pocket and drew out the photograph. Originally she intended to keep it but knowing how all individuality, all identity, was stripped from the workhouse inmates upon admission she suddenly decided she would rather pass it on to May so she would remember her. She firmly believed that, somehow, May would find a better life. Why she believed this or how she thought it would come about she did not know. There was simply something about May that, to Peg, made it a certainty - despite the dire surroundings in which the residents of the Nichol existed.

"Mistress," she called to the woman, who looked back somewhat annoyed now.

"What now? I've got a right bleedin load on me plate right now so I have." She indicated towards the morose boy, who was fiddling with a loose piece of the banister, and gave him a slap.

"Would you take this also? Will you give this to May as well?"

The woman almost snatched it, looking peeved.

"Is that all?"

"Yes, and I am very sorry to have delayed you. Thank you."

The woman nodded and wearily carried on upstairs.

Peg left the tenement block in Half Nichol Street and did not look back as it held few happy memories for her. As she made her way towards the infamous Bethnal Green Workhouse on Waterloo Road she knew this would be her last place of residence. She knew this. She was certain of this - but she was wrong.

If her time in the Nichol had run to another few nights she would not have missed May. Her eviction would, of course, still have occurred but for that one fateful night May would not have been reduced to seeking shelter on the streets and therefore everything else that happened subsequently would never have taken place. Well, not for May anyway.

Who was to say whether Ernie would have taken the same route had he been alone? Who was to say whether he would have been bold enough to approach The Man had he been alone? Who was to say whether his short life would not have ended the same way? No one *could* say but what was certain was that if everything had still occurred but without May's presence, the brutal manner of Ernie's death would have remained anonymous - unknown to all except his cowardly killer.

Eleven

May went to bed that night knowing that in the morning she would accompany Dr Barnardo to the Workhouse to rescue Peg from the monotonous drudgery of the awful place. Presumably, she would have entered the establishment closest to the vicinity of the Nichol so it was to Bethnal Green they would travel. May slept soundly. The Doctor, however, did not sleep so soundly and contentedly as she. He still nursed some considerable doubts as to the wisdom of his mission.

Christmas was now only a few days away but at Bethnal Green Workhouse there were no signs yet of festive good cheer. There would be though, by the day itself, festive decorations of holly and paper chains to at least allude to good cheer amidst the bleak squalor. There would be increased rations that were an improvement (although this would not be difficult) on the usual fare with considerably better quality beef and seasonal plum pudding. There would be beer to wash down this uncommon feast and there would be visits from the great and good, the Guardians, to spread what they considered to *be* good cheer and raise the spirits of the residents.

Having discharged this duty they would quickly scurry back to their residences, where they would spend the remainder of the day (after practically fumigating themselves to dispel any 'visitors' they may have acquired) eating and drinking in considerably more appealing surroundings, until they were compelled reluctantly, by their standing, to return. Their obligation would have been fulfilled and, for many of them - perhaps most - the plight of the residents of the workhouse would be forgotten until their next scheduled visit.

There was an irony here. Some of the Bethnal Green Guardians were also landlords of the squalid slums and some were even landlords of tenements that had recently acquired new, more lucrative, tenants. To acquire new tenants, of course, others had first to be ejected. It was, therefore, the case that some of the unfortunate residents crammed into the desperate conditions were there as a direct result of the very same 'great and the good'. The dual roles of slum landlord and Workhouse Guardian, whilst completely contradictory, were not seen as such by those who held them. They managed, perhaps too easily, to divorce the consequences of their actions as the former from what was viewed as assisting those in most pressing need as the latter. In Peg's case, although she could not know it, the link was closer still. It was a link not only with her eviction but also with May's traumatic experience and, ultimately, the fate that befell poor Ernie.

The occupants of May Cottage rose early as usual. Without a Mother to ensure order, and that correct procedure was followed, the days began in a somewhat less orderly fashion than was generally considered acceptable in the formal setting of the Village. Mothers from neighbouring cottages would call in to oversee but their duties meant the time they could spare was limited. As usual, the older girls prepared breakfast - trying not to burn the toast - then proceeded to get the younger girls ready for the day. Prayers were said but perhaps not with the same gusto that an enthusiastic Mother could command. May was ready, awaiting the arrival of the Doctor so their quest could begin.

"Where is 'e? I thought 'e'd be 'ere by now." May muttered to Lottie at just after eight as it became light.

The Doctor would come but May had to wait a while longer. She tried to busy herself with regular chores but found the time was dragging and she was becoming impatient. At last, after what seemed like forever, the Doctor arrived. When he came in from the snow, May noticed that he was not clad in his usual style of hat and coat but in other more formal attire that gave to him the definite appearance of what May considered a toff. She was actually reminded of The Man although the Doctor was much shorter and of a stockier build than the tall imposing Man.

'He is a toff after all,' thought May, her mind now made up. However, she still trusted him. She felt she was somehow betraying her mum's wishes by doing this but her mum didn't know him and May trusted her own judgement. It was not the first time and would certainly not be the last that her judgement would stand her in good stead.

"Come, May. Make sure you are wrapped up warmly, as the snow and frost are severe today. We shall first visit the Bethnal Green Workhouse on Waterloo Road to discover if it is there where your friend has the misfortune to reside as it is the closest such establishment to her former lodgings." The Doctor attempted to smile as he spoke but it was a smile that concealed the doubt he still held.

"I'm ready mister Doctor - an' look, I've put the shawl Peg gave me on over my new togs. It could 'elp 'er to know who I am like cos I looks so different now don't I? I ain't all dirty like when she last saw me."

It was certainly highly likely that Peg would have trouble recognising May as she had scrubbed up pretty well. Of course, if Peg would have trouble identifying her then so would The Man if their paths should cross again and that could only be a good thing.

May had not travelled in such a carriage before. She felt important. She felt special. She felt she was on her way to do something worthwhile.

"Mister Doctor" (May could not bring herself to call Barnardo 'Father' as some other girls did) she said as the coach left the enclosed world of the Village behind and they headed back towards the grime of East London, "They will let us take 'er won't they – if she's there like?"

"May, my dear, the citizens who have the severe misfortune to find themselves dwelling in the workhouses are not prisoners in the way that criminals are. They are not confined by physical restraints like chains or bars but by the *reason* of their enforced residence – their inescapable poverty. The poor souls have no source of income, means of support or any other place to go thus they are imprisoned *only* by the nature of their unfortunate circumstances. So, to answer your question, I think they will indeed discharge her into my protection."

May didn't understand all the Doctor had said but she understood enough to know what he meant and was pleased.

The Workhouse they were about to visit was full beyond its prescribed capacity - holding some one thousand four hundred poor souls. Some were old; some were sick and some were deemed to be 'imbeciles'. The reason for its 'popularity' was, not only did the idea of at least being somewhere off the freezing streets for Christmas have some appeal, (even though the notorious reputation of Waterloo Road was certainly *less* than appealing) but Peg had not been alone in her eviction. The agents of her unknown landlord and others like him had seen to that. The residents - paupers as they were defined - segregated by sex, age and infirmity, were at their work (if physically able) by the time Dr Barnardo and May arrived. Their breakfast of bread and gruel, barely enough to sustain them, was over as was the first part of their working time. The half an hour for dinner was about to begin. Today the residents were lucky - if lucky can be considered the right word, for they would partake of boiled meat and a potato as opposed to just bread and rather lively cheese – so often served on several other days. Before this dinner Peg had been, as usual, undertaking her mending duties. After these 'usual' matters, Peg's life was to take an unexpected turn.

Twelve

It had been some fourteen years since a damning report into the conditions at Waterloo Road Workhouse was published. Doctor Barnardo had seen this report in the Lancet as a young man and its contents had had a profound effect on him. He had read how floors were soaked with urine and how sick inmates' medical needs were served by only two paid nurses. Even these nurses were untrained and given support by others from within the pauper community itself. Now stood before the overpowering building, young May moving closer to him as she stared at the daunting structure that seemed to stretch on and on, he pondered on how the poor wretches within its walls lived now years later. Was it any better? Surely it must be. Maybe a little, but possibly not.

Outside the main door there was a huddled gathering; a motley cluster of shivering humanity – today mostly men whereas on other days it would consist mostly of women – either clutching their entry slips or just hoping, as 'casuals' for just a single night, they would be accepted. The very fact that they desired admission spoke volumes for the grim condition of their existence. The House was not a place the inside of which anyone wanted to see. That they were there at all, that what they were about to face if admitted was preferable to life outside, demonstrated their utter destitution. They watched the Doctor and May pass and he detected a few mutterings that alluded to his clothing and perceived status. To May these people were striking reminders of what she had left behind. She even thought that there were, perhaps, some familiar faces amongst the pitiful throng.

The porter, quickly realising Dr Barnardo was obviously not there to seek admission, approached him.

"Good day sir. I am obliged to inform you that it is not such time for visiting today."

"I... we," replied the Doctor, indicating May at his side, "are not here to visit. There is a specific lady we seek. A lady it is our firm intention to remove from your...care."

Whether the pause before the word 'care' – and the sarcasm it hinted at – was spotted by the porter, the Doctor did not know. He suspected, however, that it was not.

"I see, then you must speak to the Master. Follow me and I will take you to him. If he is available of course for he is a very busy man."

"As am I." the Doctor stated firmly.

They duly followed the dour-looking porter through the bleak, overbearing corridors of the vast building to the Master's offices.

"Wait here," he said as he opened the Master's door. "Who shall I inform the Master is calling?"

"Barnardo, Doctor Thomas Barnardo from Barkingside in Essex and this young lady is May, Miss Harris."

The Master spoke quietly but from outside the closed door, May could just about hear some of the conversation between him and the porter.

"I know of this Barnardo. We must allow him to locate this...lady and ensure he leaves as soon as possible with her. Show him, and that child, in."

"Did you 'ear that mister Doctor? They're gonna let us take 'er."

"As I thought they would but first we must find her and I think you are not certain as to her full and correct name May are you?"

May shook her head. The porter showed them in.

"My dear Doctor, your reputation precedes you." said the Master rising from his chair. Here was a man some twenty years older than the Doctor, and one who - by the manner of his size and appearance – did not share the meagre fare of his charges. "If you can furnish me with the name of this good lady and the date upon which she joined our worthy establishment myself and my hardworking staff will endeavour to deliver her to you with the utmost speed."

"We ain't got 'er name mister," piped up May, "I know she's called Peg, or maybe Maud but I don't know any more."

The Master looked irritated and smiled but through gritted teeth.

"I'll know 'er though mister an' she'll know me so can we go an' find 'er now?"

The Master asked the porter to summon the Matron as it was to be her task to escort the Doctor and May to the cavernous dining hall where the female residents (inmates?) were engaged in their midday meal.

While they were waiting May gazed around the Master's room.

"Right big place this ain't it. Bigger than wot your school is Doctor - and the little 'ouses like what I live in."

"It certainly is May. It most certainly..."

The Matron swept into the office. She was a stern-looking woman of a similar age and girth to the Master but not, as was often the case in workhouses, his wife. She, as did the Master, appeared somewhat irked by being taken away from her duties but upon seeing Dr Barnardo and his apparent status, her demeanour changed. It was important to present to outsiders a picture of the workhouse that was a positive one and this somewhat difficult task was attempted whenever the opportunity was seen to arise.

"Good sir," she nodded toward him "of what service can I be to you today?"

The Master spoke.

"This good gentleman, Doctor Barnardo, and this young...lady are seeking one of our throng in order to remove her from our diligent care. Will you show them to our dining hall to assist them in their quest?"

"Of course, follow me."

She flounced ahead of them to lead the way, chattering about nothing is particular but, the Doctor thought, to try to distract him from fully observing the nature of her domain. After what seemed like an age trailing through the sombre workhouse passages they arrived at the place where the female paupers were served their meals.

There the Doctor and May were greeted by a foaming wave of off-white bonnets upon a sea of faded blue uniforms. The sea stretched the full length of the hall; the women seated at long tables that were laid out in regimented rows. This throng of women all facing the same way was like a silent tide creeping in. Their expressionless faces reflected their dire situation.

"Cor blimey Doctor. All these wimmin! They all look the bleedin same!"

The Matron cast a disapproving glance at May upon hearing her swearing. The Doctor was not too pleased either but May was right – they did all appear the same despite their ages varying from twenties to, in a few cases, nineties. Any individuality they had was stripped away, along with their paltry possessions, when they gave themselves over to the strict – and harsh - workhouse regime.

Since May and the Doctor could not be sure Peg was even amongst the white-capped multitude, the only way to find out was for May to call out for her. To call her name and hope she was there to respond.

Towards the back of the hall, Peg looked up from the decidedly grey looking meat and one potato. What was this unexpected interruption? Others looked up also. Some were curious – anything, however trivial, that caused a break from the normal numbing, monotonous routine was welcome. Others, however, barely raised an eyebrow as they had long since stopped caring about or noticing anything at all.

The Doctor lifted May onto a stool so her small frame could be seen by at least some of the women and her voice, loud for such a small girl, could be heard.

The Matron spoke in a booming voice after first clapping her hands to gain the attention of those who had not looked up from their dinner.

"Listen now, listen all of you. We have here a gentleman, one Doctor Barnardo from Essex, and a young girl, who are seeking a particular lady. If this lady is here, and we have no full name so cannot be sure, they wish – if it is her desire of course – to take her to reside with them at a place some miles away called Barkingside."

The Doctor could not help but smile at the Matron's remarks – he wondered who would not desire, given the opportunity, to leave the confines of Waterloo Road for somewhere altogether more wholesome.

"The girl here is called May. If there is anyone here who is acquainted with this girl please will they stand up so they can be seen?"

May barely waited for the Matron to finish before she shouted.

"Peg, Peg, look Peg it's me. It's May. Me an' the Doctor 'ave come t'get you! Are you 'ere Peg? We want you to come an' 'elp look after me an' other girls an' all."

There was a buzz of sound as inmates who happened to share Peg's name spoke up.

"I am Peg. I'll go wi' you."

"No, I am."

"No she ain't – I am."

"Quiet, all of you. The girl knows who they seek, the rest of you continue with your food whilst you still have time."

At these words from the Matron, the shouting turned to mumbling but not yet to silence.

May scanned around the hall waiting, hoping, until...

"May? May, is it really you? I wondered if I would ever see you again and yet... here you are."

Peg moved through the crowded row to the end then slowly towards the front of the hall.

May did not wait; she headed at speed to Peg and hugged her.

"I knew I'd find you Peg. Look, I got your shawl on so you'd know me cos I look right different now!"

She twirled around just as she had when she first met Peg and was given the precious shawl.

Peg smiled down at May. It was the first time she had smiled in what seemed like an age. It was also the first time she had seen May with a properly clean face and tidy hair that did not have a life of its own. What she wasn't seeing for the first time was the determination and strength of this deceptively frail child, although she was no longer as delicate as the last time they had met. Decent, nourishing food and a warm safe place to sleep had seen to that even in the space of a few brief months.

Peg's eyes began to fill with tears.

"My dear May, I cannot tell you how pleased I am to lay my eyes on you again and to see you looking so well. This place you dwell now, is it right that you, and this Doctor, wish me to come there also?"

"I do Peg. An' the Doctor 'ere an' 'is wife. They need you they do. I need you."

She led Peg by the hand to meet Dr Barnardo. "Peg, this is the Doctor. Mister Doctor, this is my friend Peg."

Thomas Barnardo had seen the picture taken many years before but the lady was still recognisable to him.

Her demeanour was clearly one of someone who had not spent the whole of her life living from hand to mouth.

As they greeted each other the Matron looked impatient.

"Sir, I am indeed happy that your quest has been successful but I am sure you must understand we have a routine to follow. Your presence here is disrupting our ladies' mealtime. Since they will be required to return to their duties presently your reunion must be continued elsewhere."

She ushered them away and once the distraction was removed, the hall instantly returned to silence as the white-capped heads simultaneously lowered and those who had paused from eating resumed their frugal meal in silent unison.

They returned to the Master's office to go through the formalities needed to remove Peg from the Workhouse care. Her scant belongings were brought and returned to her; she signed her name – (as many who did not write could not) and was therefore free. All that remained was to cast off the workhouse uniform and reclothe herself in those shabby clothes she had arrived in.

When Peg appeared in those clothes the Doctor could see the plight that she had been living in and wondered what had brought a well-spoken and educated woman to such reduced circumstances. His doubts surfaced again and he hoped it was not because she had succumbed to the temptation of alcohol or something even worse.

"Peg, where's your cross? You've still got it ain't you? You always 'ad it on. I remember it shining round your neck. You used to touch it when you was sad you did."

The Doctor looked at Peg, anticipating her reply. Her standing as a 'good Christian lady' was of vital importance to him.

"Of course I have it May. It is the only thing I possess that holds any value to me. The only thing that gave me comfort through the hard times I found myself in."

She lifted the chain from beneath her frayed and faded bodice and the cross, simple but made of silver, shone.

"You say this cross is of value dear lady so it is true what May has told me - that you are one who has faith in our dear Lord."

"Indeed sir. My faith has sustained me through my unhappy situation and," – she looked down at May - "the hope that this young child is fortunate enough to lead a better life than that she had previously known. It seems that this hope, no this prayer, has been answered."

As they left the Waterloo Road Workhouse a downcast group remained outside. Some had been admitted and others had joined the crowd including some women and children of a similar age to May, although looks could be deceptive. Undernourished children like these would invariably look smaller than their better-fed counterparts, like for example, the children of The Man.

Peg's duties would be undertaken by another poor unfortunate soul and her mercifully brief existence at Waterloo Road would quickly be forgotten – except of course by Peg herself. And so it was that Peg left the Workhouse. She boarded the carriage, May clutching her hand, and did not look back as the coach headed towards Barkingside.

Thirteen

Upon arrival, after a journey during which conversation revolved mainly around May telling Peg of the ways of the Village, the Doctor took Peg to his office where Syrie was waiting.

"May my dear, we must now speak with this lady. Go back to your cottage and we shall be along presently."

May was worried.

"You won't send 'er back again will you?"

This was not something the Doctor was considering but formalities had to be completed. Syrie's opinion and approval was also vital.

He reiterated firmly,

"Go back to your cottage now May."

"Yes May dear, go along as my husband bids you." added Syrie

May nodded and went back through the snow to May Cottage to be greeted by an expectant Lottie.

"Did you find 'er? Where is she?"

"She's wi' the Doctor an' 'is wife now. We'll find out soon if he's gonna keep 'er, but I think 'e will. I 'ope 'e does."

Meanwhile, the Doctor and Syrie had explained to Peg the reason for her presence and what, if of course she chose to stay, would be expected of her.

Thomas Barnardo looked earnestly at Peg and spoke.

"These children, these little girls, have come to us from all manner of sad and pitiful circumstances. Some of them, as with your friend May, have no family. Some of them have families who, for whatever reason, are unable or unwilling to care for them any longer, some have led lives so despicable it is a wonder they have survived at all. They need to be cared for and nurtured. They need stability and encouragement – to believe they can become useful members of society and, of course, to serve our lord. Do you understand Peg? Do you think this a role you can undertake and perform with the diligence our Christian community needs and demands?"

Peg did not answer immediately. She was thinking carefully until she finally replied.

"Doctor and Mrs Barnardo, I have not known young May for very long, only a matter of six months or so, but I do know that she is a good child who, given the proper opportunities away from the slum from whence she came, would have a much brighter future. I am sure she is not alone in this and it would be of great satisfaction to me to contribute to this brighter future – for the other girls also. So, yes, I do understand and would undertake the role you need to fill with the diligence you require and which the girls you have taken in undoubtedly deserve."

While she was speaking the Doctor had been looking at the papers she had brought with her. He looked up and spoke.

"I am pleased Peg ... Miss Butler."

It was the first time he had used this form of address and to be referred to as Miss Butler again made Peg feel she was respected. It felt good. "I am very pleased to welcome you to our family."

Syrie clasped Peg's hands.

"Now come with me and I will take you to May Cottage which is to be your new home. You will be introduced to your charges and I will furnish you with our procedures and the duties you will need to familiarise yourself with. I am afraid your duties must commence with all due haste as your charges have been lacking a good Mother for some days now."

Peg gestured self consciously towards her clothing. "Of course, in all the rush we have not issued you with the appropriate attire or the opportunity of a bath to finally cleanse the workhouse from your person. This will be remedied immediately. I am sure your charges can wait a little longer."

"I am most grateful Mrs Barnardo and assure you that I will pursue my new duties with meticulous care."

By the evening Peg was bathed and dressed in her new clothing and, looking around the neat houses of the Village with its wide-open spaces of white, frosted grass and trees, she felt she had come home. Whether the Village would prove to be the salvation of all of the girls now residing within its confines she knew not, but having lived amongst the poverty of the Nichol did not see how it could not be better here. She pondered on her life before the sad episodes of the tenement and the Workhouse; a life she had cherished but also tried, on occasion when it became too painful to remember, to forget. Now her days would be spent in a room of a size not too dissimilar to her tenement one but one that was much cosier with an armchair, sofa and a brightly patterned carpet. And one, of course, that was much cleaner and much healthier. It would surely be her last place of residence. She knew this. She was certain of this. This time she was right.

Fourteen

Peg took to the girls, and they to her, very quickly. She was different from Hetty – more approachable but then she was not in ill health as poor Hetty had been. Peg was, considering where she had come from, in very good health and fully able to respond to any challenges - and challenges there would certainly be. Both Thomas and Syrie Barnardo knew they had made the right decision when they, despite Thomas's initial reluctance, acceded to May's entreaty.

Christmas was upon the Village in the blink of an eye and it was by turns a happy and a sad affair for May. Happy because she had a warm place to live, friends like Lottie and people who cared for her. Sad because it was only the previous Christmas that her mum had been with her and Uncle George had miraculously produced the goose for their Christmas dinner just a few days before he left to join his regiment. That was Christmas 1879 but now 1880 was drawing to a close. It had been a traumatic year for May. So much had happened. Her life had changed direction three times. At its start, she could not have imagined how different her circumstances would be by its end but she made a vow; 'I still miss you mum. I always will miss you an' I still love you I do. I know you'd be 'appy I've found

97

somewhere an' someone t'take care o' me. I'm gonna make you right proud of me mum.'

After this painful year, the one that followed would prove to be settled one for May. It began with snow and more snow – a blizzard so harsh on January 12th that May wondered how Nick and her other friends were coping; she hoped they had found somewhere to keep them safe. Maybe they had found sanctuary at a home for boys – a place something like she had found. Maybe they had. She hoped they had but wondered what would be their fate if they had not.

Over the next couple of years May would, whilst still retaining the feistiness Peg had recognised in her and Syrie Barnardo had been taken with, become fully immersed in the world of the Village. She had pledged to make her mother proud and she would do this by making sure any opportunity to improve herself, and fortunately there were many, was grasped eagerly with both hands. Her reading, her number work and her ability to manage everyday tasks improved no end. The Village teachers were impressed with her obvious desire to learn.

What was also very important to May was that she was gradually, although not entirely, losing the speech of the East End streets. She was learning to speak more like Peg – who was proving to be an excellent role model not only for May but also for the other girls in her charge. The way she spoke was so important because May had decided, even as she arrived at the Village, that she wanted a better life, a life that would have some meaning, some purpose. A life that would not consist of attending on those she was adamant were not her superiors and whom she would not accept as such. A servant's life was not for her. Speaking 'properly', she felt, brought this aim closer – made it seem more possible, more achievable. Whether it was right that people should be judged by their way of speaking was not something she considered but May could not know that this would prove to be the case, albeit in a somewhat roundabout way that she could not have foreseen.

All the while May had kept to herself what had happened with Ernie. She wanted to share her secret with both Peg and Lottie. Perhaps if she had then she may have felt better for it. She wanted to tell them about The Man. The Man whose name she didn't know and could not make pay for his wickedness. The Man she was sure she would encounter again. The Man whose face she would never forget. She would have felt better but for Peg would have come the realisation that she may also have played a part, although one she had no control over, in the events that May recounted. Peg had encountered men such as the one that would be described by May and also had reason to despise their arrogance. Also, like May, she was not ready to disclose her reasons yet. Her status as 'Mother' meant she felt obliged to retain an authority that could be compromised if her past was discussed. Generally, it was a rule that a veil was drawn over the past in the Village. Misdeeds or those perceived as misdeeds, were, for the girls, confined to history, not to be spoken about and not allowed to taint the new lives they were embarking upon. It was not considered that perhaps the past, whatever it contained, should not be entirely erased as, with May, it would help to shape the person the child would eventually become. Accordingly, Peg remained enigmatic about her own life and May realised she could not do anything about what she had seen. Not yet anyway, but one day she would. Oh yes, she would have justice for Ernie.

Fifteen

Funds were always needed to keep Barnardo's operations working. There had been financial difficulties in the past and Thomas Barnardo's ambitious vision (to some of his detractors - and even his supporters - too ambitious) had come perilously close to failing on more than one occasion. Consequently promoting the work done at the Village to further donations and enlist support from wealthy empathetic patrons was vital.

The 'before and after' photographs that May had steadfastly refused to be party to were distributed to those who had the wherewithal to pledge assistance if the sorry appearance of pitiful urchins had the desired effect. To follow on from this distribution and to reinforce the difference that could be made to the girls' lives it was a practice of the Village to demonstrate the achievements and the value of the girls to 'society' – to show what they had learned and how competently they had learned it. When old enough, the girls would generally go into service to cater to the perceived shortage of good servants and they were, actually, much in demand. This was not something that appealed to May at all. She felt she was destined for better things than, as she saw it, 'waiting on toffs'.

There was a song that the girls learned about their role as 'Little Servants' that she found almost impossible to sing with any degree of enthusiasm or belief. It was not the references to Jesus that were the problem but rather the subservience it inevitably implied. May would never do anything deliberately bad – she had a good heart but she was still the child who had told Peg:-

'I don't take no nonsense from no one I don't'

The song, she felt, made the girls believe that they had their place, that they should be docile and totally compliant. It was fixed, preordained, a station for which they had been destined and should be grateful. Of course, this life, this promised life of security, away from the ever-present (in the Nichol) scourge of crime and prostitution, was something that not all girls from the same background as May could even dream of and she was far from ungrateful. On the contrary, she believed that it was a blessing in disguise that she had collapsed outside the school and been taken in by the Barnardos. Where would she be now if that had not happened? Mrs Barnardo had told her she had been speaking to her mum in her delirious state, although she did not remember. Was her mum somehow with her, rather than an illusion, watching over her? No, she was not ungrateful; she knew education was a necessity to better herself and to her education would not be put to its best use by waiting on others; others who sometimes, like The Man, looked down on the likes of her purely because their start in life had been less fortunate.

Her doubts did not mean, though, that she was exempt from taking part in the exhibitions put on in the posh houses of the wealthy folk who resided in the better parts of London so far away in substance but not so in distance. There was no coercion however. No girl would ever be forced to participate if she did not wish to for reason of shyness or lack of confidence. These did not apply to May who was neither shy nor lacking in confidence. Whilst not happy at the prospect she felt she owed it to her new 'family' to do the very best she could. Lottie, being slightly older than May who was nearly thirteen (she thought), had already been involved in an earlier exhibition and whilst she had performed as required was also not entirely comfortable with the experience either but not for the same reason as May. Despite her initial bravado, Lottie was, in fact, both quite shy *and* lacking in confidence. She used the tough veneer to shield herself from undoubted insecurity caused by the life she had led before. It had taken May a while to realise this but it had only served to reinforce the firm and enduring friendship they had formed.

"It's not that bad really I s'pose. They ain't horrible to us – even quite nice. They had some of those pictures of us girls as we were like. They said they couldn't believe we were the same girls! And we got to have cake and that so... well... it's alright but know I how them poor blimmin performing monkeys felt wiv the organ grinders back in London!"

They laughed and May's misgivings were, for a time – until the day before the event, forgotten.

The 'better part' of London that May was to visit was that other world, Belgravia – Belgrave Square in fact. It was at number 40, the residence of Lord Fortescue – a land-owning gentleman who had, the previous November, been elected as Member of Parliament for the constituency of Tiverton in Devon that May would be required to 'perform'.

As May had never been to that part of London before she was immediately struck by the shining, stately, white buildings. Her mind was catapulted back to the foul, forbidding, black tenements and the extreme contrast between the two was overwhelming - like heaven and hell. The buildings surrounded a private garden for the use only of the well-heeled residents. This was the kind of place *real* toffs lived – like the Earl they were going to attend on. She and the other five girls were taken into the magnificent house by the special entrance for servants. The grand steps at the front were climbed only by family and distinguished visitors; the equally grand front door these people entered through, and that was opened by an immaculately turned out housemaid, was only for those of a distinctly higher social standing than the likes of a group of Dr Barnardo's girls.

In the large kitchen with its gleaming copper pans and expensive dinnerware, the girls' instructor – Miss Henley - explained again what was expected of them. This had been drilled and rehearsed many times at the Village and May was fed up with the whole thing. She just wanted it to be over. She had no intention of toiling away for toffs for her whole life and did not see the point of practising to do so.

"I don't really want to do this Peg," she had confided the day before the exhibition was due to take place. (May still called Peg by her name rather than 'Mother' as the others girls in her charge did – she only had one mother who could never be replaced – not even by Peg.)"My mum told me that toffs are no better than I am and I do not want to wait on them as if they are."

"My dear May, we all have to do things, say things, we do not like at some point in our lives. Such is this life and it is something, regrettably, that we must accept and use to make us stronger. It does not mean that these people *are* better than you and you have an opportunity to show them how accomplished you have become. Why I doubt that few of them are even capable of performing some of the tasks you carry out so well now. They could not survive what you have been through. You are a far tougher character than most of them will ever be, so feel proud of what you have achieved. Look in the mirror and see not the scrawny, dirty street child of two years ago but a capable, smart and thoroughly wonderful young person. Let *them* see that."

May felt tears welling in her eyes and hugged Peg.

"You are right Peg. I will go to this...Earl or whatever title he has, and play the game as best I can. You will, when you hear the report from Miss Henley how I worked, be right proud of me."

"I am always proud of you May, you should know that."

Peg also fought back tears as she hugged May.

So, stood in Earl Fortescue's elaborate kitchen, faced with the prospect of handling valuable china (although in reality they were not entrusted with the finest – that would be judged too risky) and singing work songs, May remembered Peg's words and her promise. She would try the very best she could. This was undoubtedly her intention but something occurred as she left the kitchen and passed through the hallway en route to the sumptuous drawing room. It was something that would jeopardise the earnest vow she had made to Peg.

She saw something in the stand near the front door. It was something that brought back dreadful memories as its shiny top caught the watery spring sunlight from the stained glass window above the door. It was a cane topped with silver – the very same cane she had seen

The Man strike poor Ernie to his death with. She froze momentarily and almost dropped the white linen tablecloth she was holding. She felt dizzy and the colour drained from her face. He was here! In no more than a few seconds she would be only a matter of feet away from him. The thought filled her with terror.

"May, May, come along. You are delaying us. We have good work to do." Miss Henley looked closely at May and saw how pale she was but put this down to nerves. "Do not worry dear; you have no need to be frightened. You are more than capable of undertaking the routines we have so rigorously practiced. Come along now." Her voice was gentle and attempted to reassure. It didn't work.

She ushered a wary May forward and she was the third girl to enter the drawing-room. The first two began singing but May couldn't bring herself to sing. She wanted to look around the room. She wanted to but she was too scared so she kept her eyes down, looking only at the tablecloth as she and another girl brought it forward to the highly polished mahogany table.

Around the room with Earl Fortescue sat four other immaculate gentlemen and five elegant ladies. May couldn't describe them; did not see them as she was afraid to look. If her eyes met those of The Man what would happen? Would he know her? Would he remember her? May told herself not to be so foolish. He probably had not given a thought to what happened that night in October 1880. He would surely have been busy doing whatever toffs like him did.

May could hear Miss Henley explaining the accomplishments of the girls as she began to lay the table. Whilst she could hear the words they did not sink in. She was preoccupied with her thoughts but somehow she managed to fulfil her role – almost as if she was somewhere else, somewhere detached. She wished she was.

The table was set speedily yet accurately with the cutlery arranged as for an elegant dinner party with equally elegant guests. The immaculate audience was impressed. Miss Henley went on to explain the other domestic tasks that the girls were able to undertake.

"Our young ladies are not only adept at laying a fine table as you have seen but can make beds, perform all manner of laundry related tasks as well as rigorous cleaning of every kind. Their cottages are kept cosily warm by the fires they set and tend. They are truly the most diligent and industrious young ladies you could ever wish to find and I have no hesitation in commending them to you."

"Miss Henley, I must laud your worthy establishment for the most thorough way you have instructed these young girls." said one of the gentlemen.

"I agree," a lady nodded, "in fact, I think that they are more adept than my own servants."

There was refined laughter and Miss Henley smiled.

"Thank you ladies and gentlemen. The achievement of our young ladies, especially considering the bleak backgrounds from whence they have the misfortune to come, is astounding indeed and speaks volumes for the dedication of our dear founder Dr Barnardo and his staff – of whom I am most proud to be one."

The girls continued to sing after Miss Henley had finished speaking then proceeded to clear away the table as efficiently as they had set it out. May kept her head down as best she could until a man's voice spoke.

"Miss Henley, these girls are indeed well trained and undoubtedly industrious as you so rightly say. I think, however, that perhaps a more cheerful manner could and should be evident for some of them, particularly the girl with the blue checked apron." May was the only girl to be wearing a blue checked apron and Miss Henley indicated towards her. "Yes, this young lady."

He spoke directly to May. "You do not have to be afraid of us girl, despite the difference in our class and status but no one - and I am sure the ladies here would agree - is happy to employ a sullen servant in their home, especially if important visitors are to be received."

May, recognising the voice but being unwilling, still, to look him in the face, stood silently. She stood silently but inside was seething with anger, resentment and hatred.

Another man, an older man with a much kinder voice, then spoke.

"It is daunting indeed for these young people to come here from the Village, where they are sheltered from society, to such a place as this. I totally understand why there should be a feeling of being overwhelmed and it is this, rather than sullenness as you suggest, that impacts upon demeanour. I propose you should be more charitable sir."

Two of the ladies nodded in agreement with Lord Cairns, whose social standing was much higher than that of May's detractor and only two years previously had held the position of Lord Chancellor. One lady addressed The Man by his name to say she agreed with Lord Cairns so now May knew his name, well his surname at least! The detractor was, it would come as no surprise to May, the same man that she was loathe to look at but now had to face. As she did so she searched his face for any sign of recognition. He had said he would know her. Did he? If he did she felt he did not show it. All she saw were the eyes of someone who thought he was so superior to the likes of her that she didn't warrant too close an observation. She was safe. Or so she thought.

The demonstration, after what seemed like an age for May, was finally over. The girls curtseyed to their audience; Miss Henley accepted the applause and thanked the audience for their attention.

"My dear," one of the ladies turned to her aristocratic husband, "when it is our need to employ more servants, and certainly, I think our household would run more smoothly if we did, the Village at Barkingside shall be our first call if it can supply such staff as these. It is so difficult to find good servants these days."

As May filed out of the drawing-room she was addressed again by The Man.

"Girl, I do not mean to upset you but you should be aware of the importance of a gracious disposition and equally gracious behaviour if you are to be a success in service in such a household as this."

Fuming inside at the pomposity of The Man she knew to be a murderer, May nodded and duly escaped from the drawing-room. As she did so she heard another lady address him (his wife perhaps?) – by his Christian name. Now May knew his full name. It was a name that, she felt, did not suit him but then she also believed no *Christian* name would be appropriate considering the most unchristian of acts he had committed.

Once back in the kitchen Miss Henley spoke to the girls.

"You did very well my girls. I am proud of you and May, do not take to heart what that gentleman said to you. I agree with Lord Cairns, who knows our dear father very well. In fact, it was he who presided over the opening of the Village that is now our home and is the honoured President."

"He is no gentleman." May muttered through gritted teeth but the others did not know she had another reason, a much stronger reason, to say this beyond his uncharitable comment to her.

Back in the drawing-room the guests discussed what they had seen and were, with the exception of The Man, full of praise.

"I take your point about nerves, Lord Cairns, but for my part I would not accept what I construe as a sullen face and attitude. Except for that one girl, I agree their manner and application was exemplary so the Village must indeed train these girls well. I understand that you sometimes visit this Village founded by Barnardo..."

"Doctor Barnardo," corrected Lord Cairns, who was one of Thomas Barnardo's most ardent supporters and being a long term friend, knew him well, "it has been my privilege to assist Thomas in his undoubted calling."

"Quite. Yes, as you support this Village I would like, on the occasion of your next visit, to accompany you to see firsthand the work, the unquestionably good work, that is undertaken there."

"That will certainly be possible and will no doubt be a useful introduction to how young girls who are products of the slums - slums that are, I feel most strongly, a deep and shameful scar upon our great city

112

– can be successfully rehabilitated despite their former degradation."

The Man nodded solemnly to give the appearance that he actually cared about the dire conditions that produced such destitute children. It was a sham, given his involvement with those very same slums, and was purely to try to ingratiate himself with Lord Cairns and Earl Fortescue in an attempt to further his political ambitions. All the while he cultivated the company of those he felt could further his career. With possible elections due in the not too distant future he would inveigle his way closer to being chosen as a candidate. He didn't want a constituency too far away from London. He didn't want to be obliged to travel too far away as he didn't trust others to monitor his lucrative, if dubious, business interests. Hackney, he thought, would be perfect and he felt his chance of being selected could be increased by, if it proved to come to pass, the possibility of new constituencies that were to be created to reflect the increasing population. He had some property there; it was close enough to allow him to visit so at least it would appear he was concerned about his constituents. Yes, Hackney would be perfect – it would allow him to play the game as *he* wished it to be played.

As he prepared to leave number 40 to cross to his house on the other side of the Square he took his cane, handed to him by the housemaid. For some reason, he paused and studied the silver embellishment as if he had not seen it, really seen it, for a long time.

As he carefully studied it his wife enquired,

"My dear, is everything well? You suddenly appear quite distracted."

"It is nothing, nothing." he said as he turned away.

His reply was, even for him, quite terse and his wife, who acquiesced to him in every way and all things, felt it would be prudent not to press her concerns. They returned to their house in silence. His mind was beginning to pull his thoughts together and he didn't like the conclusion he had drawn. He didn't like it at all. He had thought there was something about the sullen child; something vaguely familiar that he couldn't quite grasp. His silver cane was the catalyst that brought back the event that linked himself to May and he was suddenly transported back to that freezing October night in the Nichol. 'I seen you mister an' I'll know you.'

The girl's words rang through his head. 'And I'll know you, child.'

His words also came back to him and he was right – he did know her. She looked different of course but despite the passing of time he just knew it was the same child.

But what of the girl? Did she remember him? Was this the reason for her sullen manner or were her actions and attitude simply borne out of apprehension and discomfort?

Upon his return home, he poured himself a very large brandy. His wife approached him somewhat tentatively.

"My dear, the children would like very much to see you before they are taken to be given their supper. They have..."

He cut her short.

"Not now, perhaps tomorrow."

No more was said. He did have affection for his children and was keen they should take their proper place in society but today was not conducive to childish prattle of no consequence. He had more pressing matters on his mind. His wife, sensing he would be better left alone, did so although she knew him well enough to see there was something of importance bothering him. Maybe she would speak to him again in the morning or, after due consideration, maybe it was wiser that she didn't.

Josephine was a good and dutiful wife. She wanted for nothing. Well, nothing material anyway but she sometimes wished her husband was less cold, less focussed on his business and career. She didn't know much about his business; it was not her place to question him about such matters – he had made that quite clear from the beginning and anyway it was not the done thing for refined ladies to concern themselves

115

with such matters. She had been married to him for some ten years now and had borne him two children – a boy and a girl. Her family lived far away on the south coast so she saw them rarely and her husband, who was one of two children, no longer had any contact with his only brother. There had been some unpleasantness - she didn't know what – a few of years before their marriage. She had met his brother before this 'business' and had found him quite charming – more so than her then prospective husband in fact. As far as she knew her brother-in-law was an officer in the army but she knew not in which regiment or at what rank he served. Her husband never spoke of him and she certainly would not enquire.

They retired that night in silence. Josephine was conscious that her husband was tossing and turning most of the night. She knew this because sleep did not come easily to her either.

Sixteen

On the journey back to the Village May had been silent. The other girls were extremely talkative and Miss Henley commented,

"May, you must not take things to heart so much. You must not be troubled by the opinions of one man who was, you should agree, put in his place by our patron Lord Cairns."

May nodded but still chose not to speak.

They arrived back at the Village at suppertime and as May was the only girl from her cottage who took part that day, she was questioned upon her return – especially by Lottie and, of course, Peg - as to how the demonstration had gone.

"I don't want to talk yet." She didn't really need to as her expression, her scowling face, spoke volumes and no words were necessary to show everything was not well. Her mind was in turmoil. Now he knew where she lived. He could find her anytime – if he had recognised her. What would he do? Would he do anything? May didn't know – if he hadn't recognised her then he would indeed do nothing. She had wondered whether Peg would recognise her at the workhouse and Peg knew her – he had only seen her once and that was in poor light and briefly. So surely she was safe. Even though he may know her whereabouts she was protected within Doctor Barnardo's Village so what could he do to her anyway? Yet she was uncomfortable. She must confide in Peg – she would know what to do.

May waited until all the other girls, including Lottie, were asleep. Peg was quietly reading when May tapped gently on her door. She looked up as May almost slunk, silently, into the room and she did not appear at all surprised at May's downcast countenance.

"I was wondering whether you would come to see me. I could tell by your unhappy face that something is wrong and that it goes far beyond your obvious discomfort from the exhibition today. Come here, child."

She held out her arms and May solemnly drew close to her.

The only way May could explain the real reason she was so upset was to, finally, tell Peg her story. She told her story quietly and calmly, avoiding eye contact with Peg as she was afraid if she did then Peg would interrupt her and she would not be able to continue. Peg was stunned and wondered how May had managed to keep silent for so long.

"May this is not what I was expecting to hear, not at all. You are sure it was this man... this wicked man, you saw?"

"Yes, it was. I saw him Peg," she murmured in a shaky voice as she looked into Peg's face. "I saw him today. I saw the horrible man what killed Ernie. He was there, right in front of us, and he talked to me."

"Who is he; what is his name?"

"I know his name but I ain't going to say it. I can't say his name Peg I just can't."

"Why not May? Tell me. I can help you. We can reveal his terrible actions and he will be duly punished."

"If I say it, it'll be like he's a real person - like any other person see?"

"I do not understand..."

"The way he spoke. All superior like...like he was so much better than what we are. An' all the time he's a bleedin murderer. I weren't gonna swear no more Peg, truly I weren't but he's not a person to me; he's the lowest low life that I've ever known. He's worse than a turd an' I ain't gonna give 'im any ...dignity, I think that's the word, by giving him no name. And anyway, who's gonna believe the likes o'me over someone like 'im."

May had tried hard to speak better – more like Peg- but in her emotional state she lapsed back into the East End twang.

Peg now understood what May was going through and said nothing further. All she could do was hug May as her anger dissolved to sadness and she started to sob. In silence, Peg wiped her eyes and gently guided her back to bed. May climbed in, curled up and drifted off into a fitful sleep. Peg returned to her room, to her bed and, like May, her sleep was restless also. She felt that May was probably wrong not to trust her new family to believe her but it was May's choice and all she could do was support her dear young friend.

The next day May woke up feeling weary and found it difficult to drag herself out of bed. She undertook her tasks more quietly than usual. Peg decided not to speak further about the events of the previous day but it was with a heavy heart. She believed that such a crime should not be allowed to go unpunished yet felt helpless to remedy the unfortunate situation.

By mid-morning, after much confusion in her mind, May had made a decision. This Man, or 'turd' as she referred to him yesterday, was, she knew, someone who undoubtedly had power and influence. Power and influence that could affect her life if he so chose – if he knew who she was. Whether he would attempt to do so, and if so, how was something she had no control over. What she *could* control were her own actions and her own reactions. She would not dwell on him. She would not allow him to cast a dark shadow over her settled life at the Village. She would never accept that he was superior to her. In other words, basically, 'Sod him!' she thought. Well, for now anyway. When she was older...when she older then maybe the tables could be turned.

Having made this decision May's mood lightened and this lightening was instantly visible to Peg and the other girls. It was as if a dark cloud had been lifted. Peg didn't speak about the night before. She just smiled at May who nodded in return and Peg understood.

Lottie simply asked,

"You alright May?"

"Yeah," and May meant it.

"Good." Lottie was relieved. May was much better company when she was in a good mood!

Seventeen

On the other side of London in Belgravia, The Man had woken with a less than agreeable disposition. His day was, as usual for him, rigidly ordered. He had much to occupy himself and the familiar girl he had encountered the day before could not be allowed to compromise his busy schedule. Therefore he pushed her from his mind. He apologised to his wife for his aloofness (much to Josephine's surprise) and showed some interest in the recent accomplishments of his children. He had better things to do with his time than concern himself with such a worthless urchin.

Whilst he had made this decision not to be concerned about her it did not mean that he had changed his mind about accompanying Lord Cairns on his next visit to Mossford Village. This was worthwhile to nurture the caring persona he wished to cultivate and project. Although, as demonstrated by his cruel action regarding Ernie, he regarded the unfortunate progeny of the slum as inherently inferior to those of his own class. Of course, they could be trained but so could dogs so they could be useful - but beyond that? They were only fit to serve their betters; they lacked intellect, their heads contained nothing of worth or importance. They had no breeding of any value. They were products of a slum and that loathsome slum was ingrained indelibly within them; it could never be entirely erased. He knew this. He was certain of this. He was wrong.

Eighteen

Thomas Barnardo's work was in peril. Once again funds were short and there were more young people in need of shelter than were graduating into service or other worthwhile positions - so what to do?

From the confined streets of London to the wide-open spaces and clean air of Canada, was this an option? Would youngsters who had known nothing except these streets flourish, or God forbid perish, in such a profoundly different environment? This was the question that Thomas Barnardo wrestled with. It had been considered before, but a report in 1874, commissioned in order to evaluate the conditions under which the children who had been sent to Canada were living, did not paint a pretty picture. It revealed that much was not satisfactory – dire in fact - and Thomas was initially put off by this. He had, however, worked with one Annie Macpherson previously, and it was she, in an individual capacity, who had arranged the emigration of many children to Canada. In 1882 he decided to take charge himself.

Barnardo did not like to follow in the footsteps of others. He saw himself as a crusading pioneer; one who would take the lead rather than follow the path set down by others, so he decided it was time to arrange the life-changing journeys himself. He could do it better. He *would* do it better. The children deserved better. To him the welfare of the children was paramount and could not – would not - be compromised. To his undoubted relief and delight, the reports back about the progress of the first Barnardo Boys in Canada were glowing. Consequently, more boys followed.

But what of the girls who, like May, were surely destined for service in middle or upper class English families? Could life in far off Canada work for them? Girls were different; Thomas felt they needed more protection and puzzled over how this could be achieved. As so often seemed to happen with Barnardo, like with the donation of Mossford Lodge, fate stepped in and he was able to facilitate the emigration of his first cohort of girls. So it was that in the spring of 1883 there was much talk in the Village. The girls and their 'Mothers' knew of the plans but there were many questions. Who would go? Who wanted to go? How many would go? What would happen when they arrived?

For May it was not easy. She remembered the ships she had seen with Uncle George and how she had said she wanted to see the world. She still did but wondered if this was the way. She would not admit it but despite her bravado, she was scared by the idea of travelling so far away to...well, to what? What about The Man? She did not want to leave Peg, or her good friend Lottie, so that was another consideration.

As was usual for May and Lottie before sleeping they discussed the events of the day and other things that each had on their mind.

"Lottie, what do you reckon about going to Canada?"

"I don't wanna go to no Canada May. There's all sorts of creatures there. Bears an' wolves that'd eat you soon as look at you and it's such a long way. No, I ain't gonna go on no big ship on the rough sea. No fear. You don't wanna go do you?"

"I don't know Lottie, I might..."

"What for? Ain't you happy 'ere with me an' Mother Peg?"

"I always wanted to go to other countries. My uncle did and he told me about other places and I want to see other places as well. If I stay here what will I do when I'm grown? I ain't gonna be no servant for rich people that ain't any better than what I am."

"But what would you do there then? They'll surely work you 'arder over there than what they do 'ere. And there's all the other animals like cows and 'orses and pigs. Great big things you don't know nothing about."

This was true and something that May had not thought of. Perhaps Lottie was right. Perhaps instead of being a servant in England she would just be a servant, perhaps a very different kind of servant, thousands of miles away with strangers; strangers who may not be as kind as Peg.

May did not like to admit she could be wrong. She knew there was little she could do to bring The Man to justice until she was grown and by that time she would have returned to England but Lottie had certainly made her wonder whether it would be a good idea.

"Well, I don't know Lottie. I 'aven't made me mind up yet."

Lottie studied May's face and she could see that she had managed to sow seeds of doubt as to the wisdom of the idea. Lottie didn't say any more. She was happy to let the matter drop, feeling that May would be with her in the Village for the foreseeable future.

"Night May."

"Night Lottie."

Perhaps May would wait to see how the first group fared. That is what she thought but, as had happened in the past with Thomas Barnardo, fate stepped in to compel her to rethink whether this was the right decision.

Nineteen

Whilst preparations for the first contingent of girls to depart for Canada were being made, a visit to the Village had been arranged for its supporters. The visitors were to include Dr Barnardo's advocates Lord Cairns and Samuel Smith. Smith had not only given Barnardo a substantial donation especially to facilitate his emigration programme but was also the original benefactor who enabled the initial school project in the East End. Whilst a useful supporter, and now perhaps even more so as a Member of Parliament, he also had reasons beyond charity to further the Doctor's work.

A country rife with poverty and deprivation was, Smith thought, a potential powder keg waiting to explode. If emigration could help to defuse this time bomb then so much the better. With Cairns and Smith would come others who were patrons as well as those who, for whatever reason, only paid lip service to supporting the work. One such individual was none other than The Man. He was still pursuing his goal of advancement and now had the opportunity to accompany Lord Cairns on his visit - as he had suggested whilst at Earl Fortescue's residence.

The Village the group of visitors would enter in early June was a picture. The trees were clothed in myriad shades of green and golden yellow. The grass was lush and the roses in all manner of hues were blooming, their delicate fragrance filling the air as the days warmed. To describe it as a model Village was surely an understatement of its calm beauty. The contrast with the squalor of the slum, with its foul odours exacerbated by the increasing heat, was startling. Some of the girls who arrived at this time of year were stunned by this extreme contrast to the place in which they had previously existed. Some wondered if they had died and been carried off to heaven. Regrettably for some, though, their senses had been numbed to such an extent by their dismal existence that the sudden transformation had little impact. Their hollow eyes and blank faces were reminiscent of those of the sea of workhouse women. They were unseeing, uncaring and no longer responsive to stimuli. Others could not be transformed into angels by this semblance of heaven. Their behaviour and language did not change overnight and the conversion was often challenging. Barnardo did not shy away from admitting the scale of the challenge but this did not mean he wished those more challenging girls to be too visible when visitors arrived. Nothing must be allowed to cast a cloud on what he regarded as his Christian paradise – or to jeopardise much needed monetary contributions.

Whilst the Barnardos were not always present when guests were received the Doctor had made sure he and Syrie would be available to escort them personally on this fine June day. He also wished to thank Samuel Smith again for his generous contribution to his (so far) successful emigration programme. They were familiar, obviously, with some of the visiting group but had not previously encountered The Man. Lord Cairns accordingly introduced him. The Man spoke.

"My dear Doctor, I have heard much about the truly wonderful surroundings you and your good lady wife have provided for these poor unfortunate children. They are indeed as magnificent as my dear friend Lord Cairns has told me."

Lord Cairns had only met this man on one other occasion - at Earl Fortescue's house - and therefore did not regard himself as being his 'dear friend.' He had little time for sycophants and this unwarranted familiarity had further affected, unfavourably, his judgement of the man.

Dr Barnardo responded.

"I thank you for your kind comments Sir and I, together with my dear wife of course, am proud to be able to contribute to improving the lives of these poor girls – all of whom I regard as my own dear daughters. The harrowing lives some of them have lived would, I'm sure, even though you are undoubtedly aware of some of the privations they have suffered, still shock you. They have seen poverty, depravity and wickedness a fine gentleman like yourself could not imagine. Often, I am afraid to say, due to the greed of

130

those who build their own comfortable and secure lives by the exploitation of our poorest and most vulnerable citizens."

The Man nodded solemnly as if in agreement. Inside, beneath the caring facade, his real feelings lay concealed. It was a cunning, calculated, charade. Poor and stupid; undeserving and irrelevant. These were his true feelings towards the poor and yet he stood there agreeing with the Doctor. He stood there a cold-blooded murderer whose hypocrisy clearly knew no bounds.

The tour of the Village would take the party, briefly - because the heat made it not the most pleasant place to be - to the laundry. They were given a fleeting glimpse - just enough to appreciate the magnitude of the operation. The heat and the humidity were draining and the work was hard. It was still, though, the place May liked most. The aroma of cleanliness had not lost its appeal and it was here that she was busily employed as the esteemed visitors arrived. As Lords Cairns and his party were shown around by the Barnardos she was unaware that her nemesis was once again in close proximity. She would remain, for the time being, unaware as the size of the laundry building precluded their meeting. What it did not preclude, however, was The Man becoming aware of her. This time it was something about the way the girl moved. He heard her speak loudly to be heard in the noisy laundry and this louder voice was certainly familiar. He had been reasonably sure at Earl Fortescue's residence but now, even though she was further away, he was totally convinced. He did not, however, perceive her as a threat. He saw her as inconsequential and not worthy of his concern. If May had known of his contempt then her life would not be about to take such a monumental turn.

Having left the laundry the procession made its way to call on a cottage Mother. The cottage they were to inspect was none other than May Cottage and the Mother would be Peg. It would not be the first time she had received visitors as her management of the cottage was exemplary. She had been introduced to both Lord Cairns and Samuel Smith on a previous occasion but had not encountered The Man before.

Syrie welcomed them inside to an immaculately presented home with everything in its place.

"I know that our dear colleague, Miss Butler here, is familiar to some of you already."

"Indeed," nodded Samuel Smith "and I am pleased, but not surprised, to see the highest standards are being maintained by the good lady."

Peg smiled and accepted the compliment graciously.

"Thank you sir but without the industry and diligence of my young charges the cosy home you see before you would certainly not be possible."

"I believe you have not been introduced to this gentleman before Miss Butler," Syrie indicated The Man. "He is here because he too is concerned with the plight of the poor destitute children it is our mission to help."

Peg stepped forward to shake the hand of this man as Syrie told her his name. She knew not that he was the same person May had told her about. She knew not that it was his agents who had been the ones to callously evict her from the tenement. She received him warmly as she did the others and yet she sensed there was something about him she didn't like.

"It is always a pleasure to be able to demonstrate the worth of our enterprise here but if you will excuse me gentlemen I have much to do."

Peg bowed and backed away.

"Of course, Miss Butler." Syrie turned to The Man as they left the cottage, "The young residents of this cottage so well managed by Miss Butler are all busily occupied at either their schooling which, together with their spiritual wellbeing, is considered so important by my dear husband."

Thomas Barnardo, at her side, nodded,

"Or busy at their chores so they are not here to receive you. I believe," added Dr Barnardo, "that one of the occupants of May Cottage was a member of the party who performed so well at Earl Fortescue's home."

"Ah yes, the exhibition was indeed informative and encouraging. With, I recall, the exception of the demeanour of one girl. Whether it is she who resides here I do not know but I assume not, judging by the graciousness and good example set by your Miss Butler."

Lord Cairns' opinion of The Man was further coloured by his unnecessary mention of what had occurred at Lord Fortescue's house. He had concluded that he didn't like this man.

After leaving May Cottage the party encountered Miss Henley who was on the way to her teaching duties. Pleasantries were briefly exchanged and, as the group continued on, Miss Henley overheard The Man remark to another that he believed he had seen the girl he had spoken of in the laundry. She did, he said, appear to have a saving grace - as she certainly seemed to be hard working.

Miss Henley felt that this would please May. She would be happy to know that the impression formed of her by this gentleman had been altered by her obvious ability and commitment to her duties. He had evidently seen that she would indeed make a perfectly suitable servant. She would relay this information to young May at the earliest opportunity and look forward to seeing her cheerful reaction. It would come as a surprise when May's reaction was not that which expected.

The last stop on the visit was Mossford Lodge where the guests joined the Barnardos for tea, served of course by a company of girls, before taking their leave. The Man forgot about May. His thoughts were on his future. His thoughts were concerned with much more important matters as he sat to enjoy his tea with Lord Cairns. Would his association with him help further his career? He hoped so, indeed expected so. Had he known what Lord Cairns really thought of him he would have known that it was not a patronage he should count on. As it was, he left the Village in a pleasant frame of mind.

As the visit ended May was still at work in the laundry. She was tired, ready for supper, some time with her friends and with Peg. It was over supper that Peg told the girls of how the visitors were impressed with their neat and cosy home.

"I made it quite clear that I cannot accept all the praise. I told these gentlemen that it is the industriousness of my girls that maintains such high standards."

"Did you Mother? Did you tell 'em it's us what keeps it clean?"

"Well, we do don't we? Mother makes sure we do it proper like but we know what we're doing."

May was silently eating, still unaware that The Man had actually been in her house and that he had actually shaken Peg's hand.

Twenty

The next day Miss Henley took May aside.

"May, I have something to tell you that may give you some confidence and finally put to rest your uncomfortable experience during our visit to Belgravia."

May was, for a moment, puzzled and did not realise immediately to what Miss Henley referred.

"What is it, Miss Henley?"

"You will recall the gentleman who commented adversely on your, shall we say, manner?"

"I cannot forget Miss." May uttered through gritted teeth.

"Well, that very gentleman was here yesterday with our esteemed visiting party and saw you whilst you were engrossed in your laundry duties."

"Saw me?" gasped May.

"Do not worry child. He observed how hard you were working and admitted he may have judged you too harshly. I overheard him remark that he thought you could prove to be an excellent servant. Does that not make you proud and happy?"

May's previous bravado now deserted her. 'Sod him' She had said to herself. She didn't care about him when she thought he didn't know her. She thought she was safe. But now he had been to the Village and he had been speaking about her. Why had he come if not to find her? She couldn't know about his ambition or how he hoped he could climb the political ladder by association. All she thought, all she *knew* was that he had sought her out. Sought her out but for what purpose? What should she do? She knew now that this man had entered the house where she felt the safest. He would have met Peg and possibly even spoken to her. Should she tell Peg and if she did what would Peg do?

All these thoughts swirled around her head as Miss Henley spoke again.

"May, are you not proud and happy? May..."

"I gotta go, Miss, I ain't feeling very well."

May hastily returned to an empty cottage. All except Peg were at their schooling or duties. Peg, who was mending smocks in her room, was surprised at May's unexpected arrival.

"May, why are you not at your lesson?"

"I'm sorry Peg. I don't feel right well."

Peg felt her forehead and she did indeed feel hot.

"I think you may have a temperature and should take to your bed. I will fetch you some cool water if the current heat allows it."

May went to bed to consider what she should do. She did not want Peg to be involved. She would not tell her - but what to do? For all her toughness May was, after all, only a young girl. Her judgement was not that of a wise adult, despite the fact that her instincts had served

137

her well so far. The Village had been her life for over two years now; years during which she had changed physically but even so, at thirteen, she was still a child. The safe haven that had been the Village was tainted now. Her life in the cottage was tainted. The sanctuary of May Cottage had been shattered by The Man's presence and she could never feel the same again. He had spoiled everything even if he didn't mean her any harm although somehow she thought he did. Her reasoning and decisions would not always be made by her head but by her heart and therefore, lying in her bed, she came to a life-changing decision.

Later in the day, May felt sufficiently recovered from her shock-induced fever to venture once more into Peg's room. The other girls had not yet returned and Peg was about to commence preparing supper.

"Ah May, are you feeling better now? You certainly appear so. It is fortunate the fever has passed so quickly as on some occasions such a malady can endure for several days."

May did not respond to Peg's concerned enquiry but instead blurted out.

"I want to go to Canada. I need to go Peg. I don't want to be here anymore."

She had been initially hesitant about speaking to Peg and in the end, the only way was to come straight out with it. It was hard but it was the only way she could do it. What she would not do was reveal to Peg her true reason. May didn't know what would happen if she told Peg that the visitor was Ernie's murderer. She didn't know what Peg would try to do – if she told the Doctor what would happen then? May did not know how such accusations would be dealt with; she did not know how the law worked. She knew right and wrong certainly but, as she had seen in the slum, right did not always triumph over wrong and wealth and power inevitably held sway over the likes of her. Peg looked at May with shock and surprise. This was the first time she had heard of such a desire. None of her charges were due to depart with the first party of girls and for May, out of the blue, to stress how much she felt she needed to go came as a complete shock.

"My dearest child, where has this come from? I thought you were happy here with us – with me. I thought you felt safe here. Why have you so suddenly changed your mind?"

"I just have to Peg. I want to go to another country. I always have, ever since I saw all the ships when I was with my Uncle George. I was happy here but I ain't anymore and I want to go. I'm gonna see the Doctor. I am gonna try to go with the group."

Peg knew well how stubborn May could be and if her mind was made up then there was little that could be done to change it. This did not, however, prevent Peg wondering from where this sudden idea had emanated and whether, possibly, there was some link with the visit of the group of gentlemen the previous day. Only Doctor Barnardo had the authority to sanction, or prevent, her departure in little more than a month but he had conceded to May before. Peg knew her own presence in the Village gave testimony to this.

Nothing could be done this day as the Barnardos were engaged elsewhere but the following day would find May asking a question that had become very popular with girls even as young as five. "Please may I go to Canada?"

The idea did not go down at all well with a shocked Lottie given the conversation they had had and she was very upset at the thought of losing May forever, or if not forever for a very long time.

"We talked about it before an' you said you wouldn't go. Why you changed your mind? You don't really wanna go do you May? You don't wanna leave us and Mother Peg do you? You won't find no good mates like you got 'ere, you know you won't."

"I don't think I can stay here anymore Lottie, I don't want to stay here anymore. I've made my mind up this time and I won't change it back again – I can change my mind if I want. If it's not too late then I'm gonna speak to the Doctor."

Lottie knew it was pointless to say any more despite how despondent she felt.

As far as May knew there were some seventy girls who had been prepared for the first wave of emigration

– emigration was a word May had never even heard of before but was suddenly of the utmost importance. It was just over a month before their departure was scheduled and only a few weeks before one hundred boys, who were based at another of Dr Barnardo's establishments, were leaving.

She had seen some of the preparations in other cottages for no one in hers was due to go. She had seen the chests that each girl had been allocated and some of the provisions it would contain but had heard very little of what was awaiting them in faraway Canada. As May was thirteen she would be placed as a servant - the very thing she wanted to avoid - but she would be as far away from The Man as she could be. Perhaps, she thought, she could come back and he would be dead or perhaps she could tell what he had done and, as she would be older, be believed. She was determined, somehow, to try. Not just to try but to succeed in obtaining justice.

All the girls had little knowledge of Canada. A holiday Mother, Kathleen Hardy, had come to the Village from there to learn how the community was run. She would accompany the first party of girls on their journey back to Hazelbrae – a mansion donated to Doctor Barnardo by the mayor of a town called Peterborough in the province of Ontario. Kathleen felt, by writing in the charity's magazine that was published each month, she could do her duty to paint a picture of life there that was one of realism and that did not present Canada, although it had much to commend it, as some kind of paradise. A picture that recognised a new life there may not be one of constant happiness in a magical world. Kathleen knew the work could, and for many would, be extremely hard and whilst there were endeavours to ensure the suitability of the households to which the young travellers would be dispersed this could not be entirely assured. The vast distances, incomprehensible to those whose short lives so far had been confined to London locales and the Village, made satisfactory monitoring a monumental task. There had been documented cases of ill-treatment but despite these problems it was the firm belief of Thomas Barnardo that such horrors would not happen to *his* children. They would, he sincerely believed, experience lives in Canada that would be far better than those from which they had been saved.

The contrasts between English summers and winters, although stark, were nothing compared to those in Canada. Sometimes the summers, although brief, could be so hot that the sun, instead of being bright and uplifting as on an English summer day when it punctuated spells of grey clouds and rain, was almost a curse that shrivelled much that was green. The winters were harder, and longer, than anyone who had not experienced them could imagine, although roaming the winter streets of London clothed in flimsy rags was different to the stout and much more fitting attire that was vital for survival in such bitter cold.

May felt nothing could be worse than that night in October 1880. If she, as a girl of ten, could survive that she could survive anything that this faraway place called Canada could throw at her. She did wonder whether it would mean she would never see Uncle George again. There had been no word from him but how could he possibly find her even if he came back? Perhaps he had returned but been unable to search her down. She couldn't believe he would completely abandon her – especially when he learned of his last sister's death. The thought of her uncle was something that could not cloud her reasoning or her decision to leave England and somehow, at the back of her mind and in her heart, she felt he still had a part to play in her future. Somehow she was certain of this and so it would, eventually, prove in a way she could never have imagined.

Twenty one

Peg awoke the next day with a feeling of acute sadness. She knew that May, once her mind had been made up, could not be dissuaded – by her or anyone. Breakfast was unusually quiet. Lottie found it hard to look May in the face directly and Peg, despite trying to behave as normal for the sake of the other girls, was not looking forward to accompanying May to see the Doctor.

The girls, except for Lottie and May, hurried off to their tasks or lessons. Lottie remained silent and downcast, still surprised at Mays sudden change of heart. May was agitated.

"What are you looking like that for Lottie? I ain't nothing to you, not really. I know we are friends but I ain't your sister and I have got to go. I got to."

Lottie tried to hide her feelings but could no longer and her eyes were welling up with tears. Peg's were also.

"Ain't nothing to me? You say you ain't nothing to me an' I ain't nothing to you then! I know we ain't sisters, well not by blood anyway but surely we are by heart. I told you when we first come 'ere that I ain't never really 'ad a friend. You 'ave. You 'ad friends but I 'adn't. No one 'ad ever been good t'me. That's why I was so rough like. Being friends with you an' through you coming to know Mother Peg, well, this is the best life I've ever 'ad. Now you just wanna go to bloody Canada an' leave us. You ain't no good friend. You go to bleedin Canada. You ain't worth nothing, nothing!"

Lottie pushed past May and ran outside into the garden leaving May stunned.

"Peg, Peg I didn't think Lottie would be like this. I didn't, I don't... want to hurt her or you or anyone but I... but I... well I have to, I have to go."

Peg drew May to her. She could feel May's slim body quivering, could feel her anguish, could feel her shock.

"There, child," Peg quietly spoke. "You must do what you feel is in your own best interest. Of course I will miss you, just as Lottie will miss you. I owe you much May. Perhaps more than you know. Before our meeting I had nothing. It had been that way for a long time since..."

Peg hesitated, as if she was about to reveal something of her past, but then continued. "My life was empty with no one to care for and no one to care for me. You changed that. My time, thankfully brief, in the workhouse was made bearable by thoughts of you. Then, when you brought the Doctor to take me, no not take me but save me, I was somehow not surprised to see you. Not surprised even though I had become resigned to spending all of my remaining years in that awful place."

Peg could see that May was trying hard not to cry and dabbed her young friend's eyes with a handkerchief.

"So May, you have changed my life for the better. How could I attempt to deny you the chance to change yours, if that change is one you need to make? It would be selfish of me to try to hold you here. Go May, I will come with you to speak to the Doctor. I hope he will agree to your departure and we shall then have much to prepare."

Peg smiled but it was a smile that was painted on to hide her distress and to make May feel better.

"I'll write to you Peg. I will, I promise. As often as I can and you can write to me. Perhaps Lottie will write an' all. She don't hate me Peg, does she? I couldn't bear to go so far away thinking she hates me, I just couldn't..."

May's voice trailed off until she pulled herself back to deal with the task in hand.

Peg pretended to be busy tidying clothes while she waited for May to be ready to petition the Doctor.

"Let us go then Peg."

May smoothed her dress and took a deep breath to remove the lump that still lingered in her throat.

She and Peg, hand in hand, left May Cottage to cross the Village gardens, resplendent in the warm summer sunshine, to Mossford Lodge.

Outside the laundry, slumped against the wall, Lottie watched them. She wiped her eyes on her apron, sniffed then turned and went about her chores secretly hoping that the Doctor would tell May that it was now not possible to arrange her passage. She busied herself with her tasks. The enveloping steam and the oppressive heat left her no time to dwell on the possibility of losing May. When the time came for lunch she returned to May Cottage to hear, what she thought, the worst.

May and Peg were already there. Peg was busy as usual but May was quiet. She did not look happy. Lottie knew, instantly, seeing her unhappy face that her quest had not, after all, been successful. Lottie approached May in silence. May looked up.

"I ain't going. He said it's too late to change things now an' add another girl. So I ain't, I can't go. S'pose you're happy now!" May immediately looked away so did not see Lottie's shocked face. How did she feel? She didn't know, she was confused. Of course she was glad May was staying but not like this. She knew May well enough to know how obstinate and stubborn she could be so she would not easily accept a situation she did not like. She would be miserable and unhappy – not what Lottie wanted in a friend.

May in that frame of mind was not what Peg wanted either. What she wanted was to know just why going to Canada was suddenly so important. There had to be a reason. A reason that mattered so much to May that she was desperate to leave a place where Peg thought, no knew, that she had been happy, a place where she had felt safe. It was obvious from May's palpable fear that she felt safe no longer.

The girls had finished their lunch and returned to their prospective classes or tasks. Peg, who had been unable to speak properly with May on their way back from the Doctor's office, knew that something must be said. Lottie had also hung back but May appeared to be keen to escape from their scrutiny as quickly as possible.

"I am going to my work now." She did not look either of them in the eye as she turned towards the door.

"Wait." Peg's voice was firm. Lottie watched Peg's face – sensing that she was determined not to let May get away without at least attempting to extract an answer, a reason, from her.

"I gotta go. I got to go to the laundry and do my work."

"May, I asked - no I told you - to wait."

She turned to a puzzled looking Lottie "and you too Lottie."

"Now May why is... was...the journey to Canada so important to you? We care for you and you must tell us now."

"Well, I ain't. I ain't and you can't make me!"

She shrugged off Lottie's attempt to comfort her.

"Leave me alone and let me go to my work." May was shouting now and she rushed from the cottage leaving Peg and Lottie bewildered and sad.

"Mother Peg, what are we gonna do about her? I ain't ever seen her like this."

Peg, white-faced and visibly shaking, could only try to console Lottie.

"There, there child, I think we must be patient and all will be well. We must give her some time."

Inwardly, however, she was not so confident.

Twenty two

May immersed herself in her work, her mind racing. What would she do? Would she wait for The Man to come for her as she was certain he would? Would she, should she, run away? If so where could she go? Not back to the Nichol; there was nothing for her there. The only people who had mattered to her were her mum, her uncle and Peg. Mum and Uncle George were gone and Peg was here so if she left she would have no one. But...Uncle George, although he was gone from her life, was not dead - she knew he wasn't dead and if he was alive then he was somewhere. He was somewhere and she would find him! She would run away and she would find him and he would take care of her – of course he would! Where was he? Her mood lurched from exhilarating optimism to deep concern. What hope had she of finding him? She didn't even know which part of the army he had joined and it was some three years since she had last seen him. No matter. She would forsake the Village and make her own way. She would not wait for the evil, wicked Man to find her.

While she worked she planned her escape. She knew it would be tricky but it was something she could, something she must, do. She would go at night. Peg slept soundly and May felt confident she could make her way through the gardens to a place where it was possible to leave the grounds of Mossford Village unseen. She would leave the Village and somehow find her way back to London. From there she did not know, but she was a tough, resourceful girl. She had survived on her own before and she could do it again. She was older, stronger and she was able to read. She would need a couple of days to think about the details – what she would need to take – and then she would be off. She would be off far away from the friends she had made, away from Peg, away from the Doctor and his wife, who had surely saved her life. Was running away the way to thank her? No, it wasn't but as she saw it she had no choice. She had wanted to go to Canada but they had said she could not so there was no choice.

The next couple of days, as her chosen departure day loomed, were difficult for May. She tried to behave as normally as she could; tried to make Peg and Lottie think she had resigned herself to the fact that she must remain. They knew her well enough, though, to suspect that something was not right - even if they had no idea what May was actually planning.

Then, on the very morning May was planning to leave, fate stretched out its hand once more and the course of her life took another turn.

Twenty three

It had started with an early morning commotion - an arrival at the Village - that shattered the peace and constancy that was generally a feature of life there. It was an event that would cause the Doctor considerable concern. A woman had turned up at the gates shouting and screaming for her daughter. She denounced the Doctor as a kidnapper. She accused him of stealing her daughter away from her own flesh and blood to be a slave in a far off land. The Doctor was not present so the task of dealing with this most unexpected problem fell to the Governor of the Village.

The Governor, together with his wife, undertook the day to day running of Mossford Village. His concern was not with the social, the spiritual or the educational wellbeing of the girls. His concern was to ensure the mundane, practical matters that kept the Village running smoothly were properly attended to. He did not, under usual circumstances, come into direct contact with matters of welfare other than making provision for adequate food and other such essentials. All matters beyond these were the province of the Doctor and he alone – even though Syrie's support was vital.

Suddenly, on this day when the fine weather had suddenly dissolved into dismal dampness, the

Governor was faced with this woman; a woman trembling with rage and distress, shaking the gates and demanding entry. At first he tried to explain that the Doctor was not there and that it was only he who could speak with her about her daughter. This was not good enough. She demanded to see, if not the Doctor, then his wife as she was party to this kidnapping also! She was just as bad! The Governor tried again to reason with her but she threatened to slash her wrists right then and there if he did not let her in. She would do it! She would kill herself in front of him if he did not let her in to find her daughter!

Over in May Cottage and other cottages away from the gate, Peg and the other Mothers could hear the commotion but could not determine was it was or what repercussions it would have. Those nearest rushed to see if there was anything they could do. This situation was unheard of in the Village and, in an act unprecedented, the Governor with support from clearly distressed Mothers and teachers, felt he had no choice but to let the woman in. He could not have the blood of a seemingly deranged woman on his hands.

She rushed through the gardens with no clear route as she had no idea where her daughter was. She was screaming her name.

In a classroom a group of girls, the ones preparing for Canada, were being drilled in matters relating to their trip. Among those girls there was one about to receive a big shock. Emily firstly imagined she had heard her name called. But why? Then suddenly there was recognition. The voice - it sounded like her mother! She had not seen her mother for... for how long? She didn't know but her mother had not only agreed for the Doctor to take her daughter away but actually begged him to do so. Emily's mother could remember none of this as it occurred when she was lost in a haze of gin.

The shouting grew closer. Emily rose, confused, from her seat and despite remonstrance from her teacher hurried outside.

From across the garden Peg watched as the woman ran towards the shocked girl and gathered her up in her arms. Emily recognised her mother and yet there was something different about her. It wasn't that she had a different hat or a dress that, whilst old and worn, showed she had tried to make an effort of sorts, it was something more. At first though, the girl pulled away; the woman tried again; the Governor and the teachers surrounded them. Peg could hear voices were raised but could not hear what was being said. The girl was obviously speaking back to her mother. She was understandably in turmoil and yet she could not deny this woman did not seem the same as the one who had let her go without any regret at all. She genuinely appeared to care this time and the pleading look in her tearful eyes seemed to bore down into Emily's very heart.

Peg turned away; she couldn't watch anymore and returned inside May cottage. Something inside told her the outcome of this encounter would be one that would tear her in two. She knew the girl was lined up for Canada and wondered, should she decide to go with her mother - as the girls were not prisoners - would the Doctor seek a replacement? If he did then, likely as not, that replacement would be May.

May wasn't aware of what had happened until she returned to the cottage later in the day. After supper, she aimed to get ready for her clandestine departure and was extremely scared. Could she, should she, change her mind? No! She decided finally – she would go. But then, just as supper was finishing and the girls were about to clear away, there was a visitor - Kathleen Hardy. She had arrived in some haste and quietly took Peg to one side out of earshot of her charges. It was as Peg had feared.

Doctor Barnardo, on his return, had spoken with the Governor - who was understandably agitated as he had felt he had no choice but to let the woman remain on the premises. This was an unusual situation and the Governor was apprehensive as to whether Dr Barnardo would accept his handling of it. As the Doctor saw it he agreed there was no choice. Subsequently, he met with the woman, first alone and then with her daughter, Emily. Kathleen explained to Peg the outcome of the meeting and then left. It would be up to Peg to speak to May.

The girls were curious as to the reason for Kathleen's visit. Once supper was over and the clearing away done the cottage was generally self-contained unless, as it was summer, any communal evening activities had been arranged. Peg, having seen Kathleen off, returned to the girls.

"Come along my young ladies, you know what is required of you. Be about your remaining tasks. All except you May, I need to speak to you."

May wondered why Peg needed to see her. She followed Peg to her room. Lottie watched, puzzled. What was happening with May now?

"What is it Peg? What have I done?"

May was nervous. Had her plan to leave the Village been discovered? If so, how? She had told no one – not even Lottie. Perhaps her bundle had been found. Perhaps...her thoughts were cut short.

"My dear May, do not worry. You have done nothing wrong."

Not yet, May thought.

"I must ask you a question. I must ask this question but, sadly, I think I already know the answer."

"What Peg? What question?"

"Do you still wish, for whatever personal reasons you may have, to leave us to go to Canada?"

May was shocked. She was silent. This was not what she was expecting. Not at all.

"What do you mean Peg? The Doctor said I couldn't go. He said there was no room because I asked so late, so what..."

Peg held up her hand to silence May.

"I will explain, so listen."

May was impatient. She was confused but she sat down to listen as Peg bade her.

"A girl from Honeysuckle Cottage was a member of the party due to depart in two weeks. She had been residing in the Village as her mother was not able or indeed willing, to care for her. But, as sometimes happens, and all of us should be grateful when it does, the girl's mother has transformed her life to such an extent that she desires to, and is now able to, take care of her again. Her recollection of the circumstances that led to her daughter being removed from her charge is, I'm told, unclear as her mind was... confused. When she heard, and how we do not know, about the plan for emigration and that her own daughter was scheduled to go, it spurred her on to get the girl back. It was, I understand from Kathleen Hardy, quite difficult for the Doctor to convince this woman that her daughter had not been stolen as she had loudly claimed and there was no intention for her to become a slave. In her turn, the woman admitted her past...troubles and explained she had secured regular employment that would enable

157

her to resume the care of her daughter. The Doctor, still with some trepidation, however, was resigned to letting the girl return to her mother."

Peg awaited a response. May had quietly listened, taking everything in. Then, though, she began to shake and tears welled up in her eyes. She was a volcano about to erupt; a dam about to burst.

"Oh, Peg. I was gonna run away tonight. This very night! I've got a bundle under my bed and I was gonna leave in the night an' not tell you. Peg I was, I was but now I don't have to. I don't have to run away. I can go like I wanted to. I can get away."

"Away from what? Surely not me, surely not your friends? But seeing you like this I know it must be something... a very powerful reason."

May knew it was time to tell Peg why she had suddenly needed to get away.

"I'll tell you Peg. I wanted to tell you before but I didn't want you to know in case you said something an' he... he, well he might have done something to you. After seeing him at that posh house I didn't think he'd come 'ere. He came right in my house an' since then I'm scared of 'im. I know what he done. I know what he is an' I gotta get away from 'im."

May's distress was clear to Peg. She took May by the shoulders and spoke.

"I asked you his name once before May. Do you remember? You wouldn't tell me but now I think I know to whom you refer. I am sure it is the person who murdered your friend as I knew the other visitors and although I had not I met this person before, intuitively, I did not like him. I also felt that Lord Cairns had little time for him either."

Even as Peg spoke these words she realised that to try to bring this man to justice would be impossible. Peg was a pragmatist. She knew first hand from experiences in her own life that wealth and power were difficult to challenge. She could imagine The Man's response to an accusation from one such as May.

He would obviously contest the accusation: 'A murderer? How can such an accusation be made? Who is it that I, a well-respected gentleman, am accused of murdering? A boy you say – what boy?'

Having met the Man, Peg found it easy to picture the scene. There was no proof of his crime. Many people - many boys - had no doubt perished that unseasonably cold night. Moreover, who was there to accuse him? Just a young girl, a street girl, a person of no importance, the same girl who had been rebuked by him for sullenness. She had something against him, she deliberately chose him to try to sully his good name. This was how Peg surely saw the scene playing out.

"I can't do nothing Peg, not to a bloke like what he is."

Peg had reasoned why the accusation could never work; May knew instinctively.

"It is with regret May, that I have to agree with you. The world is indeed unfair to the likes of us but even so, for one such as he there must, one day, come a reckoning. I believe this. Surely such a person cannot go through his life not regretting or not being troubled by his action. Surely his conscience will eat away at him and one day he will face up to the terrible thing he has done."

"He won't Peg. Not unless someone makes him and if it can't be the law, those judges and the like, then it'll 'ave to be someone else. I know I'm only a kid but I won't always be. I'm gonna go to Canada an' when I grow up – when I know more than what I do now, then I'll come back. I'll come back an' I'll make the wicked bugger pay. I swear I will."

May said these words with such grit, such determination, that Peg shivered. She could see the steel in May's eyes. She was scared of The Man now certainly. She had reason to be Peg supposed and she understood why. As a child May was powerless but Peg could look forward into the future. She saw, she imagined, the May of the future. She saw a young woman who would, indeed, have the strength and resolve to somehow take on and thwart her murderous nemesis. Peg could envisage this and it was her dearest wish that she would still be in this world to see it.

For a short time there was silence between the two of them. The importance of the revelation and the effect on both May and Peg needed time to properly sink in. Finally, Peg spoke, gently, to tell May to go to bed. In the morning the task of preparing for Canada would have to begin in earnest.

May hugged Peg and quietly went to her bedroom where, she thought, Lottie was asleep. She wasn't.

"May, what's 'appening? What's going on with you?"

"Everything's changed, Lottie. I am going to Canada now but I'm too tired to talk anymore so I'll tell you in the morning."

"I thought that was it, I knew you'd end up going I could feel it somehow."

"Night Lottie."

May settled down, after quietly removing the bundle from under her bed - relieved she did not have cause to use it now. She slept soundly. She did, actually for the first time since she had decided to run away, but Peg did not. May was leaving and she might never see her again.

Twenty four

By the next day, the weather had changed and the July sun once again shone brightly. The drizzle of the previous day had refreshed the flowers in the Village Garden and the freshness, the seeming newness, reflected the new beginning that May anticipated.

The girls had woken early and whilst getting the younger ones ready May explained to Lottie what had happened and why she was now able to go. She didn't enlighten her about Ernie or The Man. This would be too much for her to relate again and, she felt, for Lottie to take in. How she would deal with this revelation she did not know yet she felt she owed it to Lottie, as her friend, to tell her the truth.

At breakfast, Peg made the announcement that May would soon be leaving May Cottage. Some of the little girls cried because they would miss May. They didn't understand why she would want to leave them. Did she not care about them anymore?

"I'll miss all of you, I will but I'll write to Mother and she can read to you all what I am doing all the way across the big sea. I won't forget any of you. I promise I won't and I will come back. I've told Mother, I've promised Mother I'll come back. Now come on you lot, eat your breakfast, we've got our jobs to do, our prayers to say and our lessons to be learned."

May suddenly felt grown up. She knew that when she left the Village for the other side of the world she would, despite still being under the protective umbrella of Doctor Barnardo, be on her own again. The time between her mother's death and her arrival at the Village had been comparatively short and as she was younger then she could not truly be aware of or understand all of what being on her own could mean. With the exception of the murder of Ernie the more unsavoury aspects of life in Old Nichol had not, fortunately, contrived to touch her. Some of what she saw was viewed as through a veil of detachment and, of course, her innocence. Whether this situation would have continued had May been on her own much longer who could say but that was the past. What was important now was the future. In this hopefully bright new future May would grow; she would learn, she would prepare herself for a return to London that would be instrumental in bringing about the demise of The Man. She knew this. She had no doubts.

Emily was roughly the same size as May. This was fortunate for the Doctor as it meant there needed to be no further incursion into his, as usual, meagre funds. It meant new clothing for travelling would not need to be purchased especially for May as all the items necessary were already sorted. The leather trunk, which had already been branded with Emily's name, could not be replaced as these were costly to produce. The solution was to rebrand May's name and burn out Emily's. It would look messier than the others but this was something that was of no concern whatsoever to May.

The jackets the girls had been issued with for travelling were bright red with hoods, much the same as that described as being worn by Little Red Riding Hood in her heroic encounter with the Big Bad Wolf. Red Riding Hood overcame her own powerful nemesis and there was a parallel of sorts here. No wicked wolf as such to escape from and ultimately triumph over but an equally wicked human foe who May believed was determined to make sure she would never expose him.

May would be one of the many Little Red Riding Hoods. They, although not aiming to escape from a flesh and blood enemy like The Man, were nonetheless anticipating an escape - from their previous lives. The Village at Mossford Green had been the staging post between their lowly origins and their (possibly?) exciting new future. Their Big Bad Wolf was the dark streets of the slums; the wolf's savage jaws were the vices that could close in to crush them physically, spiritually and morally. The smaller girls especially did not understand the perils of their past, or indeed, the potential perils of their comparatively unknown future. What they had was the anticipation of something better. They had been convinced that something better awaited them but Canada had wolves too – and not just of the lupine variety. There would be joy for some but disappointment for others.

Whilst some of the girls were indeed orphans, there were others, like Emily, who did have family of their own. Whether their families would ever be in a position to offer them the kind of life vulnerable young girls needed was another matter. In some cases perhaps they would be, having lives that could be turned around as Emily's mother had turned hers around. Perhaps they would regret that they would never again set eyes on their children. Perhaps, but this was something the Doctor would not concern himself with. To him, the spiritual and moral wellbeing of the girls was at least as important as their physical wellbeing – perhaps even more so. The girls were his 'daughters' and he knew, he was sure, what was best for his 'daughters'. The belief was reinforced by the Doctor at every turn was that there was a better life to come for them.

The certainty exuded by the Doctor; his total faith that what he was doing was the right thing, was infectious and there was no room for dissent. The whole Village was in a state of excitement. The Mothers whose charges were leaving were, by turn, sad to lose them but happy that the girls were looking forward to their adventure. Those girls who were not going were, by turn, regretful that they couldn't leave yet relieved that they were remaining in the secure environs of the Village. Those who were leaving were getting restless and impatient to go even though they, understandably, were apprehensive as well since their future was uncertain.

May was getting restless too. She just wanted the wait to be over. There was talk that visitors were coming again to the Village to join in the event to celebrate the first party of girls to depart. Perhaps, if this were true, The Man would again be among the number and May hoped this would not be the case. As it happened it was not – there was a celebration on the Village Green but it was entirely for those who remained, both girls and staff, to say goodbye, to wish their friends well.

The day before departure the trunks had been loaded onto carts and sent ahead leaving only small bags for the girls to travel with – bags that contained their own bibles and very little else as legacies from their life at Mossford Village. What May would not leave behind and was determined to keep with her was her shawl, which by now was almost disintegrated, and the faded brown photograph of the younger Peg. She showed the photograph to Peg before she tucked it safely into her bag.

"I'll always keep it with me Peg. All the time, wherever I go, I'll keep it until I come back to you again. And I'll write and I'll keep the letters you write back to me. You will write Peg won't you? I know you already said you would but you really will won't you? You won't forget me will you?"

"Of course I will write to you May and how could I ever forget you? You may be gone away but your spirit will still be here and I will feel it with me every single day. I will tell you all about what we are doing here, all about Lottie, if she does not write to you herself of course – but I think she will indeed! I will write about the Doctor and his work. I'll write about the news from London and, if you wish it, I will write to you to tell you what the Man is doing also. Would you wish it May?"

Peg had paused before saying The Man as she was tempted to say his name but knew that May did not wish to hear his name spoken.

"I do wish it Peg. I do want to know. I will not forget him. He may come here again looking for me and when he finds I am no longer here he may think I can no longer be a ... threat – is that the word? – to him. Let him think this. I *know* I will make him pay someday."

Peg nodded and studied May's resolute face as she prepared to go to bed for the last time in May Cottage. Peg did not doubt her unwavering intent. Not for one minute.

May hugged Peg and turned to go to her room. As she was leaving Peg called her back.

"May, I have something for you. Something I thought I would never give up but now I wish for you to have it."

Peg removed the silver cross and passed it to May.

"I cannot take this Peg. You said it was what gave you comfort when you are sad. I cannot take the one thing that gives you comfort."

"When I was living, if that is truly the right word for the terrible conditions, in both the tenement and the workhouse, I needed comfort. Now, thanks to you I am here and no longer in need of a crutch to aid me through each day. I want you to have it so when you are far away and, perhaps, feeling lonely or sad it will make you think of me and you will be given comfort also. Now please my dear May, take it."

May was unable to speak as a lump had formed in her throat. She smiled weakly, nodded and took the cross before leaving Peg's room.

The other girls were all resting now. The day that followed would, for them, be much the same as any other. Lottie waited for May to come into their room for the last time.

"After tomorrow May I might not never ever see you again. I can't believe it, now the time's come like."

"You *will* see me, Lottie. I will come back."

May meant it and Lottie could see she meant it. For the last time, May and Lottie wished each other a good night.

168

All across the Village girls ranging from a mere four years old to those of fourteen were settling down for *their* last night also. Some slept peacefully whereas others were uneasy, restless and a little scared.

The big day dawned bright and warm. Gradually the Village came to life. Normal life didn't stop because of the girls leaving. Chores still had to be done, prayers still had to be said and lessons still had to be learned - but perhaps a little later than usual.

May, along with the others, rose and dressed in her travelling clothes. They ate their breakfasts. They said their final goodbyes. They took one last look around the cottages that had been their home and went outside to join their fellow travellers.

They would be accompanied on the entire journey by Kathleen Hardy and a male official representative of the Doctor to whom they had been introduced only recently. The Doctor himself would accompany the party and remain with them until such time as the ship would depart. This would be a momentous event for him – the first contingent of girls sent to Canada entirely under his own auspices. He had to see them go. He had to give them his blessing and let them know how much he cared for each and every one. He was sure that this was the right thing to do. The problem would be that, unlike in the Village where he had complete mastery and authority, the authority would have to be delegated in faraway Canada. This bothered

Thomas Barnardo, who needed to be in control. It bothered him but not enough to dent his optimism that this *truly* was the right thing to do. Only time would tell.

The Doctor said goodbye to Syrie and their children then climbed into his own carriage to lead the convoy through the gates of Mossford Village. The girls clambered aboard the wagons that would take them first the few miles to the station at nearby Ilford, from there the train to Liverpool Street and finally to Euston. Here they would board their last train on English soil – the one that would take them to their port of departure – Liverpool. This great port was a place that until recently the girls had never heard of. The other occupants of the Village came out to bid farewell to their friends. There were tears; there was sadness but there was joy also as the convoy left the community that had been their home.

"I won't forget you May!" Lottie shouted.

Peg squeezed Lottie's shoulders and stroked her hair as she struggled to hold back her own tears and manage the lump in her throat. Despite what May had told her about coming back, something, somehow told Peg that this view of May – her smiling face and waving hands could be the last time she laid eyes on her. Peg shivered as a lone cloud passed in front of the bright sun and momentarily cast a shadow. Would time prove her right? She prayed it would not be so and hoped her prayer would be answered.

May watched as Peg and Lottie waved. She waved back with both hands, a bright smile lighting up her face. The smile though was a mask. She didn't want the last view of her by her dear friends to be one of gloom. Behind that cheerful mask, May was not only sad she was angry too. Angry at the Man. Angry that it was because of him she had to leave the place where she had been happy. She continued waving until they had passed through the gates of Mossford Village and she could see them no more. The mask then fell swiftly away.

Twenty five

Liverpool, July 1883

Kathleen Hardy stood before the Sardinian, the ship they were about to board. Leading the excited column of chattering girls was the portly figure of the Doctor, ushering and shepherding his 'daughters' onto the vessel that would be the conduit to their new lives.

The girls were all filled with a certain degree of trepidation. This was to be expected as none of them had ever embarked upon such a journey before. Only Kathleen was filled with a trepidation that the others could not share. The main reason for this was that she had made her first crossing some five years ago on the very same ship and on that unfortunate occasion there had been a fire that caused two fatalities. She had crossed the Atlantic on subsequent voyages but not again, until now, on the Sardinian. She looked at the trusting faces of her charges, eager for answers and reassurance. The ship, she knew, had crossed many times without incident since her eventful journey. She genuinely brushed off her misgivings, smiled and replied to the girls to set their minds at rest.

The questions came flying thick and fast from the company of girls. As Kathleen was the only one who had actually crossed the Atlantic before she was the target of all these excitable questions. Her male companion was making his first trip so also had doubts of his own – would he be sick? The weather was fine but, even in July this could change. Kathleen hoped, for the sake of the girls, it would not.

"It's safe Miss innit?"

"I ain't ever been on a big ship like this; I ain't even ever seen one I ain't."

"It won't sink miss will it?"

"Will it get rough out there miss, on the big sea like?"

"Will there be sea monsters and whales? Will we see 'em?"

"Well, my young ladies this fine ship has crossed the ocean many times and has returned safely. You may feel some sickness but truly you have no reason to be fearful. You may indeed see whales but as for sea monsters, well I have crossed on several occasions and never yet have I beheld a sea monster."

Kathleen laughed and the girl who had asked the question looked disappointed.

The Doctor gathered all the girls around him and requested that they sing for him one last time before he had to leave. As they sang the hymns they had learned off by heart May stepped back and instead of singing, which she avoided as much as possible, looked around the ship. From where the group stood she could see one of the masts and the funnel. She had wanted to travel, she had wanted to journey on a big ship and now this was about to happen.

As the Doctor left the girls waved until they could no longer see him. Would they see him again? Would he see them again? He intended to do so certainly, with a visit planned for the following year. Whether he would be able to visit all of his young emigrants though was debatable, especially if the homes to which they were sent were far away from the Barnardo's Ontario base. He wanted to visit as many as he possibly could and see them settled and happy. He was confident they would all, indeed, be settled and happy.

The voyage, at first, was exciting. It was something none of the girls could have imagined. After the first couple of days though the novelty had worn off as one day was much the same as the next. The six hundred passengers were mainly steerage and within the confines of the ship the same faces were seen regularly. Those who were fortunate enough to afford their own cabins did not fraternize with those of a lower class but this suited May just fine. She spent as much time as she could with Kathleen to try to find out more about what she was about to face.

"What sort of place will I go to Miss? Are the people in Canada very different from in England? Are there toffs there as well?"

The first was a question that Kathleen couldn't answer. She didn't know. She tried to reassure. Of course the Doctor would never send his 'Little Daughters' to bad places, bad people. Of course they would be well treated and looked after. Doctor Barnardo would expect nothing less and would accept nothing less. May wanted to believe Kathleen as she was a good and kind person. She knew that the Doctor was also a good and kind person – the person who had saved not just her but many others. Yes, she wanted to believe but in reality wondered if even the Doctor could make such promises when he was so far away.

May knew there was good and bad everywhere. She had seen it. She knew how closely they could exist together. She knew there would often be only a brief separation between the two; a toss of a coin. As for the other questions, Kathleen answered as truthfully as she was able.

"Well, May I must tell you that I have found the people in your new country to be very much the same as in the old. They have the same problems – how best to try to thrive, how to cope when events are not as they hoped. They have to struggle with the harsh winters and often their faith is sorely tested just as it is in England. They have the same aspirations of a good life just as people anywhere have. The challenges they face are often very different to those faced in England but they are just people doing the best, trying the best, they can. As for whether there are toffs, well there are certainly wealthy people but perhaps not toffs in quite the same way as back in England."

"Thank you Miss. Oh, and Miss, if I write a letter to Mother Peg will it be posted and reach her? I wish to tell her about the voyage as I fear that if I do not put down my thoughts now while we are still on the ship, I will forget them."

"I can certainly arrange for your letter to be dispatched as soon as it is possible. Several of the girls have asked me and I think it is a good thing to do this. I am sure Miss Butler will be pleased to hear from you - even if it may take some time for the letter to arrive. Fetch it to me after your breakfast in the morning."

In a quiet place, or as quiet a place as it was possible to find whilst quartered with so many others, May took out her pen and some paper. She began to write.

17th July 1883
Dearest Peg
I hope that this letter finds you and Lottie of course, very well. I would like to think you miss me but not so much that you are sad as I would not like to think of you sad and without your cross for comfort. Thank you for so kindly giving it me. The ship is very big Peg. I told you I wanted to go to different places of the world in a big ship but I never really thought I would you know. The sea is so big as well. It is not just a sea – it is called the Atlantic Ocean. I could not have pictured

176

it Peg. Truly I could not. I suppose you have seen the sea. You never told me but I reckon you must have. You should see the colours of it, the way it changes. Sometimes it is grey and sometimes it is blue and sometimes like a mixture of colours. Sometimes it looks calm and peaceful and then just in a blink of an eye it can turn angry and wild. I don't like it like that. It is scary then but we have been lucky and it has not been too rough. The way it changes Peg I think it is like me, like how I can change. Sometimes I can be calm and peaceful like with you in the May Cottage then something happens like with The Man when I was going to run away and I was like the sea then when it roughs up with big waves. I tried to be calm but I was all boiling and angry in my heart.

It's when it's dark that it's really strange Peg. It's like the sea and the sky join into one and it's like the ship is floating but not on water but in the air, like a feather it is. There is nothing around us just the dark, then in the morning it's just the sea again like we have not gone anywhere but I know we have. I told you about my uncle going on big ships Peg but he did not tell me it was like this. I just want to see the land again. Just want to get there. I think there are still four more days on the sea so we are not there yet.

Do not worry about me dear Peg. I will be very well really and I will write to you when I get to the place Hazelbrae. It will be a nice place I am sure. Miss

177

Hardy has shown us pictures. It looks a good place. It stands on a hill with gardens around. I am thinking of May Cottage and the beautiful gardens there and I can see them when I close my eyes. Sometimes I wake up and for a second forget that I am not there, but that I am still there. But I will be there again so I am not sad.

I am wearing your cross and will treasure it until I can return it to you and I've got your picture and all. Please know how much I care about you and look forward to hearing from you.

All my love to you May Harris

May read the letter through, smiled to herself and tucked it into an envelope. She carefully wrote the address;

Miss P Butler
May Cottage
Mossford Village
Barkingside
Ilford
Essex

She imagined Peg opening the letter. She imagined how pleased she would be to hear from her and she imagined Peg settling down to write a reply. A reply May was looking forward to receiving but knew would not be for some considerable time.

Twenty six

It was with intense relief for all the girls that land was at last spotted. As that land came gradually closer the difference between the country they had left and that which was to become their new home became apparent. It seemed so big; even the colours of the land ahead of them seemed sharper, fresher – a new world. As the coast of Ontario grew steadily closer the realisation dawned that this was it. This was their future. The eight days spent aboard the Sardinian, the eight days spent in a kind of limbo between the old life of the past and the new life to come were almost over.

There was no going back; they were in Canada with all its uncertainties, its highs and lows, to come. The party were excited, scared and full of anticipation as they left the Sardinian. With the relief of being safely on dry land again came the apprehension of a giant step into the unknown. They felt the solid ground beneath their feet. For some, who had become used to the motion of the ship, it seemed strange: for others, the relief was such that they cried out loud. Others cried for a different reason. Suddenly the epic change in their young lives was a reality. This strange land was to be their home for...how long? Would they ever return to England? Would they want to? Even if they did would they be able to or, perhaps, if they didn't want to would they be made to return? Would they be sent back to a life that seemed, already, like a dream.

Kathleen looked around her charges, sorting them into smaller groups with older ones to reassure (or try to) younger ones. Strong girls, like May, were placed with those who were overwhelmed by the sheer magnitude of their situation.

The girls stood out even without their red travelling coats that had been removed due to the heat. They were looked at by people going about their business at the port as curiosities. One girl, slightly older than May and one she hadn't really had anything to do with before the voyage, took offence at some of the looks they were given.

"What d'ya think you're looking at? What are we, animals? No, we ain't, we're girls from England and your Canada should be glad to 'ave us!"

There were murmurings from onlookers as Kathleen hurriedly steered the girls away having gently quietened down the noisy, upset child. May was reminded of her first encounter with Lottie and smiled. She missed Lottie. Did Lottie miss her? She must write to Lottie when she was settled. Settled. Somehow she wondered if she would ever be truly settled again. There were many things she wondered about. The Man was one of them. She wondered if he had looked for her again. What was he doing and had he hurt anyone else?

The long journey from the port of Quebec began by train; a train journey that was followed by the final stretch to the house called Hazelbrae by wagons, carriages and whatever vehicles were available to convey the girls. May found it hard to believe that all the fuss, as she saw it, was for them. There was a band - the Fire Brigade Band - playing a cheerful welcoming song that May had never heard before. The trees lining the way to Hazelbrae had been hung with Chinese lanterns. May had seen such things before but would never have imagined they would be used to welcome someone such as her.

"Cor is this all for us is it?" one girl remarked.

"Yeah must be as we are all that's come."

At the end of the drive was a house on a different scale to the cottages at Mossford Village and one that would mean yet another change in the lives of the girls.

Whether this change was easier to manage for the older girls or the younger ones it was difficult to say. May was one of the older girls and one who had, despite the comparatively short time she had had to prepare, tried to learn about the place to where they had come. The first few days at Hazelbrae were a round of familiarisation exercises. For some of the girls the traumatic combination of the long sea journey, the weather - it was extremely hot - and the wide open spaces were too much. One girl of ten years old had cried that the sky was too big and she thought it would

181

surely fall and eat her. Another younger girl found it hard to understand that the sun and the moon they saw were the same heavenly bodies they had seen in England.

All in all though, the transition was managed well by most. Perhaps it was that their short lives had never really been settled. They had been used to making the best of whatever was thrown at them. They had had no choice. Canada was just another step further along a road that had always been one of twists and turns, darkness and light.

May was getting restless. Hazelbrae was indeed a fine place but a fine place that was very different from Mossford Village. The grounds were extensive but there were plants and trees that she hadn't seen before. Even the air seemed different somehow. She had made friends, of course she had, but they were - by necessity - of a transient nature. Girls would be dispersed across the region to their various placements - either collected or sent by train or carriage and May herself only had a short time left before leaving for her new home. If home could be the right word. She knew not to whom she would go but had been told by the Matron that her ability to speak how they judged to be 'properly' and manage her accent should ensure she was employed by a family who set store by an attribute such as this. Despite intense teaching, some of the girls found it all but impossible to remove the often unintelligible East

End twang from their speech. Furthermore, some saw no reason to do so anyway. They were what they were. They were not ashamed of what they were and they must be accepted for what they were.

After a couple of weeks spent in domestic tasks and the schoolroom, May was summoned to be told of her fate. There was a Reverend; a churchman who lived in a town not too far – by Canadian standards - from Peterborough and Hazelbrae. His congregation was spread far and wide. His church was the spiritual centre of the county and the point where the disparate communities would travel to gather and worship for divine sustenance.

May wrote to Peg.

Dearest Peg

Well, I am here now in a big new country that I am told could have England fitted in it nearly a hundred times. I don't know if that is right but it is ever so big Peg. I thought the train journey from where we got off the ship was never going to end. Much further than from London to Liverpool it was. This land is as big as the sea or so I think.

The people are mostly nice but as you know there are always them that you don't get on with very well. I am going to be with a churchman and his wife and son. They live not too far from here. I have met the Reverend and he seems a good man. A bit like our

Doctor. Not to look at because our Doctor is short but this Reverend is tall and quite thin. I think they would look funny next to each other but would surely get on good as they both love Jesus.

I am going to be in Hazelbrae for a little while longer until I go to the Reverend's family and will try to write to you when I get there. I hope you got the letter I wrote you from the ship and I am waiting to hear from you. Miss Hardy said we should get letters from home soon as they will be sent here to Hazelbrae. If I have moved on by the time they come we have been told they will be passed on to us so that is something to look forward to.

Your friend always
May Harris

The Church was the only place where the people had the opportunity to meet on a regular basis and this hub needed a young helper who would present an appropriate face to the Reverend's congregation. He needed a young lady with a bright mind, a caring disposition and a tongue that would not cause those who came to his Church expecting piety and good manners any distress. There had been others before her but they had not lasted very long - for whatever reason.

In the past, May had recognised that language of the East End of London, the twang, the dropping of the aitches, were attributes she may prosper better without.

She did not - not at all - feel ashamed of her past, of her birth, but she was a realist and thus knew that those who spoke as she had done were often looked down upon. They were common. They were inferior. They did not deserve to climb out of the gutter in which they were born and where they surely would reside for the whole of their miserable little lives.

This would not be May, she was determined about that and with the exception of times of worry or stress her manner of speech was exemplary. It was this that caused May to be commended to the Reverend as a suitable replacement for his previous emigrant helper although the reason for this one, a boy, to leave was somewhat unclear.

The first time May saw the Reverend was as he entered Hazelbrae with the bright sun shining behind him. She could not see his features only his form, which was tall and thin - although this was accentuated by the light that seemed to both radiate from and engulf him. He was a kindly man with almost an aura of otherworldliness about him. All his life he had endeavoured to seek out the good in everyone – even in those where there was little or nothing to find. As he became more visible May judged him positively. His would, she thought, be a good household to go to, a household that could not replace her home (she suddenly realised she had never truly thought of May Cottage *as home* before) but a good place nonetheless.

185

He had a wife and a young son who was by all accounts a sickly child to whom it would be May's duty to help and give companionship.

So it was that May took up residence at the vicarage home of Reverend and Mrs Sutton. She had her own small room, which felt odd since she had become used to sharing, to always having company and never being without it. Suddenly she felt alone. She felt very alone.

Twenty seven

May gazed out of her window, casting her eyes over the never-ending landscape so different from the familiar ones of her previous life. In the distance she could see trees and cows and distant homesteads. They looked so small it was as if she could reach out and lift them with just one hand. So small because they were so far away and it occurred to May that those, unlike her, who were unfortunate enough to spend their whole lives within the oppressive confines of the Nichol would never have seen such a sight. The furthest place they had ever set eyes on, the most open space they had ever seen not crowded with tall, overbearing buildings would probably have been the park. This was, of course, if they had even been to Victoria Park at all despite its comparatively close proximity. Wide and flat although the river was at its closest part to the Nichol, it was partly covered with tall-masted ships – like tenements on water. Despite its size, it was still reminiscent of the claustrophobic slum.

Those people probably couldn't conceive the idea of such distances and maybe, in their whole lives, would never have such a revelation. Had Peg ever seen such distances? May knew she was a learned lady so she probably had. Probably, but not, May suspected, on the scale of the Canadian prairies that now surrounded her.

The dour dwellings of the slum were crushing and claustrophobic. In another way, the wide-open spaces held their own form of claustrophobia for May. She could not leave the homestead unless she was accompanied by the Reverend or his wife. In that sense she was boxed in just as she had been in the Nichol but there, within its confines, she could move around at will: so back to the idea of freedom and which is better – freedom from or freedom to. Perhaps one day. May prayed that one day, 'freedom from' would no longer be more important than 'freedom to'. For the moment and probably many more moments to come, freedom from all the bad things was far more important to May; freedom from hunger, freedom from dire poverty and most of all from fear. Fear of what The Man had intended for her should he encounter her again. For now, she would continue to grow stronger, grow wiser and grow ready to make the most of her future return to London. And she must write to Peg.

My dear friend Peg

I hope that all is well with you in the Village. You are so far away but when I see the sun and the moon I know you will be looking at them an all just the same and somehow you do not seem so far then.

You will be pleased to know that I am now living with a good Christian family. The Reverend and his wife are kind people. They have a son called Simon who is younger than me and right sickly really. I am supposed to be a sort of companion to him as well as helping with chores and things. Same stuff I did in the Village, washing, cleaning and that but course there's not as much of it. I do miss the smell of the laundry though. I always liked that smell, right from the start I did. Made me feel clean and safe in a way it did.

Saying about Simon, he reminds me a bit of Ernie. He is not as nice as Ernie was though Peg. I don't know what to make of him really. He seems a bit sneaky but his mother and father right love him and he's not done nothing to me so might be alright. The last boy here had to go because of something Simon said he did. Don't know what but that's not nothing to do with me anyway. You know me Peg I just get on with what I got to get on with don't I.

I think the Doctor might be coming out soon so if you get this before he comes you might give him a reply for me. I nearly forgot to ask about Lottie. Is she alright? I do miss her and all. You will tell her that?

I better go now. I have things to do so will say goodbye and send you all my love.

Your true friend always
May Harris

The first few weeks with the Reverend's family flew by. The summer had reached its hottest, was beginning to pass into autumn and everything all around was

189

looking somewhat tired – be it people, animals or the seemingly endless fields; the fields that were, day by day, changing colour. Day by day they turned a brighter yellow. When the winds skipped through those fields May was reminded of the sea but a sea that had magically turned to shimmering gold. It was a sight she had never seen in England and thought the whole of the Nichol, perhaps the whole of London could be swallowed up by one giant wheat field.

During these first few weeks May felt she had been accepted by the Suttons. They were good people and she considered herself lucky. Some stories she would eventually come to hear regarding the fate of others suggested not all Home Children, as they came to be called, had been so fortunate with their lot.

Whilst her relationship with the couple was developing well, it was a somewhat different story with Simon. It was as if she and Simon were doing some strange kind of dance. They were like fighters in a ring, dodging around, each trying to get the measure of the other. Sometimes when May looked at Simon she could almost see the wheels turning in his head – such was his intensity. She found it uncomfortable.

When May had first seen young Simon she was, as she told Peg, struck by the overwhelming resemblance to tragic Ernie. Whether this was because both were sickly and the frailness had a similar effect on each of them she couldn't say. Certainly, Simon was considerably better fed than Ernie but their faces were undeniably alike – pale and rather drawn with a look of melancholy about them. May's judgement had served her well in the past and she had felt, at first, that in Simon she would find someone she could help in a way that she was unable to help Ernie. Her judgement would serve her well again and Simon would be the person that made her long journey to Canada worthwhile. Hopefully.

Simon had closely studied May. His body was weak but his mind, especially for a young boy, was sharp - very sharp. Sharper than his parents knew - certainly, despite his tender age, sharper than his benign and compassionate father's. He studied her in the same forensic way he had studied previous 'companions'. It was as if he tried to peer right inside them - into their souls. May was not the first although she was the first who had been chosen from Barnardo's. The last boy, slightly older than Simon who had come from another receiving home for immigrant children, did not stay with the family for very long. There were... problems. Simon had solemnly and (he said), with much regret, explained these to his parents – sobbing as he did so. The Reverend and Mrs Sutton were doting parents who had, despite many prayers and trying for many years, been unable to bring any more children into the world. As if to try to make up for his frailty and lack of siblings they catered for their darling Simon's every whim. They decided, after hearing Simon's story, that the boy must not, indeed could not, remain. He left under a dark cloud, to the last fiercely denying the accusations that had been levelled against him. Simon would not lie though. His parents knew this – they never doubted him. They were certain that whatever he told them was the truth.

What May had noticed was that, somehow, Simon could change his demeanour in an instant when either of his parents appeared. It was as if he had two masks, like those of comedy and tragedy, which he could use to transform himself, from contented to melancholy, in the blink of an eye when he needed to. Which Simon was the real one? Was there a real one? The masks were not telling and May chose to tread carefully – avoiding being alone with Simon as much as her duties made it practicable.

It was after a spell when Simon was on his own with no companion of a similar age, that May had arrived. He thought about this new one. He thought about his previous ones. What would he do this time? He even considered why he had behaved the way he did with the others. Was it power? Was it that enjoyed the power he, a weak boy, could wield over others stronger physically than he? He really wasn't sure. He also wasn't sure how to deal with this new girl. She seemed kind but he was wary as she was harder to read than her predecessors, possibly not such a walkover.

She had told him he reminded her of a dear friend who had died. How or what actually happened to him she had not explained. If he had known her background more fully, how she had to rely on her wits and her gut feelings to survive perhaps he would have understood her better and perhaps realised she could not so easily be trifled with.

Perhaps he would 'keep' her. Perhaps, but first she must be tested. First, he must find a way to make her prove herself. Prove herself worthy. Not only worthy to be his companion but also that she would not pose a threat. Simon had wound his kind and pious parents around his little finger. They adored him.

This May, however agreeable she was, could not be allowed to usurp him in his parents' affection. For some reason, Simon actually considered this might be possible. In truth, he was insecure but also in truth this could never happen and in reality, even though he found it hard to admit, he was actually lonely.

In preparation for the harvest there was much to be done and May was kept extremely busy. She had always been a hard worker and did not shirk the duties that now came her way. Her contributions were such that praise was heaped upon her from all angles. This was not received very well by Simon who one day overheard his mother praising May to a neighbour.

"This young Barnardo's girl, May, is the most hardworking and helpful child we have ever had in our house. I honestly cannot imagine how we should manage without her now. Both my husband and I have come to regard her, even in such a short time, as a member of our family. It is our greatest hope that our dear Simon will come to value her as we do."

The lady to whom his mother spoke smiled and nodded. It appeared she had not been quite as fortunate as Reverend and Mrs Sutton and wished she had been placed with such a delightful girl. Whether the home this particular lady's child had been sent to was as welcoming and pleasant as the Sutton's was something Mrs Sutton couldn't know but she was aware that sometimes it was the family rather than the child that was the cause of disharmony.

After hearing this exchange Simon was seething with anger. May, a part of the family! She was not and never could be. He was the important one; the only one his parents should care about. He was wrong about May. How could he think she might become a friend when all she wanted to do was worm her way into his home and maybe even push him out? No, he could not have that. She would have to go. He would have to find a way.

Days passed as Simon wondered. Harvest drew ever nearer – a busy time when even sickly Simon had a part to play. His physical ability was lacking but he could count better than many of the adults and this skill was not to be wasted. He was to go to the fields, with

May as his companion and a farm worker, to help count the sheaves and record their number. This made Simon feel important. Not for him the backbreaking toil with pitchforks. A pen was his tool and he wielded it with pride.

It was on this trip that Simon felt there might be a chance to 'test' May. He wasn't sure how yet but what actually occurred changed whatever plot he thought he would come up with. It was something that would have long term consequences for both himself and May.

Twenty eight

The day was hotter than the day before. It seemed instead of cooling down as the autumn elbowed the summer away, the heat of that summer was fighting to cling on – not ready to give up its grip on the fields just yet. Whilst the heat could be oppressive, any delay that pushed the eventual inevitability of the harsh winter a little further away was welcome.

"I am too hot, May Harris." Simon complained as he fidgeted in the carriage that carried him between various points where he stopped to count the sheaves.

He always used both May's name and surname. Perhaps to let her know she was not regarded as a friend – or an equal. This is the opinion May formed. She wondered if he ever would regard her as such rather than a paid, even though she only received her board rather than direct payment, companion. She wondered but somehow doubted it.

"You must have some more water then, Master Simon, here..."

May passed him the bottle she carried but...

"It's not enough and I'm hungry too. I also need to get down from this carriage. My legs are feeling stiff – I need to stretch them. Stop the carriage. Help me down." Simon ordered their driver.

Joe the driver, a sturdy young man, assisted Simon's descent from the carriage. May simply jumped down unaided - much to Simon's annoyance.

"You may go," he ordered Joe curtly "go over there to those others working and help them. I will be all right here with May Harris."

He waved the young man away. Joe shrugged and looked at May as if to say 'you are welcome to him'. He hurried away to join others who were more to his liking having first tied the horse to a small, lone tree along the track.

May was not happy. "Don't go too far," she called after him. "you will be needed again shortly I think."

Joe turned and nodded.

May and Simon were alone. There was much activity not too far away but all were busy with their harvest duties.

"I am going for a walk."

"Where to Master Simon? Where can you walk to from here? And how will you manage in the heat? You said you..."

"I know what I said but now I need to walk. You stay here I say."

"I cannot do that Master Simon. You know that. Your father said I must be with you at all times or I ..."

Simon held up his hand to silence her. He knew this all too well. His plan was that he would wander off alone, hurt himself - or appear to hurt himself - then

May would get the blame. That was the plan but May was having none of it.

"I go where you go Master Simon. That is what I must do."

May was taking no chances. Simon was irritated but no matter, how she handled his disobedience would decide whether he 'kept' her or not. It was all up to him - or so he thought.

Simon couldn't walk very far. His legs were weak – much weaker than May's - so she had no trouble keeping up with him.

"Where are you... are we going?

"To the lake: I want to go to the lake."

He did not look at May as he spoke.

May's new home of Ontario was a land of many lakes and she knew of a large lake not far away. Not far away but further away from the others working in the fields than she was comfortable with. Also, she wondered what Simon's intentions were when he got there. She wasn't happy. Not happy at all.

"I think that is too far Simon."

"*Master* Simon to you."

Again he did not look at May as he uttered these words.

In the near distance, May could see the water shining under the hot sun. She had not been to the lake before but had been told about its size by others. She had not actually ever seen such a lake before. The only water other than the ocean and the river Thames had been the lake in Victoria Park but this was on another scale altogether. This lake was, to May, as big as a sea.

Simon picked his way shakily through the waving grass to the banks of the lake.

"Be careful Simon. Please your mother would be..."

He turned to look at May, pretending to wobble as he stood on the edge.

"I will do as I please May Harris."

He smiled and looked out across the lake then checked behind them. The only others he could see were too far to observe his actions. He would do it now. The water didn't look very deep; he would get a little wet and muddy – but not too much. Just enough that his parents would chastise May for not looking after him. It would be her fault; she would no longer be trusted and would have to go.

Except that wasn't what happened. Simon stepped from the bank but it was not as the foolish boy expected. The water was deep, much deeper than he thought it would be and despite the perishing heat, it was intensely cold.

Simon gasped. He couldn't reach the bottom. He had never learned to swim. For a boy so clever with matters of learning his practical abilities were sorely lacking. Sometimes his common sense was lacking too. This, however, was something May had in abundance.

"May! May!" Simon was struggling, kicking out to try to reach the bank. "I...don't...know how to...I can't...swim. I'm...going...to drown!"

For a brief moment, May was stunned. She knew she had to help him but the problem was that she didn't know how to swim either. For Simon there had, despite his frailty, been opportunities to try to learn. She had heard of others swimming in certain parts – perhaps areas that were not as cold as where Simon had chosen to play his unfortunate trick, but opportunities for a girl from the London slum? No. It was not something that was possible or considered.

No matter. May knew what she must do. She couldn't let Simon drown. She just couldn't.

"Hang on Simon, don't struggle so. I'll get you, I will!"

"May, help...me!"

The sheer panic in Simon's eyes was clear. In those fleeting moments as he fought to keep his head above the water he knew he had gone too far. Gone too far and was it too late?

His legs felt even weaker; he could hardly move them – they felt leaden. It was harder and harder to keep his face above the cold water. He felt this was his end; an end entirely of his own making. But then he was gripped under his arms.

"Hang on Simon," spluttered May "hang on, others are coming."

When May had first seen what had happened she had shouted as loudly as she could for help. She also used the two-fingered whistle she had learned in the Nichol; the loud whistle used to warn others of her ilk when they were about to be caught indulging in a spot of thieving. Even as she jumped into the water she had seen two figures starting to run towards the lake. Would they be in time? Could she keep him afloat until then?

Just as May's strength was flagging, just as Simon seemed to have given up, they felt much stronger arms pulling them towards the bank. Despite her exhaustion, May's first thought was for Simon.

"Is he alright?"

"He'll live May but I knew I shouldn't have left you no matter what the little sod said. Now what will happen? He will tell his parents some tale and I'll be let go. I know I will. I know what he's like."

Simon could hear this but did not respond. He was still too traumatised to speak.

May wondered if Joe was right. She indeed knew that Simon could be awkward to say the least but surely, after having been rescued from drowning? started to recover, the heat of the sun drying her clothes. She had thanked the other boy who, though wet, hurried back to his work. No doubt he would spread the word about what had happened and that word would surely reach the Reverend and his wife sooner rather than later. Joe

201

helped May and Simon to some shelter beneath some small trees at the edge of the lake.

"Wait here and I will return with the carriage. I will be as quick as I can."

He ran back to where the horse and carriage were tethered leaving May and Simon alone.

Now her first instinct of concern evaporated. May's anger at the peril Simon's action had put them in burst out.

"You little sod, you stupid little sod. You're bloody evil you are. What the bleedin hell do you think you were doing? Tell me, TELL ME!"

Simon, instead of being how he usually was - defiant and superior - collapsed in tears.

As she watched him sob uncontrollably May felt her heart soften. She actually felt sorry for him. Putting her arms around him she was aware of his delicate body quivering. At last, he spoke.

"Oh May, I'm sorry. I'm so sorry. You're right, I am evil. No one likes me and I know why."

May felt obliged to ask him why.

"I think I'm better than everyone else." He uttered between sobs, "I think I'm better but I'm jealous as well. Other boys and girls can do things I cannot. My legs won't let me run or climb or jump. My life is in my head and I just...well I don't know May, I just...I'm not a very nice person."

"Shush Simon," May knew she had to somehow make him feel better. "Listen, you are so clever. Lots of grownups aren't as clever as you. I could never be. Your parents love you so much. I never had two parents, only my lovely mum and that was only until... well until I was about your age. You are lucky having such good parents and being so clever an' all."

Simon looked intently at May. He didn't speak and May continued. "Where I come from loads of the children were far worse off than you but they had to live on the streets. In all weathers we were out - boys and girls younger than you and with worse things wrong with them than you y'know. My friend Ernie, you remind me of Ernie – right from the start you did – he..."

May paused as she thought of Ernie and his last moments on this earth. She hadn't been able to save Ernie but she had saved Simon. Emotion overwhelmed her and she started to cry.

"May, May," this time it was Simon who held her, it was her body that quivered. "What happened to Ernie?"

Not far away May could see Joe returning with the carriage. Soon they would be back home.

"I will tell you but not now. Simon, what will you say to the Reverend and Mrs?"

"I will tell them the truth May. I will tell them I ordered Joe away and planned to deliberately get wet

203

to get you into trouble. I was going to say you just left me, went off and I slipped in mud. I was going to do this May because I thought my parents liked you too much and might like you better than me. I wanted to get rid of you."

May was shocked but somehow not surprised. Now she knew what had probably happened with other companions. Was Simon so insecure he lied about previous ones? It would certainly appear so.

The carriage was almost upon them. May helped Simon to his feet. She looked at him as if to ask exactly what he would say.

"I will tell them you saved my life. You saved my life and I will be in your debt always."

May smiled at Simon and squeezed his hand. For a moment she could almost see Ernie's face looking at her. She wiped tears from her face and Simon wiped tears from his. These were the first tears he had shed for as long as he could remember - perhaps the first time he had felt anything other than selfishness. He would keep May Harris if, of course, she wished to stay after what he had tried to do. He wanted her not as just a paid companion but as a friend – his only true friend.

Twenty nine

May felt settled at Barnardos Village. She had, until the Man appeared, felt safe, felt she could learn and grow – grow into someone other than a maid to toffs.

However, she had been forced to wrench herself from that secure environment to go to faraway Canada. She had, as did all the other girls, felt a stranger in this new, very different land. Now though, having resolved the situation with Simon and been accepted by the Reverend and his wife she began to feel settled again. Gradually she became absorbed into her new life thousands of miles away from the Nichol. Her letters to Peg and the replies that were not, as yet, forthcoming would mean she did not have to lose touch with her former home. Peg was the closest she had to family even though she still felt, in her heart, that Uncle George still had a part to play in her life and he remained often in her thoughts.

She wrote to Peg

October 19th 1883
Dear Peg
I am sorry I have not written to you for a while. I have not yet received anything from you so look forward to your letter that I am sure will come. It is such a long way with trains and ships to go on so I

know it is not because you have not written. I know you will. I hope you get my letters safely in time.

Hope you are all well there. What has the weather been like there? It has been very hot and dry here but now the harvest is in and the autumn is here I think it will get colder very quickly. The winters are right cold here like Miss Hardy told us so we know what to expect.

A lot has happened here since the last letter I wrote about Simon. He is a sad boy Peg but I hope that now I can help him be less sad. He nearly drowned he did Peg and nearly took me with him I don't know how I managed it with me not being able to swim and all but I saved him I did. Two boys got us out but if I hadn't gone in the water right cold water it was, he would have drowned for sure.

He is changed now he is Peg and the Reverend and Mrs, well they was good to me before but now they treat me even better, treat me like their own daughter. They said they really wanted a daughter but couldn't have more children after Simon. That's why they make such a fuss of him I suppose.

Although he is younger than me he knows loads of stuff and is so good at his numbers and letters. He is teaching me and I can help him as well because although he is right clever sometimes he don't have the sort of common sense what the likes of me have had to have to get by. He never had to live like what I did before I came to our little May Cottage and when I tell him about the slum and the places you and me lived in before the Doctor found us he don't believe it I think. I think he believes I am making it up.

He is a lazy boy sometimes and I told him I think if he tries a bit harder with his walking then he will get stronger but course I'm not a Doctor so I don't know. Just seems right to me. But then Mrs got a Doctor. Nothing like our Doctor - to look at him. Simon said he had a Doctor try and look at him a while ago but told him to go away as he did not want him. But he let this Doctor look at his legs and he said they could get stronger if he ecercised (sorry Peg I can't spell that word so I reckon it not be right) so I was right so perhaps I could be a Doctor.

I am looking forward to hearing from you Peg with all the news. I like to write your name because it makes me feel closer to you somehow when I write it and lets you know I haven't forgotten it but you know I wouldn't. How is Lottie doing and the Doctor and Mrs B? It seems like ages ago I was at May cottage but I still look at the moon so you don't seem so far. I have tried not to think about that horrible murdering man but sometimes I can't help it especially with Simon reminding me of Ernie. He has asked me about Ernie but I haven't told him the story yet. Not ready to yet Peg. Has he been to the Village again? Has he said anything about me? I hate him. I hate him with all my heart I do. If you should see him again try to accidentally kick him for me or trip him up or the like. It is exactly three years since that horrible night. Three years but so clear in my head it is.

There is lots to do with the harvest but lots of the little farms, they are called homesteads here, are not doing all that good because they cannot get much money for their wheat. I don't know about such things except the Reverend is trying to help some of the people who are not going to be able to stay and farm. It's awful Peg because even in this big new country there are poor people struggling to get by just like at home. See Peg, I say home because England will always be my home however long I am here. You will always be my home Peg you will.

It is getting to suppertime now so I have to go as I still have chores to do and me and Simon are going to have a walk to get an appetite. It is funny though because since he has been doing more he is eating better. See I should be a Doctor. The food is good here. It is plain and simple like at home but the soup is not as good as yours though Peg. I like your soup best.

I think of you always
Your true friend May Harris

It was only the following day that May received her first, of many, letters from Peg. It had been sent to Hazelbrae and, had it not been held there for a while, would have reached May before she sent her news off to Peg. No matter. May was so pleased to have something written in Peg's own familiar hand – it made her seem no so distant.

She placed it by her bed until her chores were finished then settled down to take in everything that Peg had to tell her.

31sth August
May Cottage
Barnardo's Village
My dear May
It was with much relief that I received your letter.

The ocean you paint such a vivid picture of is indeed far larger than anything I could imagine. You are right when you said you think I have seen the sea. I did, long ago, but it was the English Channel I gazed upon with no less awe than you that first time.

I like to think that by the time you read this you will be settled with a good family. You will, I have no doubt, impress them with not only your skills but also your cheerful personality.

The Doctor and Mrs Barnardo are, as you would expect, very busy and as usual, trying to raise more funds.

You will be pleased to know that the awful Man has not ventured to our community again although as acquiring funds and patronage are so important to the

Doctor I suspect more visits will be arranged and he may therefore darken our doors again. Do not worry yourself about this May, as you are far away and safe from him.

The summer is beginning to fade now but the roses that were in full bloom when you left are, after dying away and resting, putting on a final resplendent show to guide us into autumn. As they finally wither, the trees will begin to change colour to their reds and golds so the beauty of the Village will remain. Hold it in your heart dear May – until you return. I understand the autumn in Canada is a spectacular affair with the trees glorious in their colour longer than here. I picture them clinging on as long as possible before the harsh winter takes them in its grip.

Lottie is well, and although missing you she is presenting a cheerful face to the world despite grumbling occasionally about the increasingly responsible work she is obliged to do.

I understand the Doctor will be visiting Canada next year and although that seems a long way off I am sure the time will pass quickly for all of us.

My thoughts, as always dear May, are with you and my love goes to you. I eagerly await your next correspondence informing me of your new home. I trust it will give me comfort to know you are safe and well.

Your dear friend, Peg

May thought of the roses and could remember the colours and the fragrance on the day she left. Remembered also the Village the first time she ever saw it; the mud, the bare trees so different from that day when the cart passed through the gates of Mossford Village to take her away. She thought of Peg by the sea and smiled to herself, satisfied that she had been right. The Man had not been there again so that was a good thing. The thought of Peg, or any one of her friends having to be polite to him, was not something that pleased her. May reread Peg's words, carefully folded the letter and kissed it then put it away in her little box. The first one; the beginning of a pile of letters that would grow steadily over the years that followed. Years that would see many events which, unknown to May, would shape her life in ways she could not, that night, have imagined. She placed the box in the cupboard by her bed, sighed, and went to sleep.

Thirty

November 25th 1883

Dear Peg

I was so pleased to receive your letter but that was a long time ago and I am very sorry I have not written since.

I told you I thought it would get cold very quickly and not that long after writing the temperature had fallen to below freezing. It is so cold Peg. We were told it would be but I didn't imagine it would be like this. If all I had was the shawl what you gave me I would be frozen dead for sure. They are used to it out here Peg and even Simon, who is much improved thanks to me I think, seems to take the bitter cold in his stride.

The Reverend and Mrs are getting ready for Christmas now as it is only a month away and it seems like Christmas here will be very much like the Christmases at home. I only had three at the Village Peg, same like you and I remember every minute of them I do. Our cottage, named like me, and the tree and the Doctor and his staff made it right good for us. I still have the soap you gave me the last Christmas I was there. It is in my trunk and the lovely scent keeps my clothes smelling nice.

I will miss you at Christmas but I think I will be so busy there should not be time to be sad. They are so good to me Peg and you will be pleased to hear this because some children have not been as lucky as I have. There was one boy I heard of who drowned and no one missed him for days because they didn't care. That poor boy could have been Simon Peg. I get on so well with him now, I feel he is my little brother even after just four months he is. He says I am like the sister he never had and couldn't have.

There will be a big service here on Christmas Eve Peg. People will come from all over if they can but it depends on the snow. We haven't had very much yet but as the month goes on more will surely come.

There are newspapers that we can get when we go to town for supplies and I have read about a big volcano erupting in a place called Krakatoa that I had never heard of. I suppose you have heard of it in London Peg. They say it was so big that the sky was dark across nearly all of the world. Was it dark at home Peg? I hope not because it was about the time you wrote to me about the roses.

I know the Village will be like it was when I first came now but still see it in my head as summer. I see the sun and yet I see Christmas as well. I like to think about the good things. I try Peg and then I remember my dear mum being taken and I remember Ernie and The Man and for a while I am sad again.

But I am strong Peg, you know that. You know that whatever happens, I shall come back. I shall look that

213

Man in the eyes again but this time not run away. He will know me and he will have cause to fear me Peg. He will.

I look forward to hearing from you again, hopefully with news of a joyful Christmas spent.

May the good Lord look after you.

Your dear friend

May Harris

May's first Christmas in Canada came and went. The snow did prevent some of the Reverend's widely dispersed parishioners from attending their church but many still came despite the snow that fell on Christmas Eve. Christmas Day itself was clear and snow-free – a bright yet watery sun made the snow that already lay sparkle like a twinkling white blanket covering the ground for as far as the eye could see. Two days later, at the end of a day that was somehow both tiring and restful at the same time, May wrote her final letter of 1883 to Peg.

December 27th

My dear friend Peg

Well, I have now had my first Christmas in Canada and I will say Peg that it has been a jolly affair. Of course the Reverend's service was longer than usual and I know you may not like this Peg since you love Jesus so much but I thought it was too long. A lot of the people had travelled a long way to get here so were tired and some of the children and even grownups were starting to close their eyes. It made me smile Peg and Simon saw it too but they came to life when we started singing the carols. I do like the carols. They are much better than the usual hymns although perhaps I shouldn't say that. I could close my eyes and imagine I was right back with you singing them and nudging Lottie because she was such a terrible singer. Is she still Peg or has she improved? She has such a loud voice she does.

We had a right good dinner with a turkey that Mrs Reverend had spent a whole day plucking and cleaning and the like. It was the biggest one I have ever seen in my life and was very tasty when served up to us. Mrs said she had never seen Simon eat so much and what with the pudding the naughty boy had a stomach ache. It served him right but the pudding was good and not like our one at home. I am sorry to say that it was better because it had much more fruit in it. They have things called cranberries here Peg. I have never heard of cranberries. They are little and red and are not sweet like raspberries are but go right well with the turkey meat and even in the pudding. I got presents Peg. I got some thick wool stockings that will serve me very well until the spring comes and a scarf that Mrs Reverend knitted just for me. I am looking forward to the spring because it is the only season I have not seen

215

here yet and Simon has told me after the snow has gone the grass and trees are brown and dull until the new grass starts to shoot. I want to see the new grass Peg and the planting. I will be fourteen years old in the spring and won't go to school anymore then although I haven't been much anyway and learn lots from books with Simon and the tutor that comes to him. He is right clever as well Peg but Simon is getting better and he will be going to school himself soon.

I will have more work to do and will get my own money then. I feel I am growing up and will be a young lady soon. I could never be a lady like you was though Peg and I could certainly never be a toff. I wouldn't want to be one neither. You know how I feel about toffs don't you Peg.

I hope to get a letter from you soon to tell me about Christmas there. I may not write for a while because I will have a lot to do so if you do not hear from me take comfort in knowing I am fine here and am thinking of you.

Your friend as always
May Harris

Thirty one

El Teb, Sudan, North Africa, February 29th 1884

Sergeant George Harris was tired but that was nothing unusual since his regiment had been sent to North Africa for conflict with yet another enemy threatening the interests of the great British Empire. Long days were spent travelling and then unpacking the weapons and supplies needed to supply an army of over four thousand men. It was hot despite being only February, the last day of February – the 29th as it was a Leap Year – and hotter than a summer at home in England. An England that seemed so far away it may as well have been on the moon.

They were about to do battle, the second in only a few weeks, with the forces of a leader called the Mahdi. George didn't know too much about why they were there. He was a soldier who followed orders; he would do his duty and had no further time to rest for the battle was once again upon them. This would be the battle to show the enemy what the British Army is truly made of after its brutal defeat at the hands of the Mahdi's followers that short time ago. This battle could have no defeat. This time there would be a glorious victory and George was determined to play his part in it.

When the battle was over, the dust had subsided and silence fell over the carnage of man and beast the desired victory had indeed been won. The horrific casualties would, however, temper its glory for those, like George, who saw war as far from glorious. The part he heroically played in that victory was to have ramifications that could not have been foreseen; by himself and others – including May. He was unaware of his sister's death and sometimes felt guilty about leaving them to fend for themselves on those forbidding streets. Selfish and cowardly he thought to himself now but at the time the desire to get away was so strong, so powerful that he followed his heart.

Thirty two

Spring 1884

There were other letters that passed between May and Peg in the months that followed and as the winter's (harsher by far than any in England) grip came to an end May witnessed her first, of several, Canadian springs. She found it startling. It was indeed as Simon had told her and she wrote to Peg that she had seen the transformation of the landscape. It was as if a tablecloth of pure white had been tidied away to be replaced first by a pale, dull one then one of a crisp fresh green.

She wrote of her birthday and the different stockings she was given this time – ones of cotton for the summer - and a bar of fragranced soap. This soap though, she told Peg, would never smell as sweet as that which she kept as a treasure from her.

In the newspapers in March, just before the spring had completely elbowed the winter from the land, there was news of battles that had taken place in faraway North Africa. The details were sketchy in the Canadian press – no names were mentioned. Canadians, and of course there were many who had left England or had been born and raised in this vast country, had some regard for the exploits of the army of their place of origin but for some thoughts of these were left behind and would not affect them ever again.

May had seen the newspaper and her mind turned to her uncle. Did he fight in such battles she wondered? Maybe, but she didn't know where he was, if he was alive. Simon, who as he grew stronger thought he perhaps might like to be a soldier, looked at the article with May.

"Are you interested in war and battles May? I would not have thought so but I think you could be a formidable foe and I am very glad you are my friend."

"My uncle went to be a soldier he did but I don't know anything about him now I don't. He was always a fighter Simon and a good one. He was very brave and he would win fights with his bare hands to get money so me and my mum, who was his sister, could eat better sometimes. He often had cuts and bruises but he was very tough. I wonder about him Simon and if I will ever see him again. I hope so but fear it will not be for a long time and probably, if at all, not until I go back to England."

"You will go back to England May will you? Will you leave me?"

"I am older than you Simon but as we both grow up the distance in years between us will seem less. You will be fifteen years old when I will be eighteen. We will both be free to follow whichever paths we wish I think. You may choose to be a soldier or perhaps a reverend like your father..."

At this Simon grimaced. That was certainly something he had no intention of becoming.

"...but if your health is sufficiently improved you will be able to do whatever you wish to. I well, I must return to England because there is something I have to do."

"Something you have to do? What is this May? What is so important that you must leave here?"

She had not yet explained to Simon about Ernie and her vow of vengeance on The Man. She thought it was now time to tell him. It was quiet. They had some time to themselves and May felt the need to unburden herself again - as she had to Peg. Even speaking of the events of that night, which still gave her nightmares, would undoubtedly upset her.

She related the story to a solemn Simon who could see both the pain and the hatred in May's eyes. He knew how determined May could be and didn't doubt for a second that this man would, eventually, pay for his crime. As she finished her tale, May's eyes welled up.

"You can see now Simon how I felt when I first saw you and then how I felt when I saved you..." Her voice tapered off.

"May I know you will succeed in whatever you choose to do, I just know it. You and your uncle are both strong and I am sure you will meet again. You will May."

She hoped Simon was right and could not know that across the Atlantic The Man was also thinking about her Uncle but for very different a reason.

Thirty three

London, May 1884,

The events of February 29th were widely reported soon afterwards by the newspapers back in England. The battle at El Teb was, to The Man, despite his interest in campaigns fought by the British Army as something he hoped to capitalise on as his career developed, of particular concern. He read the article in The London Gazette, which shed further light on specific deeds of bravery, with more interest than usual.

'Sergeant George Harris of the 19th Hussars gallantly gained distinction on the 29th February at the Battle of El Teb. He saved the life of Captain Richard Perryman who, whilst charging with the second line, was speared. The weapon entered the officer on the right side and upon withdrawal caused him to faint. Shortly afterwards his horse was killed. Without any thought for his own safety and surrounded by the Soudanese, Sergeant Harris managed to convey Captain Perryman out of the melee to a place of safety.'

Captain Richard Perryman. The Man had not seen or heard from his brother in many years. The gulf between them and the reason for it had precluded any reconciliation. Of course he was glad his brother had not been killed and it appeared that had this Sergeant George Harris not valiantly rescued him then death would have been almost certain.

Edward Perryman glanced through the rest of the article then turned the page and cast all thoughts of his brother, once again, from his mind. Since his first visit to Barnardo's the previous year, Perryman had continued to try to ingratiate himself with Lord Cairns but it was not going to his satisfaction. For some reason that he was at a loss to understand but was to others of a more perceptive nature all too obvious, Lord Cairn's opinion of him, formed early on, had not changed.

This was of concern to Perryman since endorsement by such a respected figure would no doubt be favourable to his aim of political advancement. His business interests in matters of finance were lucrative and his property empire in and around The Nichol brought in funds that far exceeded the costs incurred. These costs were, to Edward Perryman, negligible. The hirelings who collected the rents for him were paid a pittance; the solicitors he employed were adept at keeping his costs to a minimum and his profile low. As for maintenance, well the likes of his tenants - the odorous peasants that they were - would certainly not appreciate, or deserve, anything better. They were used to squalor so why should he lavish funds on them when they could be better used to uphold the situation and comfort of his own much more deserving family?

He avoided contact with those who also profited from the unsanitary conditions as far as possible and there were many who, as he, preferred to remain in the shadows. He was surprised that some, being of a lower class than him, had managed to acquire a property portfolio at all. Perryman from time to time, albeit at a distance when possible, encountered the Sanitary Inspector but this held little fear for him since the Inspector himself had....shortcomings...regarding properties he owned.

The unhealthy conditions prevalent around the Nichol were, at times, the subject of orders from magistrates but as yet, and for the foreseeable future at least, Edward Perryman had avoided such tiresome tribulations. He remained aloof, far removed from the day-to-day running of his empire and was determined to remain so. This was especially true since that day – when was it now he pondered? Yes, almost four years ago he recalled; the night when during his annual inspection he had come across a whining boy and an irksome girl. Since that night he had avoided personal inspections. The reason he gave to his wife was that he didn't wish to concern her; concern her for his welfare venturing to such places. Had Josephine been more fully aware of exactly what role the Nichol played in her husband's business dealings any concern she had for his welfare would probably have been different. She was somewhat naive. Blind to the contribution he made to the pitiful lives, or rather existences, of the residents of the Nichol.

What was of concern to Perryman, as a potential threat to his empire, were campaigns by Socialists or, the description he preferred - Anarchists, to disrupt the status quo. These people could prove to be troublesome with their meetings - their rabble-rousing. He felt that not enough was being done to keep these people in their place. Rallies of these idle low-lifes often occurred in Victoria Park. This should be a place of pleasant walks and fresh air and they were an affront to the delicate constitutions of those of a more refined nature.

His feelings towards these protestations and their potential effect on his livelihood, his well deserved and earned livelihood, was the main reason he still desired to gain election to Parliament as a Conservative. Liberals couldn't be trusted with the future of London. He still saw Hackney as the prospective gateway to his political career. Defence of the realm was also, in his view, imperative. The Empire was a force for good, as his self-centred eyes saw it, and therefore must be upheld by whatever means necessary

Again, and much to his reluctance, his thoughts turned to his brother and the man who had saved him; the man whose path would eventually cross his own and not, for Edward Perryman, in a good way. It was odd but the name Harris had soundly vaguely familiar to him although he couldn't tell why - something distant - but it was a common name so he dismissed it from his mind.

Perhaps, and Perryman was not happy about the prospect, having a soldier for a brother and one whose name was known beyond military circles, may be a conduit, though somewhat tenuous, through which he could gain access to potential patrons; perhaps allies more in tandem with his way - the right way - of thinking than Lord Cairns. He had decided there was no sound reason to waste further time trying to cultivate a friendship here. He would certainly not be visiting the Barnardo's Village again. At least whilst it did not suit is purpose.

No, there were others he would attempt to, no succeed in, ingratiating himself with. So, while he continued to profit from the miserable lives of his tenants in the Nichol he watched with keen interest the state of political matters in London. It was his view that the Prime Minister was looking far too favourably upon the plight, if it could be called that, of the poor. He was concerned that actions were afoot that would further strip away their self-reliance and were an infringement of the rights of gentlemen like himself to pursue their legitimate interests. Thus the Liberty and

Property Defence League gained another enthusiastic member.

The likes of those termed 'workers' having the right to vote was anathema to him; things had already gone too far in this respect. He didn't think they deserved nor wanted such a right. Allowing such people, such altogether ignorant people, to play a part in deciding matters affecting others like himself could surely only be a step along the road to socialism. Where would he be then? Whatever he could do to hold back this despicable tide he would. His campaign, his crusade, was to crank up a notch.

The next thing he could see happening was, perish the thought, votes for women. Much as he loved - if there is such a thing - his wife, he could no more see her having the intellect and critical mind to allow her to form opinions on matters of importance as he could contemplate her driving a carriage and horses.

He would proceed to seek out those in the House of Lords who held the same views as he. Josephine, whilst not being his intellectual equal of course, was a charming and most cordial hostess; he felt it was time to set out his stall and that a lavish gathering, expertly presented by Josephine, was the way to begin.

So who to invite to this gathering? Certainly only those of sufficient status to aid his advancement would be invited. There was his neighbour Lord Fortescue whose wife, he understood, had been so impressed with the Barnardo's girls that one was now in the household's employ. Fortescue was also a member of the Property and Liberty League so was definitely of the same opinions as himself. It was also understood, although as with others of high birth who dabbled with property in the less salubrious but extremely profitable areas of the capital and played their cards close to their chest, that he too was the owner of a considerable portfolio. This was someone who would welcome support in the lower chamber of an ally who could speak against the perils of socialism; an ally who could oppose legislation that would bring this evil closer. Edward Perryman's idea of evil was a warped one considering he was a murderer but this was something that did not trouble him in his comfortable world far detached from the horrors of the slum.

Perhaps it was also time he reached out to Richard. What happened to fracture their relationship was surely far enough in the past, surely far enough that they now they could resume some semblance of amity. It was time and it must be before the gathering he would instruct Josephine to plan. It would be difficult after all this time but it must be done.

Thirty four

Southampton, Netley Hospital

Captain Richard Perryman had had much time to think. His stay in Netley hospital - the soulless place to which he had been taken upon arrival back in England - was hopefully drawing to an end. He had had time to think of many things. He considered his military career – a career that once he was healed would continue until his commission period was completed or he was killed; his life before this; his brother Edward and of course George Harris - the man without whom he would not be alive. They had never met, as far as he could recall, before this event but he hoped that they would meet again under more favourable circumstances.

At night he would dream. Sometimes he had nightmares of the battlefield and would awake in a sweat amazed he was still alive. Sometimes he would be transported back to a gentler period, a time before he and his older brother became estranged. He had not seen Edward since his departure for the army - nor had he wished to. They had never been close; they were too different. Edward was, Richard thought, cold and unfeeling. He had wondered, when Edward married Josephine, how she would endure his moods; his obsession with advancement; his desire for wealth and power. It would appear, however, as he had heard nothing to the contrary, that the union had survived.

Richard had never married. There was someone once - a long time ago, some fifteen years or so, but nothing had come of it. Their worlds were too diverse in too many ways. The end was sudden. One day she was in his life albeit in a manner that was not conducive to a longstanding perhaps permanent relationship and the next she was gone. No explanation. All he remembered was that Edward was pleased and he was still certain now, as he was then, that he had played a part in making sure this relationship - this loving relationship - would not come to term. Edward had not admitted as much but it was clear. He was older, the head of the family since the death of their father and whatever Edward desired, he would ensure came to pass.

Richard had often wished he had stood up more to Edward but it was too late. However brave he subsequently became, standing up to his brother had somehow been too difficult and he hated himself for it. He reflected on his empty life. His thoughts were exacerbated by the cavernous, solemn building filled with pain and suffering. His physical pain was healing but his emotional pain was something he would never lose. It was so deep it was part of him and would be, he was sure, forever. His melancholy moods came and, although faded, never really went. Sometimes they stayed with him, in their darkest form, longer than others. Sometimes, lying in his bed surrounded by others whose lives perhaps hung in the balance, he wondered if it would not have been better if George Harris had not saved him at all.

Richard Perryman was in the final stages of his convalescence in the vast Netley Hospital when he heard he was to receive a visitor; a visitor he had wondered if he would ever see again. He also wondered whether, if this was the case, he would care.

Edward Perryman had much time to think as he made his way along the seemingly unending corridors of Netley. He had heard of the place of course as it was recognised as the largest complex of buildings in the country. Even as he anticipated the meeting with his brother he was storing away images in his head that may at sometime in the future be useful. He could see himself standing up in Parliament – a newly elected champion of Her Majesty's brave forces, someone who had seen firsthand the aftermath of battle. Yes, he would try to gain currency even from visiting his wounded brother. He found Richard in a garden and was pleased since he found the air within the hospital unpleasant, stale with no indication that the sea was close by. His mind turned briefly to the foul narrow streets that encompassed his property empire – but only very briefly.

Whilst waiting for Edward to arrive Richard pondered how the meeting would go. As he waited he considered the circumstances that lead to their estrangement. Upon the death of their father – their mother having passed away some years earlier – Edward, as the older sibling, took over the Perryman Estate. It was always his intention to build on the legacy his father had left to him.

Edward and Richard lived together in the house on Belgrave Square now occupied by Edward and Josephine. They were two extremely eligible young men but of vastly differing characters. Their eligibility meant there were many well-bred young ladies, and their parents, who viewed the Perryman brothers as ideal marriage material. Edward, before settling on Josephine as someone suitable to bear his children, had indulged his appetites with somewhat less fragrant companions. He did this despite regarding the lower classes as altogether unworthy of consideration. They had, and served, their purposes but beyond that were of no consequence.

Richard was different however; he saw those less fortunate than himself as people with the same wants, needs, hopes and fears as he. He was, unlike Edward, a caring and compassionate man. The way Edward treated the servants rankled with Richard. It was only the cook and the housekeeper - older women - whom he actually called by name; those and the male staff.

The young female servants were simply referred to, and addressed as, 'girl'. Richard considered the way Edward regarded the servants was how one might call a dog. He recalled that Edward once remarked that a dog had no surname so why should a mere servant? The more he thought about his brother his dislike and the reasons for it, grew.

Thinking of servants made Richard remember the first day he had seen Rose. Edward had employed her to assist the housekeeper and Richard was immediately struck by her. She seemed shy yet strong and the attraction, despite their differing stations, was instant. She, in turn, looked fondly upon him but was in no doubt of her place so quickly turned her gaze away. Yet, despite this awkward beginning, the relationship, against heavy odds, somehow blossomed. Richard only ever knew her as Rose. As he recalled that time a voice, still familiar after many years, spoke.

"Good afternoon... Richard."

Edward paused before addressing Richard by his name, finding it difficult to speak it after such a long time. Richard looked upon his elder brother. Older of course, perhaps more distinguished with the greying hair but still with the same air of superiority he recalled was a constant and not very endearing feature. It was clear from his appearance - his attire and deportment - that here was a man of wealth and confidence.

"Good afternoon Edward." There was no pause in Richard's address. "You are looking well brother."

Edward examined Richard, who was sitting in a bath chair with a blanket covering his legs. Even though the day was not chilly, he was still sufficiently weak to need the extra warmth. For a moment Edward remained standing, forcing his brother to look up to him, then he sat down opposite - deliberately brushing down the wooden chair before doing so. His brother looked much as he had done the last time they met but was, of course, thinner and older although not as pale as he was expecting. The exposure to the North African sun on his face had not yet faded and gave the impression he was perhaps healthier than he appeared.

"I was sorry to hear of your injury brother. I have, of course, read about the battle during which it occurred and it is indeed certain that had you not been rescued you would surely have perished."

Richard nodded, not knowing what to say to his only brother after so long. There was a silence broken by gulls and crows chasing each other; a contrast of black and white. Edward looked up and commented.

"The gulls show how close to the sea we are yet from within the hospital it cannot be seen."

"The wards do not face it more's the pity, and so when the weather is fine I like to sit out here for as long as possible in the fresh air."

"Indeed the air inside has a somewhat sour odour to it. I was struck by it almost immediately upon entrance."

Both brothers were uncomfortable and aware that such small talk could not continue. Richard spoke first - and candidly.

"So why have you come here Edward? All these years no contact yet here you are having torn yourself away from your considerable business interests in London to come down to Southampton. Unless, and I am afraid it is something I doubt, you have changed, then I feel there is some self-serving purpose to your visit."

Edward fidgeted. Even after all this time, Richard had the measure of him.

"I am sorry you have come to such an unfortunate conclusion. Can a man not visit his only brother who has suffered greatly in the service of his Empress without that visit being viewed with suspicion? It is purely due to concern for your welfare that I have come. I feel it is time that the past is laid to rest and that you must, after your period of convalescence is completed, come to London to stay with myself and Josephine until such time as you may resume your regimental duties."

He waited for Richard's response.

"Why is it that your sudden concern for my welfare strikes me as so hollow? There have been other occasions when I have been in comparatively close proximity to you – even in London when duty required my presence – but never before have you sought me out. To be truthful I was not perturbed about this. I have never ceased to believe that you were behind Rose's sudden disappearance."

Richard noticed that Edward's expression turned from apparent concern to one of vague recollection.

"I can see from your face brother that the name means something to you or rather you hazily recall it. You knew how I felt about her. You knew it but could not bear to see the Perryman name, in your eyes, discredited. I know not what you did, what lies you told, but it is my firmly held and constant belief that it was your intervention that caused her to go. Go to lord knows where. And I, just off to the army, could not search for her. She may have, probably, left believing I did not care, that I had abandoned her when it was of your doing."

Edward tried to speak but Richard raised his arm as if to silence him and continued. "So, my dear Edward..." he almost spat the words, "I do not wish to come to your home. I do not wish to accept your frankly and obviously false concern but I do wish never to set eyes on you again for as long as I am destined to remain in this world. I have had cause to wish Sergeant Harris had never saved me and now looking upon your face, the duplicitous face I remember so well, I further believe it would have been better if he hadn't. Now leave...please."

Edward was taken aback by Richard's reaction. Surely, after all these years he could not still regret his lost love? Love? How could she have been his love? The likes of the Perrymans do not love servants. Edward had assuredly rendered Richard a favour by removing such a creature from his life. It had given him no pleasure informing her that Lieutenant Richard Perryman had instructed him to advise her that his feelings were not as he had apparently led her to believe. She had been a plaything for him and could not possibly expect a gentleman to commit to such a lowly girl as she.

He didn't remember her shock and horror. He didn't remember the tears as she rushed away. And he didn't remember the look on her face as she turned to flee never to be seen by either of the brothers again. He didn't remember because her feelings, nor Richard's, were of any importance to him. Nobody else's feelings ever were.

Thirty five

Peterborough, Canada 1884

May's life in Ontario had settled into a pattern. She had always felt, and loudly announced, whilst in the Village, that she would never become a servant to toffs. Despite undertaking domestic duties, she did not feel like, nor was treated like, a servant but a valued member of the family. Other girls she encountered while in town or at church (when they had the chance to speak candidly) had different tales to tell. Some had been moved from place to place hoping that their next situation would be better. Sometimes they were lucky but other times definitely not. May heard stories that would not have seemed out of place in the Nichol; girls being taken advantage of or discarded when they could not work through illness or accident.

The plight of such girls was brought home to May when one she had become friendly with - on the brief occasions they encountered each other - from another farm, suddenly was no longer around. The owners of the farm, even the Reverend commented, were not the most agreeable of people. They, he said, outwardly pious and godly yet did not appear to act towards others in the way that supported this piety and godliness.

One day the girl, Margaret, was with them but the next time they arrived at the church she was not. She had, it transpired, been rendered deaf when she had somehow fallen into a river. A deaf servant who could not instantly respond to commands was of no use to them so she had been sent away. It was as if, May thought, her friend had never existed in their eyes. She had obviously not been viewed, as May fortunately was, to be a person with feelings and a soul but as a chattel to be cast aside when no longer of any use. May had travelled thousands of miles to a new country but found that inhumanity and ill-treatment were not confined to the streets she had left behind.

May did not get to see the Doctor when he came over to Canada in the summer of 1884. The great distances over which the girls were spread made visiting more than a handful impossible, much to his regret.

She did not hear much of his visit except from those who had encountered him - either at Hazelbrae, one of his many lectures or if he had visited at their residence - when they came to church. When he returned to the Village Home the Mothers were told of the success of his enterprise. He told them he knew there were some issues to be resolved but this, he felt, was to be expected in the early stages of his venture and had no doubts that the scheme would be a success.

Peg wrote to May in late summer of 1884. It was a long letter that she hoped May would fully understand.

My dear May

I trust and hope that this letter finds you well. I know it has only been just over a year since I saw you but can imagine you grown and looking more like a young lady all the time.

I am well, a brief spell of fever but that soon passed and I am much recovered. The girls in my care were kind and helpful to me. Mrs Barnardo also assisted when needed.

The Doctor himself travelled with the next party of girls. They also left in July, as you did and you may remember Alice Smart, I am sure you do, who was one of our number. She was one of those who departed with him. Maybe you will come across her sometime although given the vast size of the country this is unlikely. It is my dearest wish that she finds herself placed with a good family, as you have.

We were told about Canada when the Doctor spoke to us all upon his return. The picture he paints is a bright and cheerful one of a land of fresh air and healthy surroundings. As you know May our Doctor is a sober and religious man so was at pains to point out that wherever he visited he was not offered, nor did he see, beer or wine. I suspect he stressed this to reinforce the importance he places on sobriety but do wonder if perhaps our dear Doctor is somewhat unworldly in believing the vices that exist here do not exist in Canada. No matter, as usual, his enthusiasm has, it

241

seems, prompted goodwill and support from many quarters despite some stories to the contrary that appear in our newspapers. I fear it is too easy to criticise such work as his. He told us he was so disappointed he could not meet more of his girls but his schedule of meetings and talks was heavy and exhausting.

But enough of our life here dear May and forgive me for running away with my news. I have not heard from you for some time and like to think this is because you are finding your time with the family so agreeable you have little inclination to dwell upon your friends so far away although I know you hold us in your heart.

Perhaps by the time I receive my next welcome letter from you we shall be once again approaching Christmas, The time seems to go by more quickly with each year that passes and as I grow older - although not quite in my dotage my dear - I am grateful that my time in the workhouse was brief. Briefer than my time residing in the tenement block where I had the misfortune to be living, if living is the right word, when I had the pleasure of my first encounter with you.

Regarding that slum from whence we came, I have heard there are certain moves afoot by reformers to improve the conditions there. But it is and I fear always will be, those with money, power and influence - perhaps those who benefit from the conditions we

*once endured and which others still do - who hold
sway.*

*It is my wish, although I believe it is something that
will never come to pass, that the whole area of those
black streets is rendered to rubble to be replaced by
altogether less harsh and foreboding homes for the
poor. Perhaps one day my dear May.*

*The country you have left has many problems and the
politicians, as usual, find it hard to agree on the most
advantageous way to settle them. I feel changes are
coming and whether Mr Gladstone will remain as our
Prime Minister for much longer I do not know. All of
this is of no concern to you my dear but I know you will
return, as you have told me, and so wish you to be
acquainted with the country to which you shall. I will,
of course, inform you of any matters relating to the
person whose name you do not wish me to commit to
paper.*

*Well, that is all I have to say to you for now. I look
forward to receiving news from you as soon as you are
able.*

*My love to you always
Peg.*

Peg folded the letter and placed it in an envelope
addressed to the family home of the Reverend Sutton
ready for it to begin its long journey across the ocean.
As she did so she could not know that Edward

Perryman was preparing the way, laying the foundations, of his entry into the contentious world of politics and how close she was to the truth with her opinions.

Thirty six

London, Belgravia 1884

Josephine had heard her husband leave early on the morning after her elegant and meticulously arranged gathering. His mood as the guests left was hard to gauge. He appeared, she thought, as two people - presenting a different face to them than to her. Had it gone well, as he hoped? She couldn't tell if his silence, when they were alone, was one of contemplation - weighing up and analysing some of the conversations he had had or... well she just didn't know. They retired immediately and little was said. As usual, Josephine thought it better to maintain silence until Edward saw fit to share his thoughts with her.

He had been affable she must admit; perhaps more agreeable than she had seen him for a while and certainly since he returned from visiting Richard in Southampton. The first she had heard from him as he entered the house on that occasion was a tirade at the maid for not taking his coat promptly enough. This did not bode well she had thought and decided to wait until he spoke for fear of saying the wrong thing and incurring his displeasure - or even his wrath. His first words to her were not of greeting.

"The man is a fool. I hoped perhaps after all these years he would, with the responsibilities he shoulders as a leader of others, have developed an altogether more fitting attitude. Alas, this is not the case. The man lives firmly in the past, still hankering after..."

Josephine looked at him as he tailed off. 'Hankering after what, who?' she thought.

She had attempted to speak, to question, but Edward had not waited to hear. He did not even look at her but said there were things he must do. He had hurried away to his study where he remained for the rest of the day

It was after this episode that Josephine knew Richard would not be attending their party. She was disappointed. She would have liked to see him again after so many years. She was not going to find out from Edward what had passed between them and perhaps, she was hoping, she would have found out from Richard. This was clearly not to be. Whatever the issue that had led to their estrangement, it had not been exorcised by time.

After his earlier than usual start, when there had not been time for any discussion of the events of the previous night, Edward did not return until much later in the day. Josephine was beginning to think he would miss the time he scheduled with the children and maybe even dinner but upon his return, he was in better spirits.

"My dear, apologies for my somewhat late return - forgive me. I shall see the children. Then, over dinner, I shall relate to you the good news that will, without any doubt, further our progress."

She did not have time to answer before Edward left the room calling for the nanny to fetch the children to him and was somewhat stunned by the change in his demeanour. Josephine was all too aware how his moods could change. It would appear that whatever had happened with Richard had been cast aside and his path was on course as he wished it.

As they sat down to dinner Edward related a summary of what had transpired the previous evening and that day. His mood was buoyant.

"I must commend you, my dear, for the most excellent occasion you provided for our esteemed guests last evening. I noticed that you appeared to find Lady Anne most amenable and I am pleased since her husband Lord Elco is an extremely worthwhile ally to help further my political ambitions." He paused to begin eating. "Once again the meal is outstanding. We are fortunate to have engaged such a fine cook. Well done my dear."

Josephine moved to speak but was pre-empted.

"Since Lord Elco - Francis - has taken his seat in the Lords he has watched with dismay some of the antics of Parliament. He agrees with me that our country is in danger of being taken over by those with little or no

247

regard for our fundamental freedoms. This was something he has been aware of for some time and why he founded the Liberty and Property Defence League, of which I now count myself one of its number. It is also why, after boundary changes next year when new constituencies are formed, he will endorse my candidature. It even appears that Hackney is to gain another seat. It is to that seat that I aspire."

He paused again, once more enjoying the dinner. This time Josephine had an opportunity to respond.

"That is wonderful news, my dear. I know how much this is something you wish for. It is my only concern that, along with your other business interests, you may - if elected of course - spread yourself too thinly."

Edward dabbed his mouth on the crisp white table napkin and waved his hand dismissively.

"My dear, do not worry on my account. There is nothing that I shall be required to do that will necessitate my being spread too thinly as you so quaintly put it. And please do not speak of 'if' I am elected but 'when'. Now, since that dinner was first rate I am expecting a dessert of a similarly high standard to follow it. And when we are finished we shall open the very best brandy in celebration."

Josephine smiled and nodded. Edward, it seemed, was on his way.

Thirty seven

Barnardo's Village, September 1884

Peg wrote again to May with news that had stunned her and, she knew, would stun May also.

My Dear May

I know it is not too long since my last letter and, of course, I have not yet received a reply from you.

I am writing again so soon to let you know some news that has recently reached me. It is something I read in the Illustrated London News and whilst I cannot be entirely sure if it is the same person so would not wish to build up your hopes, I feel that it is.

Dearest May you have told me about your Uncle George being a soldier and how you wondered what had become of him as he was unaware of his sister's death. I know it was, and I'm sure still is, your fervent hope that there should come a time, praying he is still alive of course, that you would be reunited.

In the newspaper under the headline 'Soudan Heroes' was an account of events that took place at Windsor Castle on the 3rd of July. It was when the Queen conferred honours on soldiers who had performed heroically in battle in a faraway place called the Sudan. I am vaguely familiar with its location and since you and Simon are keen to learn about all manner of subjects, including geography, I suspect you may be too.

There are many names May but one that stood out to me - Sergeant George Harris. I believe this could be your uncle, I truly do. And there is more my dear; the name of the officer he saved, despite being surrounded by the enemy, was Captain Richard Perryman. I do not have to tell you who it is that shares this surname.

We cannot know if Richard Perryman is cut from the same cloth as his relative or even if indeed they are related but we now know that it appears George is alive and may still be in London although by now he has probably rejoined his regiment. This is very good news May I am sure you will agree. If there is any more word of him I will of course let you know with as much haste as the distance between us permits.

There is nothing else that warrants your attention here except to tell you that since my last letter Lottie has left us to take up employment. Whether she will adjust readily to her new station is something we must wait and see. I have a full complement of girls under my charge and whilst most of them are agreeable enough, even though as you know everything does not always run smoothly here, you will always be at the forefront of my mind and of my heart.

God bless you and keep you

Peg

250

This letter was received with much joy by May and her reply was swift.

October 1884

Dear Peg

Your last letter has just reached me and I am very pleased by your news. Can it really be that Uncle George is alive and a hero as well? I knew he was brave Peg I told you didn't I how he would fight and often get hurt to buy us food.

Him and my dear mum were very close when I was little and I think I told you about Violet who died of cholera. I don't know what happened to their parents Peg as I was never told anything about them but I suppose they died. Loads of people were always dying in the Nichol Peg - like you know I'm sure. Mum said George looked out for her and Violet although he was younger, then they got positions as maids or something like that, like what I didn't want to do it was I think. I don't rightly know the whole of it except mum wasn't in the posh house when I was born. Don't know more than that I don't Peg because she never said nothing about my dad. I never had one. Uncle George never knew neither about him so he couldn't tell me nothing, he just come back from being at sea and there I was - born. That's all he could tell me and mum wouldn't tell him nothing and all.The last time I saw him was just before poor mum passed away so even if he come back

251

he wouldn't know how to find out what happened to her or to me but I have always felt he was still living Peg. I just feel it somehow I do.

As for the man he saved well it might be that evil man's brother or something but we won't ever know I suppose and even if he is he might be alright.

I would have written to you anyway Peg even if you hadn't told me this and it was good to hear that something may happen to the Nichol but I am like you because I don't think it will either.

It did make me smile when you said what the Doctor told you all about beer and wine. I know there are lots of drunken people here just like back in London. I hear what goes on because of the church. Reverend Sutton does not drink, only a little bit of wine on special days but he comes across men what hit their wives and children when they are drunk. The Doctor is a good man but I agree with you that he can be a bit blind to what goes on although he did get one girl taken away while he was here because she wasn't being treated right.

I will go to bed happy tonight and sleep soundly but then I always do Peg. And I do remember Alice Smart. Little and thin she was with right curly hair. If I do come across her I wonder if she will remember me.

God bless you Peg
Yours always
May Harris

252

Thirty eight

For the next year, there was no news of George Harris that Peg was able to relate to May and their correspondence was of day to day matters for both of them. Peg, for her part, recognised May's ever-evolving power of communication. This became more evident with each letter; the young girl who had, through fear, fled to Canada was no more. As she approached an age where she could determine her own path, it was clear to Peg that May's pledge to return and avenge Ernie was not something that had evaporated. If anything her resolve and confidence, aided by Reverend Sutton, his wife and young Simon had grown stronger.

It was not until October of the following year that Peg's letter contained something other than general gossip.

October 1885
My Dear May
I hope and trust this letter finds you well. All is much the same in the Village but I have heard news that will no doubt be of interest to you. Our little world here is, as you know, a peaceful island set against the lives led by those less fortunate. I was once one of these of course - we both were, and it is not always easy

keeping up with what goes on beyond our walls. As I have, perhaps, more reason than most to keep myself acquainted with what is happening among our supposed betters in the political realm; I read whatever news I am able. Without this, it would not have been possible to tell you the good news about your uncle. Regrettably, I have found no more mention of him to reassure you of his continuing survival but if, as I hope, you are both of the same steel then I am sure he is alive.

I have digressed, although I am sure you will forgive me. The newspapers, together with information I have gleaned from the visits of various dignitaries, suggest it is very likely that a general election will take place sometime in November. I shall not be able to cast a vote as we women are not, as yet, although surely the time will come, deemed fit to contribute to the running of our country. What I have heard is that he whose name you will not speak is standing for election in one of the new constituencies in Hackney as, to be expected, a Conservative. Whether or not he will be elected is, of course, uncertain but if he is then I fear for the poor people who are unfortunate enough to dwell there. His regard must surely be for his own advancement or to protect the wealth and influence he already has. That a man such as he could aspire to an elevated position with no doubt the aim of climbing higher says a great deal about the dire state of our nation.

I know you intend to return and it is a day I am looking forward to my dear May, to see your face again, your smile again and I hope the England to which you return will have seen some improvements to the lives of the poor. You have not told me much about Canada beyond your own experience and situation. I would, however, like to think that a new country, although modelled on our own, has not inherited the division and inequality that is so prevalent here.

If I do not hear from you before Christmas is once again upon us I will be writing to you soon after with news from the election. I am sure the Reverend is well informed and ensures news from England reaches you so you will probably already know the outcome when my letter arrives.

Know that, as always, you are in my thoughts
God bless you,
Peg

****

Peterborough, December 1885

Dear Peg
Thank you for your very welcome last letter despite the reason for it and the news it brought. I am always pleased to hear from you and am glad you are well.

We have had news of the election here and see that Mr Gladstone has been replaced as Prime Minister by Lord Salisbury. Although he is of the same party as my enemy this does not mean, I know, that he has been elected in Hackney but something tells me Peg, and I cannot say why, that he has. My stomach turns when I think of him. Like you, I look forward to the day when we women will be able to have our say in deciding who runs our country. We are just as capable as men Peg, I know we are and stronger too I think. I have spoken about this with Simon and he is of agreement. He is such a clever boy and I believe he will be a great man in the future. He has told me he is very fortunate to have my companionship and is full of regret for the way he treated me when I first came here. No matter, that is past now, we are good friends and will remain so I am sure, even when I return to England.

Once again we are preparing for Christmas and as usual thick snow is carpeting the ground. I wonder if you will have snow this winter Peg? I remember my first sight of it at the Village. Pure and clean it was unlike the grey sludge in the Nichol. There the whiteness was gone almost as soon as the snow had fallen. I can still see the snow that night – over five years ago now – still see the awful deed.

But I will talk no more of gloom. Now let us think of Christmas and give thanks for what we have. May yours at Barkingside be peaceful and joyous as I am sure mine will be. I pray that 1886 will be a good year for all of us.

Much love to you

May Harris

Ps You have not mentioned Lottie recently. I hope she is well and perhaps, if you are able to communicate with her you can pass on my address here. I would very much like to hear from her.

Thirty nine

Edward Perryman could never have been described as modest. Josephine knew this from the start but back then was attracted by his self-confidence, his unshakeable faith in his own abilities. She was envied by friends, for Edward was a handsome man whose attentions any woman would be pleased to receive and he had chosen her; chosen her so she was special. He had made her feel that whatever happened, she, and any children they had together, would be looked after in the material way that was deemed so important to a woman of her class and standing. Not that she was a weak woman but she was pragmatic.

A woman's life was inextricably bound up with that of her husband. It was just the way things were and how they were forever likely to remain although she wished it was not so. Since this was the way of the world then it made sense to ensure she had a man who could provide for her in a comfortable fashion. As the years went on after their marriage Josephine couldn't help but become a little less accepting of Edward's self-important and even somewhat denigrating ways. Certainly, he praised her but the praise was usually tinged with a degree of condescension she found increasingly difficult to overlook. Upon his election by 'the good people' of Hackney the pomposity had, inevitably - as she suspected it would – become harder to tolerate.

Coming as it did just before Christmas his success meant this one would be unlike any other so far. Instead of a somewhat subdued affair, although of course resplendent with enough food to feed many of his new constituents for several weeks, there would be a party to celebrate his success. Josephine wondered if Edward would extend the invitations beyond his circle of influential friends to Richard. This had not been the case before but perhaps, with Christmas approaching and with Edward basking in the glory of his new prominence, he may. She hoped he would but had no idea of Richard's whereabouts and if Edward had then it was not information he chose to share with her. Would Richard even accept anyway? It was necessary, it always had been but since his triumphant entry into Parliament even more so, to broach certain subjects to him with care. Over the years Josephine had become adept at correctly judging Edward's erratic moods.

She sat drawing up plans for their party, absentmindedly sketching and waiting for her husband's return. He was late; later than usual and this could mean one of two things. Either good in which case his disposition would be also or bad in which case he would be insufferable. As she pondered, the nanny came in; Josephine did not expect her to knock but

Florence would not have entered thus had Edward been in residence.

"Excuse me madam but as it is quite late now and the Master is not yet home do you wish me to put the children to bed?"

Josephine thought for a moment.

"Yes Florence, certainly. I would not wish their sleep to be compromised by waiting to have a brief visit with their father."

"Very well madam."

"I will come along to say goodnight presently."

Florence left and Josephine wondered what time Edward would return. The time he devoted to his children had diminished even further and Christmas was not something she was looking forward to. She would never tell Edward but she regretted the new role he had so eagerly embraced. She stared at the ornate mantel clock and considered how such a simple matter as telling the time could be embellished to such exorbitant proportions.

It was not something that had crossed her mind before but now she saw such excess as pointless. Much about her life was gradually being exposed as pointless. What was she? An adornment; an accessory; the obligatory gracious hostess? Did she still love her husband? Had she ever loved him? The question was increasingly eating away at her. She gazed into the mirror over the fireplace, behind the elaborate clock.

Again this was something far more ornate than it had any reason or need to be, and did not see a happy woman. Staring back was someone who wondered if she would ever experience real happiness again. Perhaps the only time she had been truly happy and content was when her dear children were born. When they were grown - what then? What would the future hold for her? Perhaps it was better she didn't know.

Forty

Richard Perryman would not, even had Josephine attempted and managed to contact him, been able to attend his brother's victory gathering. Nor would he have wished to. The gulf between them remained too strong, too indelibly ingrained to make such a meeting possible especially after their last one at Netley Hospital.

The news of Edward's much-lauded (by himself) new role had reached Richard in despatches regarding the General Election sent from London to the Sudan. Once again, there, he was about to go into battle. Once again he would face the same enemy and wondered when this conflict would ever finally be settled, lasting as it had some four years already. As 1885 neared its end, Richard speculated what 1886 would bring. More battles, more lucky escapes? Or perhaps there would be no more lucky escapes; no one to rescue him - to save his life. Perhaps his death would come. If he did survive, leave the army and return to England when his commission ended, what would he do? He had no family other than Edward, Josephine and their children. He was an uncle to children he would most likely never see. He doubted he would ever have children of his own. How different his life might have, probably would have, been had Edward not thwarted his chance of happiness with Rose. Whatever became of dear Rose?

His brother had, seemingly, all that Richard wanted for himself but he was not envious. Something told him that Edward would never be satisfied with his lot. He would always crave more and strive to obtain it by any means. Such a man could never be truly happy nor, Richard suspected, could he make anyone else truly happy. He thought of Josephine and doubted that her life with Edward, despite her material comforts, *was* a happy one.

As Edward prepared to embark on his first year serving, as he somewhat ironically chose to describe it, his constituents in Hackney, Richard was a world away riding through dry, dusty palm groves at the head of his mounted infantry. Armed with bayonets they drove their enemies, the Dervishes - by now much diminished in number, back until they fled into the desert and vanished into clouds of swirling sand. This day at Ginnis, Richard was not one of the ten killed or the forty or so injured but there would be more battles to come. And not all would be military. Faces from the past would reappear in Richard's life and Edward would, although he could not have guessed it, take centre stage.

Also serving his country at Ginnis this day was George Harris - although this time their paths were not destined to cross. After fighting their way through the narrow streets of the town, George and his compatriots forced the Dervishes out into the palm groves for them finally to be routed by none other than Richard's company.

The two men were in some ways alike, both with the same purpose and both - once the victory had been secured and the dust cleared - of a similar mind. George was also wondering what his life would be like when he left the army. Would he leave it at all or re-enlist indefinitely and die a soldier? The life was hard but there was a camaraderie that he had not known many years ago back in England. If death were to come in battle then he saw it as preferable to rotting in some awful slum as was the Nichol. When he returned to England to be presented with his Victoria Cross he had not ventured there. It was something he wanted to do but time and duty did not permit it. What of his sister and his young niece May? She would be almost sixteen years old by now. He wondered how she and his sister were managing. He felt bad that he had not made more effort to try to find them. Five, nearly six years had passed. This was a long time and recently his thoughts had turned to them more and more.

When he left, it was always his intention to keep in touch but this had proved more difficult than he had envisaged. Letters were written to the last address he knew but the transient nature of life in the slum meant whether they reached his sister was uncertain - he couldn't know. Perhaps they had and been replied to - replies he had not received - or perhaps they were never received, never opened, never read. He knew his name had appeared in the newspapers and hoped they had seen it. If so they could at least be reassured that he was still alive. Maybe post from them would reach him via his regiment at some point but nothing, so far, had been forthcoming.

George, like Richard, doubted he would ever have any children of his own. May would possibly be the closest to parenthood he came. There was another year to serve before he had to decide whether to sign on again or leave, return to England, and try to make a life for himself again there. If he left he would remain a reserve so the army would not be out of his life completely even then. By this time May would be eighteen - a young woman and his sister, well maybe she had married and had more children. He hoped it was so. She deserved to be happy, so did May as her start in life had been...difficult.

He shivered. It was cold as the day drew to a close but not as cold as he knew it would be in London. He shivered not just because of the cold but because a feeling of disquiet had suddenly beset him. Such a feeling often followed battle but this, somehow, was different.

A couple of hundred yards or so apart George Harris and Richard Perryman were both seriously considering their futures. As stillness descended in the eerie aftermath of the battle, each eventually drifted off into a restless sleep.

Forty one

May's third Canadian winter was nearing its end. The first had been a shock – its ferocity had been such that nothing she had been told could equip her for it. The cold seeped deep into her unprepared English bones. The second winter was not such a surprise and therefore somewhat easier to cope with. As this winter drew to a close, despite being hit with a hard blizzard that eliminated all colour, May was stronger. Her whole being was immersed in the extremes of the Canadian climate. She was not only mentally stronger but physically too. So was Simon and this gave her great pleasure. They would spend time outside together when duties and lessons allowed. May couldn't help but wonder how the confines of London, and especially the slum, would seem to her after the fresh air and space of her, albeit temporary, Canadian home.

Of course, the Village would still be the same peaceful, calm place it had been when she left - at least she hoped and supposed it would. Nothing she had heard from Peg suggested any different. Would Peg remember she was fast approaching sixteen? Surely she would for Peg remembered everything. Sometimes May had seen in her face a flicker of sadness or even pain when she was, for some unknown reason, reminded of events in her past. When May returned, as a young woman with more knowledge of the world, she would try to persuade Peg to share some details of her early life. Despite their undoubted closeness, May knew little about Peg other than that which she had discovered from the faded photograph - which she still had and treasured. What she did know was that Peg was a good, kind person. She knew Peg would get along with the Suttons very well and it was a pity they were never likely to meet.

Easter was late that year - only a couple of weeks before May's birthday. The Suttons were busy with preparations for it but despite their industry May was touched by their kindness and generosity to her. Her birthday fell on a Saturday and Mrs Sutton had arranged a small party for her, inviting others of a similar age that May had befriended. The day was bright and warm for early May. The light held the promise of a wonderful summer to come. A dress had been specially made for May in a vibrant shade of emerald green and white. Mrs Sutton had stitched it herself in secret - May having no idea. She was also not aware that emeralds were the birthstone of the star sign under which she had been born - that of Taurus the bull. May could be stubborn so this star sign was quite apt.

May would wear the dress proudly and intended to adorn it with the silver cross given to her by Peg. No word had come from Peg by the day before her birthday but May had no doubt she had remembered... she must have. As she helped herself to breakfast she saw the postman's coach stopping at the house. She watched as Simon collected something from him and, smiling, hurried back to the house.

The beaming boy came into the kitchen and presented May with a small parcel.

"This is for you May. All the way from London it is. I think it must be something very valuable as it has been so carefully wrapped."

Simon held the small rectangular parcel just out of May's reach.

"Come on Simon, give it to me."

May smiled as Simon darted away, waving the parcel - teasing her with it.

"Simon!" called his mother "You give Miss Harris her parcel forthwith. She is a young lady now who will not wish to be included in childish games. Isn't that right May?"

"I suppose I am a young lady, but in truth, I do not feel like one and if I should be inclined to play childish games now and then it is not something of which I am ashamed. On such a fine day as this games and joyfulness should be encouraged I think."

They all smiled and Simon handed the parcel to May. Before opening it she studied the hand in which it was written. It was, of course, from Peg and May was sure that, whatever it contained, there would be a letter also.

"Do not let your breakfast chill further. Those are good eggs laid fresh this morning. Your parcel is not going anywhere."

The anticipation of discovering the contents was as great a pleasure as opening it would be so May placed it on the table whilst she finished her breakfast.

"I have a present for you too May." said Simon "It's a wonderful present I am sure you will like very much - I chose it myself. I will fetch it while you eat."

Simon left to get his gift. May finished her last mouthful and picked up the small parcel. Carefully she unwrapped it, struggling a little with the string and needing a knife to cut it. Inside was a box. Inside that box, together with a folded letter, was a shiny silver frame. A frame that had two openings and was just the right size for the photograph of Peg May cherished.

This was something very special. May's eyes filled up. A lump formed in her throat. She unfolded the letter.

My dear May

I hope and trust that this letter and my little gift find you well. It is hard to believe that the thin child I first encountered at the rag shop is now sixteen years old. I wish I could see what a fine young woman you are becoming. In my mind, I see a clear and wonderful picture of you. Your cheeks will be pink with health and you will, of course, have grown taller. By how much I wonder?

I desire and believe I will see you again and by then you will have grown even more. I see my charges here bloom, well most of them at least, into fine young women and cannot help when I look at them to consider how they might compare with you.

I do not seem to have changed very much; perhaps to others, if gradual changes are noticed, but within my head I remain much the same as many years ago. If there were no such things as looking glasses none of us would see how we change, how we age. Perhaps this could be a good thing I think. Then what we do would be governed not by how we look but how we feel.

But enough of me. Your birthday will, I hope, be a jolly affair. You deserve it to be my dear May. The month in which you were born and after which you were named is surely the most joyous month of the whole year. The spring had given us her yellow daffodils and then May is the glorious bridge between spring and summer - full of the promise of that which is to come. It is always my favourite month at our Village. I wondered if you could remember it so that is why I have sent you, together with the frame - which I acquired at a very reasonable price in case you are

271

concerned about my circumstances - a photograph of the gardens here. You can just see your old home in the background.

May paused from reading the letter to unfold another piece of paper within which was the photograph.

As you can see the roses are delightful as usual. This image was taken last summer but I am sure this year's blooms will equal their splendour. It is a pity we are not able to capture the wonderful colours. Maybe in time such a thing will be possible but we can use our imagination, and I know yours is a magical one, to paint the colours we choose.

I think the picture you have of me will fit into the other side but please if you have another - perhaps of a young man - whose image you would like to display then please do not feel obliged to use mine.

There is little news here but it may be that another general election will take place this summer although it is so soon after the last one. I wonder whether he whose name you will not speak will be re-elected? I suppose, since it has not been long enough for him to cause too much damage, he may well be.

Preparations have already begun for our Queen's Golden Jubilee next year, assuming, of course, she lives to see it. If so I doubt it will be a very jolly affair as widow's black, which is all she wears, it not associated with celebration. I am sure we will mark the occasion here at the Village as, no doubt, will Canada since she is Queen there too.

Well, May I have kept you long enough with my ramblings. Please accept my best wishes for your birthday.

I am, as always thinking of you.
Your dear friend
Peg

May put down the letter and studied the frame; a picture of a young man? There was no young man and even had there been Peg's place in the frame could not be usurped. She examined the picture of the gardens, concentrating so hard that the colours she remembered of the roses came to life before her eyes. So many things were seeming to change in the world that she was sure it would indeed not be long before images could be produced in true colour rather than the gaudy hand-painted tints that were supposed to enhance them.

Simon broke May's reflective mood as he rushed back into the room holding a package.

He was expectant of May's pleasure at his gift.

"Here you are May. I hope you will like it. It is, you may have guessed, a book. I think it will be special for you because it was published the year you were born, or close to it at least and it is about a girl who..." Simon broke off realising he was about to give away too much and spoil the surprise, "I do hope you like it dear friend May." He said again.

He passed it to her and waited eagerly as she took it from him.

"Easier to unwrap than my present from Peg." May smiled as she opened the package.

"You haven't read it have you May? I hope not."

May studied at the cover of the book - a young girl and a looking glass. Before anything else came to her mind or she spoke to Simon she thought of the sentiment expressed in Peg's letter.

"'Alice Through the Looking Glass' - thank you, Simon. I have not read it and I am sure I will like it very much."

Simon was pleased with her reaction.

"I am glad, but now May you must come as guests for your party will begin to arrive shortly and my mother is expecting you to be ready to greet them wearing the dress she made for you."

The afternoon of her birthday passed happily for May. The sun shone on the little gathering, her dress was admired by all, and Mrs Sutton was commended for her skill. Mrs Sutton was a humble woman but May could tell she was delighted by the praise she received. In turn, the Reverend took pleasure in his wife's joy. May took pleasure also in the happiness of the couple who had taken her in and cared for her so well. Her sixteenth birthday was one she would always remember - no matter what the future might hold. She wished Peg could have seen her and of course, her Mum. May thought of both of them and smiled. Smiled then but later, alone and beginning to read her book, other less happy thoughts crept in.

Reflections on her life so far. She began to read the story and found she could identify with the girl who left her familiar world behind. The description of the snow by Alice could have been written about winter in Canada; the trees 'covered in a snug white quilt to sleep until summer wakes them and clothes them in green again.' May imagined how it would be if she, like Alice, could step through the glass of her mirror. She imagined how it would be if she could jump through and find herself, not in a Looking Glass room, but back in the Village.

Reflections of her mother came to her mind. How did she look when she was sixteen? She had no photographs of her and was sad, even guilty, that how she looked, how she sounded, how she smiled was gradually evaporating. She had become a shadowy figure, harder and harder to cling on to. As May grew up would she grow to resemble her mother more? She wondered, if, should she - and she hoped she would - be reunited with Uncle George, he would see his sister in her.

The year continued uneventfully. Letters passed, as usual, between May and Peg. News of Edward

Perryman's re-election came as no great surprise. May envisaged his arrogance being increased still further, if that was possible, by being a representative of a party who had won the latest poll by a landslide. Despite a reluctance to leave the Suttons May's return to England could not come quickly enough.

Forty two

London, June 1887

George Harris was uncomfortable in his uniform waiting in the hot sunshine. Discomfort in uniform was, of course, nothing new and at least this particular discomfort was not a precursor to facing the guns and bayonets of whichever enemy the British Empire was engaged with at the time. He was waiting, along with other recipients of the Victoria Cross who were lining the route of the Queen's Jubilee Procession.

He hoped this would be his last outing in the uniform. The decision had been made not to re-enlist. He had no desire to be a soldier any more He had chosen to attempt to make a life for himself as a free man; albeit one that could be called up to the Reserves if his Queen and country deemed it necessary. He still had his health - which was much more than so many had. He had survived where so many had not and he was still comparatively young. Young enough to build a life that did not involve violence, although as a Reservist being called upon for conflict could mean this was not possible.

The Victoria Cross gave him a pension of £10 a year which, whilst not much, was something not many others had. The younger man who once sought excitement and adventure was no more. He now wanted a quieter, more peaceful life. George wanted to find his sister and his niece and that, when the Jubilee Celebrations were over, was what he would do.

First, there was to be another meeting. A grand gathering had been scheduled in the gardens of Buckingham Palace and those who had fought so bravely to save the lives of their comrades - those who held the Victoria Cross - were to attend.

So it was that a month after the Jubilee procession George was once more in the uniform he hoped he would not wear again. The scale of the party was so vast, some six thousand people, that the only other time George had seen such numbers in one place was on the battlefield. The men who were not soldiers wore a uniform of their own - elegant black suits, as did some of the older women; the younger women wore white. They moved around like a giant chess game; the monochrome broken up by the deep green and purple favoured by others among the older ladies. George thought the colours were more suitable for a funeral than a celebration.

The unease at being at such an unfamiliar gathering was relieved only by the company of the other soldiers who shared his honour. Together they presented a fine crowd who drew admiration from all quarters as they awaited the arrival of the Queen. As if commanded by the Queen herself, the clouds parted and the sun shone on the vast crowd as she appeared. In unison, all hats were removed and all heads bowed as she passed along the line that formed across the lawn. How proud his sister would be. She should be there with him. Just as pretty, he was sure, as any of the fine ladies present.

Major Richard Perryman was also attending the Garden Party - as part of the military guard contingent. He too looked around at the elegant women in attendance and imagined Rose dressed in such finery. His mind drifted back to all those years ago - how many now? Seventeen, eighteen? He felt he should remember exactly but the passing of time had clouded some of his memories. Some, but not all and the feelings he had, how he was hurt through Edward's doing, had certainly not faded.

Richard was jolted back to the present as the Queen's Carriage and her Guard paused alongside the gathered rank of the Victoria Cross holders. She waved and nodded in acknowledgement of their service and they, in turn, bowed to their Monarch. As he looked around from high on his horse at the faces in the crowd, Richard recognised someone; someone to whom he owed his life - George Harris. He would search him out when his role in the Queen's protection ended and he was no longer on duty. Despite both being involved in battles since Richard's life had been saved, they had not met since the ceremony when George received his

Victoria Cross and then only very briefly. Richard fully intended to remedy this.

George had thought he would like to reconnect with Richard Perryman also. There were some things in George's life he was not proud of; his failure to maintain contact with his sister for one - but knowing his bravery had allowed another to live was certainly the best thing he had ever done. So, he thought, it was likely to remain.

Later as the crowds began to dwindle and Queen Victoria was once more secluded from her subjects, Richard Perryman, now off duty, and George Harris finally came face to face. They shook each other's hands and began to get to know each other.

Forty three

George was now a free man. He could set about finding his sister and his niece. This was of the utmost importance to him and something he was determined to accomplish.

His first port of call was the Nichol where he had last seen them - where he had said goodbye. The place had not changed. If anything it had become blacker, more depressing than he remembered - and he had left them here. Deserted them; left them to whatever fate. There was some talk of renewal - of the slums being razed to the ground to be replaced with dwellings fit for people to live in but as yet nothing had been done. The darkness, the dirt, the oppressive atmosphere covering the place like a grey blanket - it resembled an all too familiar battlefield which, to the unfortunate residents it surely was. Living like this with no end except death, no hope - it could not be right. He could taste the despair in the very air. Of course there were smiles. Of course there were laughs. Of course there was merriment. There had been even on the battlefield but these were more a testament to the strength of the human spirit against overwhelming odds than reflections of happiness. The contrast between the finery and wealth on display at the Garden Party, the abundance there, rankled with George.

He returned to some of his old haunts where he had fought for money to help feed little May. Some remembered him. Those who did (those who still lived - for many of the people he knew were dead now) gave him the news he least wanted to hear. His sister was dead. She had died not too long after he left, killed by a disease brought on by the conditions in which she existed.

The guilt George felt on hearing this seemed to shrink and age him instantly. He should never have left them. Never. What had become of May? Now, more than ever, he needed to find her. Now, he had only recently discovered, there were two reasons.

"George the 'ammer 'Arris, as I live an' breathe. Is it you?"

George had heard this many times since his return but this time the speaker would prove useful to him.

"It is me right enough. Back from the army and hopefully will never be asked to fight again."

"If I recall George you was always good in a scrap. Still got the scars to prove it I 'ave. Scars wot you gived me."

He pointed to his face. George studied the shambolic figure smiling at him. He didn't recall the man's name but the battered face was just about familiar. The nose had been broken once, maybe twice more. How George had managed to avoid the same fate despite all his fights he didn't know.

"Wot you doing back 'ere then 'Arris? Didn't fink we'd see you again round 'ere. You know your sister snuffed it doncha? What 'appened to 'er kid? Wot was 'er name?"

"May."

"Yeah right, May. Skinny gel she was. You seen 'er?"

"No, and it is her I seek. Do you know anyone who could help me?"

George tried again to remember the man's name but the years had drained him of such memories and his mind was purely focussed on May.

"She ain't bin round 'ere for years, well I ain't seen 'er. Be grown up now I s'pose so lord knows wot she's up to...if y'know wot I mean."

The man smirked and it took all of George's self-control to prevent himself from striking him - the implication of his remark clear.

George remained silent, put his head to one side then said,

"So you can't help me then?" He turned away.

"Wait 'Ammer." The man picked up he had said the wrong thing and not wishing to antagonise George further, called him back. "There woz a little gang of scamps she went around wiv. Some of them ain't around no more - one poor little sod was found stone-cold dead when we 'ad all that awful early snow. When was that? Cor must be seven, eight years ago nah.

283

Anyway, there's one kid, Nick yeah Nick that's 'im. That's wot he's called. Well, he's got a sister - bit of a trollope she was but I fink she's alright nah. Doing sumfink for that Barnardo bloke."

George's patience was wearing thin as he listened to the man who was, he realised not only punch drunk - in spite of the early hour.

"What about May?"

He took the man by the shoulder as it appeared he was about to fall over.

"Oh yeah, where was I? Yeah well, that Nick he's done alright an' all. He was always a smart one he was. Smart by name an' smart by nature. Funny that -'is name like. Anyway, yeah 'e got a place... gawd knows how, but like I said - he's a smart one, always thought he'd do alright..."

"May, please, what about May?"

"Okay, Okay "Ammer, I'm gettin' there." George wondered if he would ever reveal anything of use; his frustration was building. "Yeah so 'e got a place on the papers he did. He does reports on local stuff he does. Bet he'd know wot happened to 'er. Nah wot paper was it? Oh yeah 'Ackney Gazette, not that I read the bleedin papers. So George, wot yer bin up to in our old Queen's army? Killed lots of them foreign bastards 'ave yer? Shafted 'em good I'll bet. No messing wiv you mate eh?"

By this time George had already left the man behind. Soon, he was sure, his informant would have forgotten their encounter and gone in search of his next drink. Now he had to find Nick, whom he did vaguely remember. Who was the boy who died? He thought he was probably one of many who met their end on these forbidding streets due to illness, disease or hunger. Murder, of a child, was not something he considered.

George was familiar with the Hackney and Kingsland Gazette. Perhaps once a week, if possible, he would glance through one of its thrice-weekly editions, so he knew where to go to try to find Nick. His pace quickened as he hurried up Shoreditch High Street towards Kingsland Road and the newspaper offices. Would Nick even be there and if he was could he really help? He had already heard the bad news about his sister, what if there was similar news about May? He just couldn't think about this. Somehow he knew she was still alive. He had to find her. He had to tell her the news; the news that could change her life forever - whatever that life was. The only thing that concerned him was that despite all the odds stacked against her, May might have found a better life that did not need changing. No matter - the important news he carried must be shared as soon as possible.

As George approached the print works two young men were leaving. One was hazily familiar. He exuded the same confidence George had seen in him as a boy all those years ago. The two young men stood together to say goodbye then turned in different directions.

"Nick?"

Nick looked surprised as this stranger called his name.

"Who's asking?"

Suspicion was written all over his face.

"George Harris. May's uncle. I remember you as a boy. I'm looking for May."

"George Harris. Fancy that. Pity you weren't around back then when her mum passed away. She could have done with you then."

George was in no mood for anything other than information and nothing Nick implied about his leaving could make him feel more remorseful than he did already

"Well, I'm here now and can you help me find her or not? Do you know where she is?"

Nick could see George was in no mood for obstruction and his attitude softened.

"Come across to the Bull," he said "we can talk there. I'll tell you what I know."

George nodded and followed Nick across the road and into the pub.

"Ale or porter? I'm paying, George. Earn an honest crust now - well if you can call some of the stuff that I write honest."

"Ale, thanks."

George waited while Nick got the drinks. After what seemed like an age he set the beer down and began to speak.

"May is in Canada, George."

"Canada?" George was shaken. "How...?"

"Well, she was in a bad way. It was just after poor Ernie died - in the snow it was. She got taken in by Doctor Barnardo...you've heard of him?"

George nodded.

"She went to live in that Village of his in Barkingside – out in Essex it is, in the country - then off to Canada." Nick took a drink and waited for the news to sink in then he spoke again. "I know this because my sister Aggie... you remember Aggie?" George nodded again and recalled the remark made about her by the man who put him on to Nick. "Well, Aggie had a kid see. It happens a lot don't it? Well you know - like with your sister having young May."

"Yes...about May."

Nick paused to take a long drink of beer...too long for George.

George drummed his fingers on the table then he suddenly picked up the half-full glass and banged it down, his impatience building.

"Whoa, I'll tell you!" Nick sat back, shocked at George's action but it was clear he was on a mission and anything other than information about May was of no interest to him whatsoever. "So Aggie managed to

287

get herself and her child into Barnardo's new mother and baby place out at Barkingside - you know, where I told you May went - and she found out and told me that May... she asked if I remembered May and I said I did because we were friends back then and..."

"For God's sake Nick, just tell me or I swear I'll..."

George stood up as if to grab Nick but managed to restrain himself - he had learned much about restraint in the army.

"May went to Canada with the first lot of girls Barnardo sent there. '83 it was. Never found out why she wanted to go but go she did."

"And then what happened to her? Where is she now?"

"One of the House Mothers, the one that looked after the cottage, lovely they are - better than the bloody slums round here, told Aggie - as she knew that Aggie had known May - that she is with a good family and is happy with them."

"When was this Nick, this latest news? How long ago?"

"Not long. Not long at all. Don't know if that lady has told May, because she writes to her apparently, that Aggie is there."

"And the last time this lady heard from May she was good yeah?"

"Yeah, look George I'm sorry you won't be able to find her but she is alright and probably better off over there than in this shithole. Working on the paper - some of the stuff I see and hear, you wouldn't believe it."

"Oh, I reckon I would Nick. I reckon I would. And thank you...sorry I've been a bit rough on you... you understand yeah?"

"Course I do mate and if there's anything else I can do you know where to find me. What are you going to do now?"

"Go to that Village, find out more, find that lady. Got to Nick. It's really important; May needs to know."

"Needs to know what?"

George didn't answer. He just finished his drink, smiled and left the pub. He was heading to Barkingside – wherever that was.

Forty four

It was mid-afternoon by the time George arrived at Ilford station; the closest one from where he could get to Barkingside. Then he would walk, having been directed to the Village, which was well known. It took him just under an hour to walk there. The open spaces between the growing town of Ilford and the Village were in stark contrast to the grime he had left behind. George, though, hardly noticed as he hurried along the straight road past scattered dwellings. His mind was set on finding the lady. He did not know her name but was certain he would find her - he had to. So much was at stake for May that any other outcome could not be considered.

The trees were in full leaf. The roses were in full bloom. As George approached the gates of the Village and had his first glimpse of the cottages, he remembered Nick's words. It did indeed appear idyllic in the afternoon sunshine. He smiled and thought of May here. It had to be better than the Nichol, but then again, that was not too difficult.

George pulled the heavy bell at the gate and soon a man came to see who the visitor could be and what his purpose was. Visits to the Village were generally arranged in advance. The man who answered the bell was the porter.

"Good day sir, May I ask the reason for your visit? We are not expecting any guests here this afternoon."

"My name is George Harris, Sergeant of Her Majesty's Army and I come seeking information about my niece, May Harris, who I understand lived here before leaving for Canada."

The porter seemed to accept George's reason but asked him to wait outside whilst he made enquiries.

"I am sure you will understand sir that the Village Home is a place of safety and security which must be strictly maintained at all times. I will endeavour not to keep you waiting for too long."

George nodded and looked around whilst he waited. All the time that had passed since he last saw May and now, he fervently hoped, there would be something solid, something positive. Just beyond the gate he could see cottages that appeared newly completed. This was clearly a place that was expanding. Presently the porter returned with the Governor whose residence lay just behind the Porters Lodge.

"Sergeant Harris," he said as he opened the gate. "I hear you have come to enquire about your niece, May."

"Yes, I have been given to understand that she was fortunate, and having seen the surroundings here I am certain that she was indeed, to live here for a while but is now in Canada."

The Governor, who had held his post for some years, was reminded of the first emigrants and the incident

291

that caused an additional place to become available. When the porter informed him of George's arrival he had consulted the Doctor's meticulously kept records and found that May was, indeed, the girl chosen to replace the one who was removed by her mother. She was the very girl this man was inquiring about.

"Sergeant Harris, I can confirm that your niece did reside here and that she was among our earliest group of girls to depart for Canada."

"Thank you, sir. I believe that May does not know that I still live and now having left the army, on a permanent basis at least, I wish to remedy this situation. It has only recently become known to me that her mother, my sister, is dead. There is also important news I need to tell May with all haste."

"Miss Butler, the House Mother of May Cottage, is the lady you seek. The cottage is just around here to the left."

George followed the Governor past some of the immaculately kept gardens. In front of him was the Village Green and then, the second house from the end of the row, there was May Cottage.

"When you were announced I consulted our records and found that your niece came here in 1880. This cottage, bearing the same name, was only completed the previous year."

George was struck again by the contrast to the Nichol and tried to imagine May, at ten years old, setting eyes on such a dwelling, and one that even shared her name.

It was suppertime so Peg and the older girls were preparing their food when the Governor and George arrived.

"Miss Butler," Peg was surprised at her unexpected visitor. Who was this person who somehow looked familiar, with the Governor? "Miss Butler, I know this is a busy time for you but this gentleman is someone I think you will be keen to meet."

Peg looked on expectantly.

"I will?"

"This is George Harris, the uncle of May Harris."

Peg was speechless. May's uncle, her brave uncle, here at last seeking her. George smiled and held out his hand. The Governor also smiled, nodded and left.

"I will leave you to your conversation."

"Girls, I have an important visitor here. You know what is expected of you so please continue whilst I receive him." The girls were not used to having a man in their cottage other than esteemed visitors or staff so George's arrival caused some excitement; they were quickly quietened by Peg who then led George to her sitting room. "George Harris... this is a most unexpected pleasure. I had informed May of my belief you were alive when I read of your rescue of a fellow soldier and your subsequent gallantry award. Now to have you here, in my home - the home I would not have but for May, is something I did not think I would ever see. Please sit."

"Thank you, Miss Butler, you have a fine room here and I am interested to know how May and indeed yourself, came to dwell in such surroundings."

"I will fetch some tea. Presumably, you have walked from Ilford Station so are no doubt thirsty - and hungry too - I will arrange some supper for you. And then I will explain the circumstances by which we both came here."

Peg served George tea and bread with cheese then began to relate the story of both her and May's separate arrivals at the Village.

After listening, George paused then slowly and quietly spoke.

"All of this happened while I was away. I knew nothing of my sister's death until but a few days ago; that I was absent, that I was not here to help, weighs heavily upon me. I must try my utmost to make up, if I ever truly can, for not being present when I was needed most."

"May did not blame you Sergeant Harris, She always held you in high regard and was so proud of your bravery."

"Please, call me George."

"And you must call me Peg, as May does." Peg had not, so far, mentioned the name of the man whom May had fled to Canada to escape. Nor had she or George mentioned Richard Perryman. Then..."I feel I must tell you, George, that the man of whom I spoke - he who is responsible for the death of May's friend, shares a surname with the man whose life you saved. They are both called Perryman."

At hearing this, the cup slipped from George's hand and he visibly paled.

"George!" Peg was concerned; he looked as if he had seen a dreadful apparition. "George, are you all right? Do you feel unwell?"

"I am sorry Peg," he stuttered as he tried to wipe the spilt tea from the chair with a handkerchief. "This is something I could not have expected. Major Richard Perryman is indeed the brother of this Edward Perryman and knowing Richard it appears that they are as far apart as two brothers could possibly be. I am shocked."

"Please do not worry about the spillage. It is something I can easily remedy. I wondered if they were related and suspected it was so, but siblings are not always of the same manner or temperament; it is something I am all too aware of."

Peg was thinking back to her own life before the slum but did not elaborate further.

The news George carried was originally intended to be shared with Peg, but now he had changed his mind. It was news he must tell May in person when she returned to London. The following year she would be eighteen years old but would a return be possible then or would it not be so until she turned twenty-one? Such a delay was something he could not imagine. He composed himself as best he could and rose to take his leave.

"Miss Butler, Peg, it has been a great pleasure to meet you. I am so pleased that May is happy. I would appreciate her address so I can try to write to her myself but I am sure my writing of English is not as good as yours and I would struggle to put into words what I wish to say. Will you write for me? Will you tell her I am sorry I was not there for her and I eagerly await her return? As for what you have told me about Richard's brother, well, this requires more thought."

"I shall write to her directly George and I am pleased to have met you. I am sure we will meet again when May returns. I will escort you to the gate and leave you to your thoughts."

As they walked round to the gate and the Porter's Lodge the talk was of the Village; its gardens, its colours and fragrance but George's mind was elsewhere. The blood link between Richard and Edward Perryman - whom he now knew to be a murderer - was not something he could easily dismiss. He couldn't dismiss it at all. Not now. On the way back to Ilford Station George had much to think about – his mind was whirling.

Forty five

As well as George's mind reeling from Peg's revelation so was hers from his. Something did not sit well with Peg. She could not understand why the fact that Edward Perryman was Richard's brother should affect George in quite such a way. Yes, it would certainly be unnerving to find someone you counted as a friend had a murderer for a brother. Of that there would be no doubt and yet Peg could not help sensing that there was more; something she had not been told - something important.

She would write to May to tell her the good news about her uncle. Of course, May was already aware of the probable connection between Richard and Edward but beyond that, beyond what she knew for certain, she would not share her unease.

Peg began to write her letter once the girls were settled and the cottage was quiet. Interruptions to the routine were rare and it was to this unexpected disturbance that Peg attributed her sudden, but increasingly common, feeling of sickness, of distraction. She would surely feel better in the morning. Yes, of course she would.

August 1887
Dear May

We are in high summer with all the roses and the numerous other flowers resplendent as you, I'm sure, would expect. There is one thing though that you would not expect, neither did I until today when it happened. Something you have wished and hoped for a long time my dear.

Your Uncle George came to the Village seeking you. Yes, it is true. It was such a surprise as you can imagine. I could see the resemblance, see it right away. He had traced your whereabouts to here from an old friend of yours called Nick whose sister, whom you also know, is happily settled in our new mother and babies area. Babies' Green it is called but more of that another time, let me concentrate on George. He has now left the army although there are times when he may be called upon again should the Empire require it.

He was pleased and relieved that, after your mother's death, you had the good fortune to arrive here and it was clear the guilt he felt at leaving you and his sister is a heavy weight he carries. That you are in far away Canada was of great surprise to him and when I explained the reason why you chose to go his anguish became even stronger. I told him, to try to reassure him, that you bore him no ill will but I think the events that occurred whilst he was away will continue to be a burden.

The Man is indeed the brother of Richard Perryman but it appears certain that they are vastly different in character. What George will do next, whether he will reveal Edward's dark deed to Richard, remains to be seen although I do not think he will be content to let such a despicable crime go unpunished. He was, of course, interested to know when you will return to England. I have made him aware of your desire, your firm intention, to see justice for Ernie - but whether he would be prepared to wait to assist with this upon your return or endeavour to confront Perryman himself I do not know. Since Perryman is a rich and powerful man and without a witness to his crime, I doubt there is very much that can be done until you return. However, George did not make his intentions clear.

Such a day it has been for both myself and George. A day that leaves me very tired and in need of sleep now. I must, as usual, be up early in the morning as I must prepare a new contingent of girls for laundry duties. Do you remember the laundry May? You loved the smell. You said it was a clean, warm, pure smell that drove the memory of the stench of the Nichol away. I am sure you will remember.

I am pleased I can bring you such good news and hope that you and the Suttons are all well.

My bed is calling. Goodnight my dear May

My love always Peg

The post from England to Canada was, as a rule, quite reliable. Transport across the Atlantic developed and the expanding railways with their special mail cars meant correspondence arrived more quickly despite the long distances involved. This, however, was not always the case and one unfortunate incident caused May to remain unaware of George's visit and Peg's reaction to it. Most of the letters between them were not of great importance but the one containing the news May had hoped for was destroyed, along with many, many others – perhaps of similar significance. The train, and particularly its mail coach, was badly damaged by fire. Some post was saved but the majority of the contents, including Peg's letter, were lost.

May's next letter to Peg, of course not referencing that of which she was unaware, was sent in late summer. Another followed the busy time that was harvest. But May hadn't had a reply from Peg for some time and she was worried. Peg's letters were regular. Sometimes there was nothing of note but they were a connection with what May still regarded as home. As the winter that spanned 1887 and 1888 began to fade and her eighteenth birthday drew closer May could wait no longer. She wrote again to Peg - wondering why her last letters had gone unanswered.

My dear friend Peg
I have not received a letter from you for much longer than the usual gap between them. I have written to you several times with no reply. It is with concern that I

write now as I am anxious to know that everything is all right with you.

My eighteenth birthday draws near Peg and although I know I could be made to stay until I am twenty-one it is then that I shall be at liberty to leave Canada. The Suttons are such good people and they know of my desire to return to England - they say they would not dream of keeping me when I wish to leave. It is something my feelings are somewhat confused about. My dearest wish is to see you again - and the Village - but leaving the Sutton family will be difficult. I truly believe I have been the most fortunate girl Peg. I have heard more terrible stories since the other ones I have told you. Things that are done sometimes are awful and I think of the poor children. It is not only the children though because sometimes they have done bad things too. It is surely that all over the world there are good people and bad people. England is not a bad country and Canada is not a good country. They are both a mixture they are but I do want to see England again. It must get better there. I think one day it will. Maybe even one day me and you will be able to vote Peg. It would be good to do that, not to be below men. Many men are nowhere near as clever as you Peg and I think I am getting quite clever myself but you might scold me for not being humble because Jesus was humble. I am not as good as Jesus though because I still have anger in my heart for Ernie and would never

301

turn the other cheek for that Man. Understand me Peg. I think you do.

It is now a long time since I have had any news of my uncle and he remains in my thoughts as does he to whom I will deal revenge. Of course Uncle George is remembered fondly whilst The Man is only remembered with hate. He has been on my mind a lot recently Peg and I am dismayed by my lack of any kind of plan regarding him. Nonetheless, I am sure that as the time grows closer, with my resolve as strong as ever, a way to realise my aim will become clear to me.

Please Peg reply to this letter as promptly as you are able to settle my mind and reassure me. The next time I correspond with you may be to tell you of my forthcoming return.

Yours as always
May Harris

Forty six

March 12th 1888

My dear May

Firstly let me apologise for the delay in responding to your kind letters. In truth, I have not been well. This is the only reason that would prevent me from replying to you.

I am feeling a little better now and am trying to run our happy cottage in the way you have such fond memories of. This has proved difficult though and whilst I am still in charge - as you know I like to be - I have a young lady helper who is a great asset to me and my girls.

This young lady, Agnes, is someone I believe you know. She resides in the new baby area with her child, having been removed from the Nichol and an altogether unsuitable situation for a young mother and baby. Of course, she could not run a cottage by herself but is a great support to me.

She has told me about her brother Nick, or Nicholas as I prefer - much more gentlemanly - whom you also know. He has, despite many hardships, become a trainee newspaper reporter and is, by all accounts, doing very well. I am sure you will remember them both.

It is the thing I most desire - to see you again - and hope that my current malaise has passed by the time of your return.

Forgive me for such a short letter when there is much more I would like to say but I am very tired now and Agnes has instructed me, forcefully I might add, that I should rest.

My love to you dear May, Peg

It was early April by the time this letter came and May was instantly struck by the handwriting on the envelope. It was undeniably Peg's but unlike her usual style which was neat and firm. The words appeared to be written by an altogether different hand despite May's certainty that it was from Peg. This hand was not firm; this hand was not straight; this hand was erratic. May could tell from the method of writing more than the contents of the letter that all was not well with Peg. The word malaise was not one May was familiar with so she looked it up in the dictionary she had brought with her from England. The meaning she found suggested that Peg's illness was not too serious. But May wondered - she was still worried.

She was surprised to hear about Agnes and Nick. Of course, Peg had mentioned them in her earlier letter - the one May did not receive - so was unaware of the duplication. Had she seen the earlier letter she would have wondered why Peg appeared not to remember referring to them before. Agnes had always puzzled May when she was younger and she wondered what Peg had meant about the unsuitable situation. That a child was involved, now May was worldlier than she had been, was not much of a surprise. Perhaps the path Agnes appeared to be taking led to this inevitably.

As for Nick, well he had always been smart and much more adept at dealing with life on the streets than May. She was glad he had found a way to use his shrewdness in a way that did not involve petty crime. She felt happy for them both. There was no mention of her uncle so May assumed that, given her wish for information of him, there was none to be conveyed. Surely, Peg would have informed her if there had. What May did not know was that Peg had, during the months that followed her last letter - the one that was so regrettably lost - become increasingly forgetful and the visit from George had faded from her mind.

May hoped that another letter would swiftly follow, perhaps and hopefully, one that found Peg in an altogether improved situation; this was May's fervent wish but somehow it was something of which she was doubtful.

It was not too long after that another letter did arrive. This time she did not recognise the handwriting at all. She left it on the hall table. Those for the Reverend, Mrs Sutton and even one for Simon were removed to be read. The letter for May remained there - she somehow sensed bad news. She wished to delay opening it as long as possible so to not make whatever bad news it contained, real.

It was not until the evening when, her jobs done and other tasks completed, May picked up the letter and took it to her room. She laid it on her bed and looked at it; she could put off opening it no longer. The letter, written in an assured hand, was from Mrs Barnardo.

Mossford Village, Barkingside
Dear May

It is with sadness that I am obliged to write to you. I know that ever since you were instrumental in my husband liberating Miss Butler from the workhouse and even before, that there has been a deep attachment between the two of you. I understand in the last letter Miss Butler- Peg - wrote to you she informed you of her illness although I am told by Agnes that the full extent of its seriousness was not conveyed.

Whilst Peg remains with us there is no doubt that the further inevitable deterioration of her condition will result in her passing in a relatively short time; surely and sadly no more than a few months. She may not last beyond the summer despite our best efforts.

I know it has always been your intention to return and, knowing your bond with Peg, am sure that you will endeavour to hasten your return to meet with her before she is no longer with us. It is her wish to see you and I truly believe it is the powerful desire to do this that is giving her the strength to keep going, although how much longer this inner strength can sustain her I do not know.

If you are able to arrange passage then we look forward to receiving you as soon as possible. We know you are on extremely good terms with the Sutton family and am sure they will afford you every assistance.

I am sorry to be the bearer of bad news. My husband and I remember you fondly and are thankful for your part in bringing such a wonderful person as Miss Butler to our Village.

Yours sincerely,
Mrs S Barnardo

May threw down the letter then, after a short pause, tentatively picked it up again. She didn't want to reread its awful contents but had to be sure she had not misunderstood it on first reading despite knowing full well the sad news it contained.

She slumped down on her bed, expecting to cry but no tears came. May was numb. Peg was going to die. She would die and May would be alone again. Even with the distance between them, May had not felt alone because she knew Peg was always in her heart and she in Peg's. Despite the warmth of the Suttons and their inclusion of her into their family the bond she had with Peg could never be replaced. Her mum was gone. Her uncle was perhaps no longer living. Now Peg was nearing her end.

I am selfish, May tortured herself. *I think only of my situation, how I will be affected. I should think of Peg – she is such a good person with so much more to give to her girls. It is not just me who will miss her.*

Finally, tears did begin to fall. May was drained with emotion. She fell asleep, fully clothed, whilst still sobbing.

The next day May showed the letter to Mrs Sutton. Again she started to cry. Simon heard her crying.

"May whatever is wrong?" He rushed to comfort her but his mother shook her head and he was quiet, holding back.

"My dear May, this is indeed terrible news for you. Since you have been with us the affection in which you hold Miss Butler and the good reasons for it have been abundantly clear. We are so sorry and, of course, as Mrs Barnardo so rightly says, we shall assist you in every way we can to enable you to return to England. We shall do this in as much haste as possible."

Mrs Sutton held May who in turn reached out to Simon. Through her sobs, her voice faltering, she managed to speak.

"Mrs Sutton, dear Simon. Thank you so much for your care and kindness towards me. I came here uncertain what to expect; a child in a strange country whose fate could not be known. When I first wrote to

Peg about my life here it was, of course, when Simon and I..." she looked at Simon who was on the verge of tears himself "...had not formed the friendship we have now but later, when we became settled, I could feel Peg's relief in my soul I could. I will tell her of your gentleness; of the Reverend and his benevolence; of you Simon, and how your cleverness has helped me."

Simon interjected,

"That is as maybe but it is your strength and commonsense that has helped me just as much. You have made me a better person than I could ever have been had you not come here. I will miss you so much."

May had yet to speak with Reverend Sutton himself but for now, overcome with emotion, she would return to her room.

"I will talk with my husband and we will arrange passage for you. Write to Mrs Barnardo. Tell her you will be returning forthwith." Said Mrs Sutton as May turned to go.

Later that day when she had composed herself May wrote, as the adult she felt she now was, to Syrie Barnardo.

Dear Mrs Barnardo

I was most upset and saddened to receive your letter. It did explain much as I had felt for some time that all was not well with Peg. Our correspondence had always been regular and when so much time had passed before I finally received a letter from her, together with the manner in which it was written it made me believe my fears were correct.

I have today spoken with Mrs Sutton although not yet with the Reverend himself but, and I have no reason to doubt her, she assures me all will be done to speedily organize my return. It is with a heavy heart I will leave the Sutton family. In truth, there could not have been a finer situation for me and I count myself as blessed.

My biggest regret is the circumstance under which I am leaving. I knew I would go back to England but imagined a joyous departure. It would be a happy affair, a leaving party perhaps and the belief that one day we would meet again maybe in England, where I know they desire to visit. I know this, them going to England, could still happen but I so wanted them to meet Peg.

While Canada is a country I have come to love and I shall miss, I still call England my home. The Doctor has been here so he knows the contrasts between it and England. I honestly believe there is good and bad everywhere and I have written to Peg of this in the past. When I come back, and I pray I am not too late to see my dear Peg once more, I will endeavour to seek out what is good and thwart, as far as I am able, the bad.

Since leaving five years ago I am in some ways a changed person - in good ways I think - but in others I remain the same child you rescued from the streets. I am eternally grateful to you, and the Doctor, that you welcomed Peg into your Village as well. Not only was my life saved but I am sure, as was she, hers too.

I will write again when my passage is confirmed but perhaps, and hopefully, I shall return before this letter is even received.

Yours sincerely
May Harris

Forty seven

The return passage was, as they had promised, swiftly arranged by Reverend Sutton. Her conversation with him had been brief but it was clear he would miss her as much as his wife and son. The goodbyes were subdued. There was no celebration, no good cheer, just sadness at the reason for May's hasty departure.

As May stood waiting to board, coincidentally, the same ship that had brought her to Canada - the Sardinian - she couldn't know what exactly would happen upon her return. Of course, she would proceed as quickly as possible to Barnardo's Village but that would not be for many days yet. She hoped the voyage would give her time to think, time to plan. Once onboard May opened a letter that had been given to her by Simon with instructions not to read it until her journey had begun.

My dearest friend May

I know how much you like to read and I know that you hold England in your heart as your home, so please take this poem I have copied with my finest pen for you. It is by Thomas Bailey Aldrich. He is American but this poem about England will prompt thoughts of your home on the journey. I wish I could give you his whole book of poems but it is quite new and I need it for my studies.

England
While men pay reverence to mighty things,
They must revere thee, thou blue-cinctured isle
Of England—not to-day, but this long while
In the front of nations, Mother of great kings,
Soldiers, and poets. Round thee the Sea flings
His steel-bright arm, and shields thee from the guile
And hurt of France. Secure, with august smile,
Thou sittest, and the East its tribute brings.
Some say thy old-time power is on the wane,
Thy moon of grandeur fill''d, contracts at length—
They see it darkening down from less to less.
Let but a hostile hand make threat again,
And they shall see thee in thy ancient strength,
Each iron sinew quivering, lioness!

It is my aim, my firm intention, to come to England when I am all grown up and able to pay my own way with funds earned by my intellect and my wits. I am sure we will meet again my dear friend.
Simon

There had been no further correspondence from Mrs Barnardo since the letter informing of Peg's illness – at least nothing that was received before Mays's departure. May had written to Mrs Barnardo immediately she knew her date of arrival so at least they would be aware of when to expect her but another letter had crossed with this one and so arrived in Peterborough when May was already aboard the Sardinian.

Mrs Sutton felt she had no choice but to open it although, whatever the contents, there was nothing she could do. She hoped it did not contain news of Peg's death for if it were so then the thought of May returning to such a sad situation affected her deeply. She held her breath as she opened the envelope but, upon seeing its contents, exhaled in relief. Peg was still holding on; waiting for May, or at least she was when the letter had been sent, but there was more news that May could not have been aware of. Mrs Barnardo wrote of May's uncle. She had been surprised there was no mention of him in May's last letter since she knew Peg had informed her he was searching for her and had been to the Village. This had happened many months ago but recently he had been in touch again so had learned of Peg's sickness and May's imminent return. He would, Mrs Barnardo wrote, be waiting at Liverpool when the Sardinian docked. This was wonderful news but news that Mrs Sutton had no way of communicating to May. How May would feel though, how pleased and surprised she would be, to be unexpectedly greeted by her uncle. Would she recognise him? Would he recognise her - a young lady on the verge of her eighteenth birthday - after so long? The ship was due to dock in five days. In five days May would be reunited with her only living relative.

Once again after five years, May stood on the deck of the Sardinian looking through the darkness at the merging sea and sky. It was as if no time had passed. She was thirteen again. She was going into the unknown. She was Alice going through the looking glass into a world that was familiar and yet not. Simon's poem was tucked inside the Alice book he had given her and she found them both a comfort - a link to the life she was leaving as she returned to the place of her previous one. What would greet her there? Would she be in time to see her beloved Peg again and how would she face Edward Perryman? She was still unwavering in her resolve to avenge Ernie yet no plan had been formulated. Her mind was torn between Peg, justice and her uncle. As the end of the voyage drew nearer May found it more difficult to sleep. Her heart would race. Her mind was bursting with thoughts jostling for position. She was scared of what she would face. Her anxiety grew and grew until, at last, the ship docked at Liverpool.

Disembarking was frenetic; shouting, banging, whistling - all manner of noises as the passengers set foot on English soil. The crowd swept May along with it. Through the official channels she went in a daze until, her head spinning, she was back. She was properly back in England but what to do now? She must get the train to London. From there to Ilford and if no transportation was available she would walk to the Village. However tired she would make it. She would make it to Peg.

Suddenly, and at first she thought she had imagined it, she heard her name. Just beyond a jostling crowd, she caught sight of a board held aloft by a person she couldn't see. On the board, she could just about make out, was a name - her name. MAY HARRIS. She pushed closer until she stood face to face with the man holding the board. He lowered it and spoke softly.

"May, May my dear niece, after all this time. It is truly you."

May stared at George then overwhelmed by the extraordinary situation, she fainted. George quickly gathered her up and moved her to a place where she could sit.

"May! May... give her some air here, move away! My niece needs air!"

A woman nearby produced some smelling salts and offered them to George. He swiftly passed them under May's nose causing her to wake with a start. She looked into George's face noting the changes since she had last seen him but having no doubt this man was her uncle.

"Uncle, is it really you?" She hugged him and both, after such a long separation, sobbed.

During the train journey to London, George explained about his visit to the Village and it soon became clear to May that an important piece of correspondence had gone missing. But that was the past. She was back and no longer alone - she had an ally she could trust. Not just one though, George told her of his friendship with Richard, of how he had met with Nick and how they would all support her in her quest to bring Edward Perryman to justice. The other news that George still desperately wished to tell May lay heavy on him but the time was not yet right. Soon, he hoped, it would be.

Forty eight

May and George now stood at the gates of the Village at Mossford Green. The porter smiled as he opened the gate. May looked around the grounds; they were as she remembered except the trees had grown taller and the flowers were even more abundant in the warm sunshine. If she was Alice then the journey through the Looking Glass was not to a world of contrast but one that remained much as she had left it. She clutched George's hand as the porter began to lead them towards May Cottage. She shook her head. There was no need for guidance. The path to her former home was not one she had forgotten. As they approached, a girl of a similar age came out of May Cottage. Upon seeing May and George her face lit up and she rushed towards them.

"May, oh May thank goodness you are here." The girl hugged May tightly, then brushed tears from her face. "Do you remember me May - without a label on?" she laughed - recalling the first time they had met.

"Of course I remember you, Lottie. How could I ever forget such a true friend?" Lottie had changed little, her features sharper maybe and hair neater but there could be no mistaking her.

"It is so good to see you again but the circumstances are so sad. Come quickly to see Peg. Mrs Barnardo and

Agnes are with her. The Doctor is away but has been tending to her as much as he is able. He says there is little that can be done other than making her comfortable until..."

Her voice tailed off as they entered May Cottage. It, like the grounds, had changed only slightly. There were new furnishings - and the girls seemed very young to May. Lottie opened the door to Peg's room. Mrs Barnardo and Agnes turned to see who had entered. May and George were expected, yet no precise time was known as the journey from Liverpool was a long one.

"My dear May." Mrs Barnardo reached out to her and clutched her hand. "I am so pleased you are here. Please, come forward. Peg is drifting in and out of sleep but speak to her. Let her know you are here. I am sure she will respond."

May steps were small - almost fearful - as she tentatively approached Peg's bed and looked, for the first time in almost five years at her face. It was pale, her cheeks sunken, her eyes closed.

"Peg, Peg, it's me Peg. It's May. I have come back to see you. I told you I would. I promised you didn't I and now here I am... dear Peg." She gently took Peg's hand. She was shocked by the frailty of it; her skin was papery; her veins clearly visible. Peg slowly opened her eyes.

"May? Is that you May? Are you really here or is it a dream all in my head." The voice, whilst still recognisable as Peg's, faltered as if even speaking was painful for her.

"No Peg you are not dreaming. I am really here; really back with you."

Peg managed a weak smile and tried to clasp May's hand but there was not enough strength in her fingers.

"You have been in my thoughts so much May. It has been my dearest wish to see you again before I join my Lord Jesus in Heaven."

Her voice was shaky; the emotion plain.

"I have always held you with me Peg. See here..." May reached into her blouse and pulled out the silver cross Peg had given her. "See Peg, I still wear it. I shall always wear it - close to my heart as you are. No, you are *in* my heart. You are in my heart and will be forever."

Once again Peg tried to smile.

"But what of your quest? What of Edward Perryman?"

Peg's memory was erratic. Sometimes she would not remember what had happened from day to day but Edward Perryman had stayed in her mind - he had not been forgotten.

May was not certain how to respond to this question as she had no plan but knew that this was important to

Peg. She must reassure her that justice would be served.

"Do not worry Peg, Ernie will be avenged. I have my dear uncle and he has assured me that Richard Perryman, despite being that man's brother will assist and Nick will too. We will make sure he does not remain unpunished." May noticed, as she finished speaking, Peg's eyes closed - a faint smile on her lips. "Peg, Peg!"

Agnes came closer.

"Do not worry May. She merely sleeps again. This is what happens. I have seen how death comes and this know this is not its time. Not yet. Come..."

May turned away from the bed.

"Agnes, thank you for all you have done to help her. She wrote to me of how your assistance enabled her to continue serving her charges for so long and now, of course, Nick is helping George also...therefore helping me."

"We both remember Ernie. Nick remembers that night when you came to the arches - that night in the snow. He remembers how you were and then, suddenly, the next day you were gone. Much happened to both of us in the years that followed but now I, and my child, are safe here and Nick, well, Nick is doing very well. Do you remember how we were always running away from the police? Well, one policeman – Nick called him Fred, cheeky devil that he was and still is - took to Nick. He saw something in my brother that made him think he could do better than thieving and helped him get into working at the newspaper. Never looked back and making quite a name for himself he is. Now you must rest. We have a room for you."

"Yes come dear." Mrs Barnardo led May away as she paused to look once more at sleeping Peg.

Outside George was waiting. He could see May's anguish instantly. He could also see her relief that Peg was still living despite being resigned to her friend having little time left. He reached out to comfort her.

"Oh uncle, I fear her end is coming ...I can't..."

"Sh, May. You made it back in time and Peg knows. You must take comfort from this."

"What of you, Uncle, what will you do?"

"I have arrangements to make in London. If all goes well I will have spoken with Richard and Nick. You rest now and very soon, on Friday, we shall together confront the other Perryman. I will arrange to send a telegraphic message, if that will be acceptable to Mrs Barnardo..."

"Of course, Sergeant Harris and our carriage will be available to convey May to Ilford Station for the train to Liverpool Street."

"It will not be long May, before you can tell Peg your quest has been successful."

George said goodbye and left May wondering what the plan could be. She was, of course, anxious to ensure Perryman faced justice but was torn whether to leave Peg; what if her friend passed away whilst she was not present? May could not bear to think of Peg meeting her end without her. Also what part would she play in any plan? The quest was hers. What part for any of them, especially Richard, whom she was very keen to meet. She had heard much about him. George had called him 'the finest of fellows' so he really must be the opposite of his brother. She also wondered, had George not come back into her life how on earth she would, despite her resolve, have managed to accomplish her mission. May had never believed in fate; never believed the paths we travel are mapped out for us but now it seemed that ever since she had first vowed she would get justice for Ernie wheels had turned to ensure it was so. Somehow to ensure she would not have to achieve her goal alone.

She slept soundly despite her head being full of swirling images; Lottie, Agnes and of course dear Peg. Thank goodness she had been in time. Her next wish was to be able to tell Peg that Ernie had been avenged. May spent much of the next day reacquainting herself with her surroundings. As well as the laundry, where the smell evoked many memories - mostly good ones despite the work being hard - there were new buildings too. Agnes took her to Babies' Green and the cottage where she lived with her child. The boy was almost two years old now. Agnes did not speak of the circumstances of his birth and May did not press her for details. These, she thought, Agnes may prefer to keep to herself.

Lottie wanted to know all about Canada. She asked if there was a young man in May's life as she had in hers beyond the Village. The Village was no longer her home but her presence here had been arranged to enable the reunion with May as well as visiting Peg. No young man May told her. She was too focussed; perhaps when her quest was over. Perhaps then, but not before.

Friday morning found May readying herself for whatever plan had been formulated. She looked in on Peg, who was sleeping peacefully so did not disturb her. May was loathe to leave her - fearing Peg would pass while she was not there, yet May knew Peg would wish her well on her quest.

The message came. Her carriage awaited. At Ilford she boarded the train to London. She sped towards the resolution that had been so long coming. She would meet Richard. She would see Nick again. She wondered about both of them. Would Richard look like his brother? Would Nick have changed much - would she recognise him?

When she disembarked at Liverpool Street she looked around and George was coming towards her, waving. The man with him hung back a little. Was he nervous? He was about to challenge his own brother so, despite knowing the extent of his guilt, she could understand his anxiety. What other reason could there possibly be?

"Richard Perryman I would like to introduce you to my niece - May Harris. I have told her much about you but, of course, there is much more to know."

May shook hands with Richard. His grip was firm. He covered her hand with both of his.

"I am so pleased to finally meet you May. I feel as if I know you already but look forward to finding out more about your stay in Canada, which is a country, despite my travels, I have never had the opportunity to visit. My brother is, you no doubt know, nothing like me and I am ashamed I share the Perryman name with such a person."

"Richard, I do not hold you responsible for the actions of...him." She was not yet ready to speak the name of her adversary and the next name she spoke was....

"Nick!" she recognised him right away and hurried towards him.

"Sorry I'm a bit late, got caught up in the press room and well, I'm here now. Cor May you look different from the last time I saw you. 'Course you had reason to back then but you didn't tell me what had happened. You should have told me, Should have told me...Give us a hug eh." She duly did. Nick hugged May in return then said "Come, we must make our way to

Westminster. The route along the river will, I think, be busy and we must not be late for the Chief Inspector has agreed to meet us."

"A Chief Inspector?" asked May "Does this policeman believe my story? You have told him?"

"Well he's not exactly a mate of mine but he used to be a copper in Whitechapel back when I was...a little wild shall we say. Instead of a clip round the ear, he kind of steered me on a more righteous path. Tea boy first..." he spun around obviously proud of his clothes and position, "then I made it to trainee reporter, so here I am. Me and Fred Abberline go way back."

"Yes, May," said Richard "both myself and your good uncle here have, with Nick's help, been able to gain access to the ear of Chief Inspector Abberline, currently based at no less an establishment than Scotland Yard. He is willing to accompany us although requires proof - in the form of a confession - before anything can be done to apprehend my dear brother."

Now May knew her role. She must, and this was what she probably always intended, compel Perryman to confess.

Forty nine

Edward Perryman's mood was jaunty. His life as an MP, even though it was for Hackney - a place he had little taste for - was proving extremely satisfactory. He made connections; he found previously closed doors open to him and, of course, this pandered to his innate sense of superiority and importance. He would go far. His aims were high and he could see nothing preventing him from the cabinet position he richly deserved. He thought this but thoughts do not always convert to reality and desire is no guarantee of success.

It was a Friday and Perryman was looking forward to tea on the terrace of the Palace of Westminster before the sitting began at two o'clock. There he would pontificate on matters of great importance - mainly to himself. Conversations with others of a similar mind would follow then, in the Chamber, he planned to take part in the debate; a debate that was of particular interest to him as it covered efforts by those of a too liberal nature for his liking to reinforce the rights of tenants. They had enough rights he would argue. Any extension would be against the principle of the rights of the landlords. It was their property, so theirs to do with what they wished. Some of his tenants, although he would not go so far as to say this in the House, were scum who deserved no better.

At every opportunity, Perryman aimed to thwart any measures that might see his lucrative empire impacted. The scum had no vote so to him were of no consequence at all. He had a spring in his step as he bade farewell to Josephine.

He didn't know, as she waved him goodbye, that Josephine had herself a purpose that day. She would deviate from her normal somewhat monotonous routine; there was something she had long wondered about. Today she determined to wonder no more. A more auspicious day she could not have chosen.

Perryman arrived at Parliament, greeted some fellow members and strode through the lobby towards the terrace. Even though he had been an honourable member for over two years now and had sauntered along the corridors many times it still gave him pleasure. The heart of his great country, unquestionably the greatest in the world, and he was a part of it. What a legacy he would hand down to his children. Perhaps young Rupert would even follow him into politics. Perhaps he should begin teaching him the ways of his world. The Perryman name must be assured of its place in history.

What of Richard? Well, he had served his country in another way, but what legacy, what contribution to the family name, would he bring? He had no children and wasn't likely to - still dwelling on that wretched servant girl after all this time. By now, surely, he should have moved on. No, it was up to him, Edward, to climb the ladder of society. The uncomfortable fact that Josephine appeared to be becoming less than enthralled by his ever-expanding interests must be an irrelevance. She was, there could be no doubt, an asset to him. She had charm, she had grace and she was certainly a good mother but lately he had detected an air of restlessness about her. Also, she was showing interest, more than was seemly he thought, for this ridiculous campaign to give, heaven forbid, women the right to vote. Suffrage was the term. Suffrage indeed. It would be the husbands, sons and brothers who would suffer if this ever came to pass. Unthinkable.

From the Terrace on the pleasantly warm day, Edward took tea and watched the waves of the Thames gently lapping below. He was glad of the light breeze that moved and freshened the air. He remembered the foul odour from the river some thirty years previously and certainly would not have wished to be a Member then. On a fine day like today, though, he was eminently pleased with his lot. After tea with a nod to colleagues, he proceeded to work on what would prove to be his last day in the Chamber.

Fifty

Outside the Houses of Parliament they gathered - May and her company. It was a building May had not seen before and she was struck by the grandeur of it. Would women ever be able to take a seat there as a Member rather than purely a visitor she wondered? May hoped her wish would one day become reality. They would go through the Public Entrance, through Westminster Hall eventually to the Stranger's Gallery where they would watch the debates unfold; to watch Edward in full pompous flight. Each of them looked around the vast cavern that was the Hall. None, except Chief Inspector Abberline, had entered it before. Nick would take his place, not in the Stranger's Gallery, but in the area specially reserved for reporters. May would go to the Ladies' Gallery, as women were not allowed elsewhere. George's travels had shown him so much of nature that he was no longer impressed by anything built by man and Richard wondered what sort of country allowed a man such as his brother to determine the fate of others. Chief Inspector Abberline had been taken there once before by Scotland Yard business. He was weary after a busy week and just wanted to get the whole matter over without too much bother.

It was May whose heart beat the fastest; she who had the biggest stake in what would happen next. This day had been a long time coming. This day was one she had imagined facing alone but she was not alone. She had her uncle, she had Richard, she had Nick and the support of a senior policeman who was accepting of her accusation - but needed proof. Would she obtain the proof she needed? She had to. She had to get justice for poor, helpless Ernie.

The accused was a powerful man who would not take May's accusation lightly. He would undoubtedly dismiss it and without proof, well... May's agitation was palpable. Her heart was pounding. She clutched George's hand and almost did the same to Richard but suddenly held back.

Nick would speak to Edward first. He was a reporter. He came from the Hackney Gazette, Edward was the MP who served the constituency and Nick had questions to ask of him. Upon taking his place in the gallery to hear Perryman speak Nick was struck by how alike all the men below looked. The unofficial uniform was one of a top hat, a long black coat and usually whiskers. He thought they looked like undertakers.

The view from the Ladies' Gallery, high above the Speaker's Chair, was not a clear one. May knew Perryman would not be able to see her. The ladies were seated behind a grille - separated from sight - but even if he could see her he would not know her after so long. Yet the grille afforded protection – protection she did not need but still welcomed. She wondered if she would be able to hear his voice. She wondered if she would remember his voice. She wondered but was sure, that when he began speaking, she would have no doubt.

George, Richard and Abberline got ready to watch the debate. Richard had not seen Edward in full flow before but found it easy to imagine. This was the perfect setting for his brother's hubris. They did not know how long it would be before he spoke, but the session, as it was Friday, would finish promptly so the Honourable Members could hurry back to pursue their other interests.

The speeches were, for the most part, dull and boring. Boring in their delivery yet the core of what they contained, here so far away from the lives of the ordinary people, impacted on those lives. May found it strange; the likes of her were pawns - pieces in a game. Were they viewed as real people with feelings, with problems - so many of which were caused by the actions of those men she was watching? Here she was in the Ladies' Gallery. Did any of the other, mostly fine looking women, see anything wrong in this? Were they happy to be kept to one side - behind a grille?

Mostly the ladies were in pairs but there was one other who was alone. She was looking down and arranging her skirt carefully as if to give herself something to do. May thought the lady looked uncomfortable. Uncomfortable but she had, as did May, a purpose. May nodded to her and the lady nodded back. The lady spoke first.

"This is an unusual place to find myself. I have not ventured here before. And you? You are a very young lady to be concerned with the discourse undertaken here."

Despite how easy it would have been for May to feel patronised by this, there was something about the woman, a look of melancholy that meant her reply was conciliatory.

"I also have not ventured here before and after this day when my purpose is achieved, I have no intention of ever doing so again unless circumstances change to a greater extent than I can ever foresee. My youth, I am eighteen years old lady, does not mean I have no interest in the matters that are discussed here. What those men decide is what my future, and yours - although you are a fine lady - depends on."

May did not go further but the lady leaned towards May and she could see she was intrigued.

"It is correct what you say and indeed I share your opinion - although it is not always viewed favourably in my circles to air such opinions. My husband, you see, is one of those who decide. It is he I have come today to hear. He does not know of course. He believes such things are beyond our intellect but this is not my belief. I too think the way forward for this country is for women to have the right to participate in its governance."

Others in the Gallery overheard this. Some nodded in approval whilst others appeared shocked.

The lady continued.

"That we are in this Gallery at all - like a cage - is a fitting metaphor for our position in society I think. I am afraid my husband believes not only that we lack intellect but are not of the correct temperament to participate in such matters. That we allow our emotions to dominate and therefore cloud our judgement."

"You obviously do not agree with your husband then."

"No I do not, yet I cannot help feel powerless, even feeble, and it is not a situation I wish to continue but my husband is a strong man."

May smiled, all was not lost if women like this lady held the same views as she. She would tell Peg. Peg would like to know this if...

Her train of thought was interrupted as the lady spoke again.

"Ah, my husband has been called. I must listen although I suspect there is much of what he says I do not concur with."

May froze. The name called was Edward Perryman. This lady was none other than his wife. She had given no thought to Edward's family. She knew Richard of course but beyond him, no thought had ever crossed her mind. Now here, in front of her, was his closest family member. May had encountered her before but the recollection of events at the grand house where Perryman admonished her did not include his wife's appearance.

Suddenly May felt pity for this woman. Not only did her marriage appear not to be a happy one but her husband was actually a murderer. May could not speak nor could she bring herself to listen to Perryman's pomposity. She left Josephine to her thoughts as she watched her husband and wondered how this poor woman would deal with the events that were planned to follow.

Fifty one

Edward left the Chamber before the conclusion of the debate. His voice had been heard. He had made it clear any further concessions on tenants' rights or indeed the right to vote should not be countenanced if the order of society was to be upheld. He had noticed more nods of agreement than shaking of heads - even on the opposition benches and had found this encouraging. Now he would take his leave and return to a pleasant late spring afternoon with Josephine. Matters of state or business were not for her ears. He remained unaware of her presence just a matter of yards above him - above him in the cage. This was how she felt in her marriage - caged - but any irony of the situation would surely be lost on Edward.

By the time he emerged through the Members' Entrance into the Palace Yard and the sunshine, May and her party were waiting out of sight around the corner by the Public Entrance.

Nick approached Edward, offering his press card. His manner was deliberately deferential.

"Good day Mr Perryman, sir, Nicholas Smart from the Hackney Gazette. I heard your contribution today and wondered if you have any further comments I might add to my report to be included in our next edition... sir."

Perryman cast a curious glance over the young man standing before him. His opinion of this reporter - with his hat perched at a cocky angle - was not a favourable one but he was used to dealing with such people as part of the role he had to play.

"Well, young man, there is really little more I can add. It is a regrettable fact that many of my constituents, whose welfare of course concerns me, do not have the wherewithal to understand the complexities of what is involved to maintain this great country, no, Empire, of ours. Whilst they may feel, may believe, they have a contribution to make I fear interference from those unused to power would, instead, be detrimental. The State is a benevolent father who recognises it is not always what appears to be for the good of his children that is actually of benefit to them in the end."

Nick was scribbling. He was fidgeting at the talk of children.

"Mr Perryman you express concern for children, do you not?"

"Of course, young man. I have children of my own who are very dear to me. That children are nurtured to become useful members of society is of the utmost importance to me."

May, George, Richard and Abberline were still out of sight of Edward. Now Nick raised his voice. It was May's cue.

337

"Thank you, Mr Perryman, sir. I am sure the article I write will be of considerable interest to our readers."

Nick dropped back and Perryman turned to leave. May came from around the corner and was now only yards from him.

"Edward Perryman."

She spoke his name for the first time. It was difficult. The anger, the resentment that had festered within her all those years was concentrated into those two words. It was as if they had been trapped inside her waiting for the right time to escape and now, at last, the time was right.

"Edward Perryman." She said again, more loudly.

He did not expect to hear his name again and turned suddenly. May caught sight of the dreaded silver-topped cane. It caught the light as it had done in the hallway of the Belgravia mansion.

"Who are you girl? Why do you address me in such a disrespectful way? I do not know you."

"You do know me. Not only do you know me but you yourself told me once that you would. You said it many years ago on a freezing night in a dreadful slum that still, shamefully, remains."

"I do not know of what you speak girl. I must be on my way."

"Do not dismiss me so readily sir for I am indeed acquainted with you. I know your crime. He meant nothing to you. You beat him with the very cane you still wield today."

"Once again girl I do not know of what you speak. You try my patience. Leave me alone or I shall summon a constable."

"Edward Perryman," this time May practically spat his name, "I am just a girl and I am, as you can see, alone."

She gestured around. Her companions remained out of sight but just within earshot and the only others in the Palace Yard were preoccupied with their own business.

"Admit it to me. What can someone such as I do to you? You are a rich and powerful man. I am nothing. Just, sir, let me hear it from your own lips that you acknowledge what you did. I say again, how can I possibly hurt you?"

May hoped that Perryman's smugness, his high standing, would mean such a humble entreaty would appeal to his vanity. He would be so sure she could not hurt him. What did he have to lose by giving her some small measure of satisfaction?

He stood straight in front of May fingering the silver knob of his cane. He spoke slowly with the merest hint of a cruel smile on his face.

"Much has happened since that night, which is one I do in fact recall... yes that boy. The boy was without a doubt a thief intent on robbery. I was merely defending myself as any gentleman has the right to do against a low-life, a pickpocket. It was his own fault. Yes, I struck him but what else would I be expected to do? That I struck him several times was because I was in fear for my life. Why, after all this time should you still care about it?"

"Because the boy you beat was killed that night. You killed...you murdered him! That is why. He was helpless, he was my friend and you murdered him." Perryman had suspected as much but did not consider the boy worthy of his concern. "Say it, Perryman. Say it to me. Say you killed him. Say it! Say you struck him with that cane until you killed him!"

Perryman looked around. There were no others close by that he could see to hear him.

"Very well girl. Yes, I hit him and it appears, as a consequence, he died. There, are you satisfied now? You have your confession and there is nothing you can do about it. No one will believe the word of a girl like you against that of an Honourable Member of Her Majesty's Parliament."

From their hiding place, the Chief Inspector, accompanied by Nick, emerged. They had heard everything. George and Richard remained there. Richard was visibly shocked by what he had heard despite already knowing what had occurred that night.

Again Edward's name was spoken but this time by the Chief Inspector and with authority.

Edward looked confused as the reporter and the other man came forward whilst May dropped back.

"I am Chief Inspector Abberline of Scotland Yard and together with Mr Smart here we heard every word you spoke to the young lady. We are left in no doubt as to your guilt. You have affirmed what Miss Harris told me about the events of 19th October 1880. On that night, you did cruelly strike down and murder an innocent boy of ill-health who could never have posed a threat to one such as yourself. I therefore arrest you, Edward Perryman."

Perryman was stunned.

"What nonsense is this Inspector? Surely you cannot believe these lies. Why, I only said what I did to humour the girl. She must be of feeble mind, she - for whatever reason - has made up this ludicrous story and I simply played along to indulge the poor deluded child."

Then Edward heard a familiar voice, in fact two familiar voices - neither of whom he could possibly have expected. The shock drained any remaining colour from his face.

The first voice belonged to Richard.

"Edward, my brother you may be but you are the most despicable human being it has ever been my displeasure to meet. I believed the account of your crime even before hearing it from your own lips but now, even if doubt had ever existed, it would be gone."

341

Perryman was rarely speechless but now he truly was. After Richard spoke, the other voice he heard was Josephine's. She had come upon Richard and May as she left the House, intent on returning home as quickly as possible to greet Edward without him knowing where she had spent the afternoon.

"Edward..." she tried to speak but no more words would come. All she could do was turn to Richard for comfort.

"Come with me, Mr Perryman. Come with me now,"

Two constables had joined Abberline and they attempted to manoeuvre Edward toward a police carriage that had turned into the Palace Yard.

"Richard. I have always had great respect for you, you know that, how can you possibly believe this girl over me? Whatever you appear to think of me I am still your brother! She is nothing to you."

As Edward was being led towards the Black Maria, Richard glared into his eyes.

"You are wrong Edward. She is something to me. More to me than you have ever been or could ever be. Do you remember Rose - whom you lied to about me causing her to disappear? Rose, who I have never forgotten and truly loved? Well, brother, this girl is Rose's daughter; *my* daughter and therefore sadly your own niece. You have wronged us both. You have ruined my life and Rose's caused one child to die and another, May, to suffer hardships that no child should ever have to endure. At last, you will pay."

Edward somehow managed to break away from the constables when they were almost at the carriage. Beyond the gate crowds were gathering. Carriages were arriving to collect those members who had stayed until the close of business. The street outside was noisy and dusty. Edward felt all eyes were on him, burning into him. He couldn't, he wouldn't, get into that black carriage. He could not tolerate being humiliated by his peers. He must run, get away; get lost in the crowd.

He managed, using all his strength and driven by sheer will, to push the constables away. He ran. He ran through the Palace Yard Gate to the street. There was shouting. His own brother shouting at him! In his haste, the cane slipped from his hand. It fell to the ground and as it did so, his foot somehow caught behind it. He tripped, staggered forward and fell. Fell into the path of a carriage drawn by two large black horses.

The driver couldn't hold them. They were startled. They reared up. Edward was now on his knees in the road, looking upwards. In a moment, hooves came crashing down upon him as he tried to clutch his cane to try to defend himself. But the attempt was futile. The cane was kicked from his hand, broken in two by the hooves that then caught his head. Then another blow struck him, then another...until finally the powerful horses were brought under control. Perryman lay still, silent, his body also broken - as was, all those years ago, little Ernie's. The silver knob of his shattered cane was still catching the light and shining.

Abberline rushed forward to examine Edward. He turned to the others and shook his head.

May tried to approach but a constable held her back. She could see there was blood on the cane but this time it was Perryman's own blood. This was not how she had imagined their confrontation ending. Yet for Perryman to meet his end in such a way, due in part to the cane that killed Ernie, was surely fitting.

Amongst all the noise, all the frenzy as the body was removed, May stood wondering if she had actually heard the words Richard had spoken to Edward - the last words he had ever spoken to his brother. Those words had shocked Edward so much that he had dashed, unseeing, into the path of the carriage.

Her associates were all looking at her, speaking, but she could not hear their voices. Their lips were moving but silent; their faces full of concern. Then a fog began to appear; the same fog that had hidden her mother from her that night. It gradually enveloped them. She could not see. Everything went dark. For the second time in only a few days, May fainted.

Josephine held on to Richard trying to maintain her composure although she didn't know why, in such dramatic circumstances, she would be expected to.

"Richard is this true?" she asked as he, George and Nick tried to rally May. "You really are this young lady's father? I can't...I don't understand. How...?"

"I will explain everything to you later Josephine. I am so sorry you had to see this...find out in this way."

"My children! I must get home for my children, my poor children they..."

A constable waited with Josephine while George and Richard spoke. May was coming round. Nick comforted her as she opened her eyes and looked straight at Richard. The revelation had shaken her. She would never be the same again. She had a father but why did he leave? If he was such a good man why did he leave her mother?

She attempted to get up, to challenge him, to find out why but Nick restrained her gently.

"Wait May, there is much you need to know and you will be told soon enough. It was not intended to be revealed to you this way. Just try to be patient a little while longer.... we will get you back to Barkingside and..."

"May I am so sorry you found out in this way." George interjected "Before I knew of Edward's crime it was my intention to tell you about Richard but then, when Peg told me his brother was responsible for the murder of Ernie - it was something I couldn't do."

Richard spoke next,

"I have so much to tell you, so very much but for now just know that I loved Rose dearly. So much, and if it were not for damned Edward we may have been a proper family. I have so many regrets, so many."

The police carriage left with Edward's body. The crowd had gradually dispersed. It was time to return to the Village; time to let Peg know that when she was gone, May would not only have George but a father too. They thanked Abberline for his contribution and he remarked that he hoped the remainder of 1888 would be good and peaceful for them. Nick hurried back to write what he thought would be the biggest story of his career, although this would prove not to be true as the biggest story of the year, for him and Abberline, was yet to come. Richard escorted the devastated Josephine home to help her deal with the traumatic situation she must face. George and May sped to the Village as quickly as they could. May had to get back to Peg.

On their arrival, by now it was evening, they were met by not only Mrs Barnardo, but also the Doctor himself. He was as May remembered him, perhaps a little more portly, perhaps the whiskers were longer but he remained much the same. Without delay, he took May by the hand and hurried to the cottage.

"My dear child, you must come quickly for I fear Miss Butler is nearing her end and I pray you are not too late."

Inside both Agnes and Lottie had plainly been crying; their faces were stained with tears.

"I think she has gone May, I fear you are too late." Lottie sobbed.

"No, No Peg!" May looked down upon her dearest friend. She looked serene, she was still, but no, she wasn't dead. May saw her eyes flicker.

"She remains with us but only just." Said the Doctor " The end cannot be long. Take her hand May."

May gently took Peg's hand once again jolted by the papery skin.

"Peg, it's me, Oh Peg we did it. We got him. He's gone Peg. Trampled by horses he was and that cane, the one what killed Ernie, that cane helped to do for him but that's not all Peg.....Peg? Oh no, I think she's gone. Did she hear me?"

May started to cry but then, almost imperceptibly, Peg's eyes opened, she smiled faintly and with the last scrap of strength left in her frail body squeezed May's hand. Her eyes closed. Her hand went limp. She was gone. The smile, however, remained on her face.

May buried her head on Peg's chest, weeping. She would never know Peg's own story. The story she had hoped, one day, she would learn and Peg would never know that Richard was May's father. Doctor Barnardo put his hands on her shoulders.

"Peg heard you May. She has gone to meet our Lord content and in peace. You have made sure her passing was a happy one. Come away now child."

"I don't want to leave her. I have been away so long and have spent so little time with her." She could not believe dear Peg was dead; Peg who had been so much like a mother to her. She turned away, wiping her tear-stained face.

Fifty two

The following week May wrote to the Suttons. There was much to tell them and she was determined to leave nothing out. She had never told the Reverend and his wife directly what had happened to Ernie but as Simon had said he would tell them, the conclusion of her quest had to be explained.

Belgravia May 25th 1888

Dear Reverend and Mrs Sutton and Simon

I am sure you have been eagerly awaiting news from me. I am sorry it has taken so long to write to you but as you can imagine, lots has happened - far more than I could have ever thought. I will describe the events to you duly but first must tell you that I arrived in time to meet with my dear friend Peg and hold her hand. She smiled at me, a weak smile but nonetheless it showed she had heard and understood when I told her Ernie had been avenged. She slipped away peacefully and for this I am most thankful.

Doctor and Mrs Barnardo have arranged her funeral. Peg will be laid to rest in the City of London Cemetery. We have chosen a tree, one that will produce pink blossoms in spring, and there will be a plaque to honour her. She will be sorely missed. I will miss her very much. Even though there was an ocean between us I always felt close to her - like she was with me. But now she has gone to be with the Lord she firmly believed in so I should not be sad.

My friends, I have other news to share with you. News that is so unexpected and exciting that I still cannot truly believe it myself. Having Uncle George waiting for me at Liverpool was wonderful and what a great help he has been. Without him I could not have fulfilled my quest. The other news is that Richard Perryman is my father. It is true, he really is. Not only did his brother Edward Perryman kill my friend but he was responsible for my poor mother raising me alone. I would not wish death on anyone else but I am glad Edward Perryman is dead. Do not fear kind Suttons, I did not kill him. He fell under two strong horses pulling a carriage because he tripped over his cane - the same cane he beat Ernie with - and was trampled to death.

The Perryman family employed my mother and Richard fell in love with her. He did but Edward lied to her, he told her Richard wanted nothing more to do with her, that he didn't love her and she believed him. We cannot know what went through her mind but perhaps she could not understand why someone such as Richard would love a servant girl so she ran away. Edward lied to Richard too. He told him she had just gone away. What else could he expect from someone of her class he told him. The man was hateful. Richard did not know, maybe even my mum did not know, she was with child when she left.

All the years my poor mother struggled; all that time she could have been happy and I could have had a wonderful father. I am in a big house now. A beautiful house it is, Josephine's house now and big enough for myself and Richard to live in. Big enough for many families I think so I feel guilty. I cannot help it. Josephine was Edward's wife. She is a good woman, living with him cannot have been easy and she has children too. They are polite children, a boy and a girl, but I think it will take a while for them to accept me as their cousin, for that is what I am.

I have also become reacquainted with old friends from my time in the Nichol and at Barnardo's Village. One, Nick, was instrumental in the plan to trap Edward Perryman and I have seen much of him lately. He is very sharp and would, I think, get along very well with Simon. Perhaps one day they will meet.

So, my dear Suttons, this is all my news. My life has turned out so differently from how I could have foreseen it. I have a purpose that has been shown to me by all the things that have happened. There is much in England that is not right; there is so much unfairness, so much suffering that should not be allowed to continue. Josephine agrees with me that women should have a voice. We can help to change things for the better. We can if we work together and that is what we will do. There is a movement here to try to get women the vote. It is called Suffrage. I and Josephine will join this movement.

Thank you for the care and kindness you showed to me. I will never forget you and one day hope to welcome you to my new home in London. A fine home the like of which I never thought I would see.

I must go now, Richard - my father - and it is strange to say these words, is calling me for there is much to do.

God bless and keep you all,
Your friend always,
May Harris

Thanks for reading.

Are you wondering how Posh Peg ended up in Old Nichol?

May would never know, but you can.

Peg's story will be revealed....but not until next year.

For news about
'An Enigmatic Woman '
check out
www. JaccquelineSHarvey.com
There is also flash fiction changed regularly. This is new material that does not appear in my collection 'Never know...and other stories'.

Comments welcome

Printed in Great Britain
by Amazon